Those Lake View Wives

also by Charles Cohen

FALLING OUT

SILVER LININGS

DADDY

THOSE LAKE VIEW WIVES

BY

CHARLES COHEN

DONALD I. FINE, INC.
NEW YORK

 Published in the United States of America by Donald I. Fine, Inc. and in Canada by General Publishing Company Limited.

Library of Congress Cataloging-in-Publication Data

Cohen, Charles.
Those Lake View Wives

I. Title.
PS3553.0419T48 1989 813'.54 88-46156
ISBN 1-55611-143-6

Manufactured in the United States of America

10 9 8 7 6 5 4 3 2 1

DESIGNED BY IRVING PERKINS ASSOCIATES

For Tad, who heard every word.

THOSE LAKE VIEW WIVES

June

S	M	T	W	T	F	S
					~~1~~	~~2~~
~~3~~	~~4~~	~~5~~	~~6~~	~~7~~	~~8~~	~~9~~
~~10~~	~~11~~	~~12~~	~~13~~	~~14~~	~~15~~	~~16~~
~~17~~	18	19	20	21	22	23
24	25	26	27	28	29	30

July

S	M	T	W	T	F	S
1	2	3	4	5	6	7
8	9	10	11	12	13	14
15	16	17	18	19	20	21
22	23	24	25	26	27	28
29	30	31				

August

S	M	T	W	T	F	S
			1	2	3	4
5	6	7	8	9	10	11
12	13	14	15	16	17	18
19	20	21	22	23	24	25
26	27	28	29	30	31	

Chapter One

THE NIGHT Elizabeth Siegal shot her husband was not all that unusual. It was, of course, somewhat difficult for Marty Siegal who laid on his thick white bedroom carpet with a bullet lodged securely inside his heart. But, for the rest of Lake View, it was just another very warm night. It was the first of June.

Theories abounded about Elizabeth Siegal's motive. And why she wasn't in jail. All the usual reasons were cited: jealousy, greed, hysteria, menopausal madness. But somehow it was all kept quiet, swept under the rug. The Chicago papers were too busy covering a sting operation involving half the City Council to make anything out of a suburban murder. And the Lake View *Gazette* always went into a kind of shocked silence when something untoward happened in town. So it was all very hush-hush. Accident was the official explanation. But the cause of that accident was never explained. And nobody I knew had asked. There wasn't even a funeral. A "quiet cremation" was the official announcement. No memorial service. Nobody liked Marty Siegal all that much.

Elizabeth didn't have many friends in town, nobody she confided in, who would then confide in the rest of us. She wasn't very friendly with the other wives on our block. She didn't have coffee in the morning. Or play tennis in the afternoon. She did her nails, went to the hairdresser, and shopped by herself. So no one I knew ever really came out and asked her. I did though, on a ninety degree Saturday a couple weeks later when I was mowing my lawn and Elizabeth was laying out in her backyard bronzing her Kewpie-doll body.

"Why'd you shoot Marty?"

She looked up slowly. Took off the sun goggles and gave a pull to the top of her pink bathing suit. It took her a while to focus on me and my lawn mower. When she realized that she was talking to her next-door neighbor she reached over for the diet soda on the table next to her chaise. She took a long sip and then leaned further forward.

"The guy was an asshole."

I turned off the lawn mower and nodded. "He wasn't warm."

She fell back and replaced the goggles over her eyes. She talked to the sky. "He was a major shit."

"But why'd you kill him?"

"It was an accident."

"In the heart?"

"Yeah, the jerk fell to his knees begging for forgiveness. I was aiming for his crotch. If he didn't try acting humble for once, he would have only had a wounded nut."

My body seemed to huddle around my groin. "Too bad."

She gave a slight shrug with her chest. "No big deal."

"If you go to jail it's a big deal."

"I don't figure on going to jail," she said calmly, reaching for the can of soda. I took pity on her fruitless search and walked the fifty feet from my yard to hers and handed her the soda.

"Here it is."

She took a long pull and then handed it up in my direction. I put it back on the small round table and stayed where I was, looking down on Elizabeth Siegal's well-tanned body. It was on the zaftig side, but there wasn't much fat. For a woman rushing recklessly toward forty, Elizabeth Siegal was in fabulous shape. A few too many hennaed curls, but lying down, without makeup, the bursts of rhinestones and the shoulder-padded dresses, she exuded the sexuality that made her the center of male attention at our infrequent neighborhood gatherings.

"Why aren't you going to jail?"

" 'Cause," she said calmly, as a cloud came by to cover her sun. She sat up and stared at me.

" 'Cause why?" I asked, noticing that her heavy breasts seemed to float on her chest.

"Not 'cause why," she explained, "Cause. Reason. That's why my attorney tells me I'm going to get off."

I looked up and watched her take the goggles off and lay them next to the diet soda and bronzing gel.

"Self-defense?"

She shook her head. "No, better."

"Insanity?"

"Temporary." She pulled the towel around her shoulders and threw her feet over the side of the chair. She searched around for her pink-heeled sandals. I was going to go over and help her, but her pale pink toenailed feet discovered them first. "The man was a sickie," she finally said. She reached for her soda and held it in her hand. She seemed to be reading the label.

Marty Siegal may have been obnoxious, but he never struck me as sick. I never knew exactly what he did. He just seemed to own things. If someone on the block was looking for a car, Marty had an interest in a dealership. You needed a new refrigerator, Marty could get you twenty off. Whether it was clothes or air conditioners, Marty Siegal would get you a deal. Nothing wrong with that.

Elizabeth went on without prompting. "I knew he was strange, but not that strange."

I tried to force my mind to remember every word, so that I

could repeat it for the rest of the block. So far she hadn't sworn me to secrecy. "The man was fucking my mother."

I had a feeling I wasn't going to forget.

Elizabeth went on as if she were giving me a tuna casserole recipe. "He had this thing for old ladies. The more wrinkled the better. Sort of like early necrophilia. My mother explained it to me after I caught the two of them." She paused dramatically. "In flagrante delicto." Another pause, very pregnant. "If you know what I mean."

I nodded and sputtered. "So she . . . your mother . . . in bed . . . so it was she who was there?"

Elizabeth sighed and looked toward the cloud that was covering her sun. "Yeah, it was very dramatic. Sort of like Lana Turner and her daughter."

"Cheryl Crane," I said, proud of my knowledge of trivia.

She nodded seriously. "Except that I don't think I'm going to jail like Cheryl did."

"Positive?"

"That's what my lawyer says. Even the DA doesn't want to prosecute me for murder."

"Accidental homicide?"

She nodded. "By reason of insanity. With probation. They're waiting until the whole thing dies down before they go to the judge. I figure sometime around Christmas. My lawyer is great at delaying."

"Congratulations."

She stood up. Her breasts appeared to float up along with her. "Yeah, I guess I should throw some kind of party." She nodded in agreement with herself and followed her chest back into the house.

As it turned out, Elizabeth Siegal's "Victory" party was the highlight of Apple Tree Lane's June. Everyone was there. Not that everybody was all that much. There were just four houses on our block of Apple Tree Lane. The Siegals, now the Siegal, the Bernsteins, the Redfields, and the Kleins. I was part of the Kleins. Jack Klein. Dr. Jack Klein. I specialized in allergies.

The party was fairly uneventful. Elizabeth had ordered in. Ribs and chicken. After dinner we separated into our usual two groups. But, for once, Elizabeth Siegal wasn't surrounded by the local males. She was with the women. They had set the table for her. Filled the dishwasher for her. And now, they were seated around the kitchen table with her. There were only four chairs around the table. And they weren't about to make room for any more.

It was all very strange. For years the other wives had looked on Elizabeth, if not with disdain, then at least with an "attitude." Why did she bother living in suburbia? In Lake View? On Apple Tree Lane? She didn't have kids. Didn't even want them. Didn't work. Or own a dress shop. Sell real estate. She didn't even join the other wives for lunch in town. The only reason she was a neighbor was because Marty liked the suburbs. She wasn't one of "them." Until tonight.

So, Dave Redfield, Frank Bernstein and myself stood outside. Watching our wives sitting at the table. The men had usually spent summer nights talking about baseball games, and winter evenings discussing the state of professional football in Chicago. But now there were just the three of us doing it. No more Marty to argue with Frank. We seemed to have left a place for him and Elizabeth, who had always stood there scratching Marty's back. She wouldn't say much, the subjects obviously bored her, but she would smile every once in a while, especially when one of us checked out the state of her bust. She would give the looker a barely raised eyebrow and a smile. Frank or Dave or even me, very occasionally, would quickly look away. Trying hard, for at least five more minutes, not to glance back at her.

So now that the Siegals weren't here, it was as if the picture was not quite balanced. Everybody had always had their role. Short, nervous, argumentative Frank. Tall, shy Dave. Aggressive, athletic Marty. Elizabeth the affectionate, obedient wife. And me. There was nothing unique about me. Nothing to single me out. "He looks like a nice guy," people said. I was average height. Average weight. Maybe my light brown hair was growing thinner. And there were wrinkles to show my age. Still, I had "a cute smile," my wife once told me. So I was happy.

It was another hot, humid evening. I could feel the molds growing all around me. Tomorrow was going to be a big day at the office. People's allergies always reacted to the heat. I thought of writing a paper on it sometime, because, in fact, it really had very little to do with pollen and mold growth. But, nonetheless, many of my patients felt that a hot summer meant more sneezes, more asthma attacks. I still hadn't written the paper, yet. But soon.

"I never liked the guy," Frank Bernstein said, taking a quick swallow of his drink. Frank was an accountant, a short stocky fellow, who took little swallows and gulps of everything. He was very nervous, always looking around for someone, or something. Even when, like tonight, there was nothing but yard to look at.

Dave Redfield pondered Frank's statement. Dave pondered everything. He was the vice-president of the Lake View bank. The bank his father had run for forty years. Unlike his father, Dave didn't want to get anybody mad at him. Dave finally got his words out. "Marty did have . . . his friends."

"Face it," I looked up at Dave and then down at Frank. "The guy was terrific for favors."

"He got you that stove," Dave said eagerly, looking down from his six foot six inch height to accountant Frank Bernstein's five feet seven.

Frank shrugged the stove away. "So what." Quickly he searched the yard for intruders. When he didn't discover any, he turned back to us. "I only saved a couple hundred bucks. Big deal." And then, in a mean sort of mumble, "I never liked the guy anyway."

"You loved his wife's breasts," I said to get him. I knew the statement was worth at least three looks around the yard. It turned out to be five.

Dave coughed while Frank did his number. Finally, Frank got it out. "Well, I mean everybody looked, what's the big deal, I mean like I'm a regular guy. Ask your wife about that," he said to me, standing up on his toes, and thrusting his finger at my chest, as if he were James Cagney. "Yeah, ask her if it isn't normal for a normal kind of guy to look at a woman's breasts? Go ahead, Mr. Doctor, ask your wife. It's perfectly normal, I'm telling you guys, it's practically un-American not to look at a woman's breasts."

My wife Barbara was getting her degree in psychology. She had been getting it for ten years. So far the only people she had treated were our neighbors, who were not sure they wanted her to finish. It was cheaper this way.

I could feel Dave blush. "I don't think we should be talking . . ."

I gestured towards the kitchen window, where the four women were sitting around the table. "What do you think they're talking about?"

Dave quickly glanced over, and then back to us. He took a long swallow. "Women's things . . . I guess."

"I bet it's the murder," I said with certainty.

"Nah," Frank Bernstein derisively waved away my idea.

"Ten to one, it's the murder," I said, with growing confidence. I took a look at the table. They were all hunched forward. Our wives leaning toward Elizabeth Siegal, who was pointing to the part of the anatomy she had told me she was aiming for. "Yeah, absolutely."

Frank shook his head and took five birdlike swallows. He ate constantly to keep up his overweighted figure. "Fran doesn't talk about that stuff." He leaned forward, probably to see if his wife Fran was participating in the conversation. "Told you," he said to each of us as he made sure his wife wasn't talking. "She's thinking about the Farmer's market on Tuesday. Trying to figure out if they'll have any of those blackberries I like."

I turned around. Fran Bernstein was riveted. Her mouth was slightly open. Taking in everything Elizabeth Siegal said like a vacuum cleaner. Blackberries were not on her mind.

* * *

Barbara and I walked home around ten. Even though it was summer and both our girls were away at camp, we still thought of Sunday as a school night. We were the first ones to leave. Barbara kissed Elizabeth good-bye. I just smiled. Elizabeth seemed as calm and unruffled as she had the day she told me about the murder.

Our block of Apple Tree Lane was the shortest of the two mile street that wound through all of Lake View. A small street in a small suburb of Chicago. We were at one end of the street. Almost an afterthought. The result of a rich man's sudden failure in the grain market and the selling off of his property to make three new houses. We had bought the Grain King's Georgian fifteen years ago, when I finished my residency in allergy. I chose Lake View for its trees, molds, and abundance of pollens.

Now we had two girls, eleven and fifteen, who were at camp like everybody else's child on the street. All of us had moved in at the same time. In our early thirties, ready to start careers and children. We had all grown into our forties together, and while ordinarily we might not have chosen each other for best friends, proximity had made us close.

"What were you guys talking about?" I asked as we walked the fifty feet to our house.

"Stuff."

"The murder?"

"The accident." She turned to me and gave me a look that, even in the dark, I could tell was sharp.

"Okay, the accidental murder." I took her hand and held it as we walked up the long brick path to our front door.

She nodded. "We talked about it."

"And?"

She turned to me as we got to the screen door. "And, I think she's remarkably calm about it."

I opened the door. Barbara walked in ahead of me and started up the staircase. I stayed behind to turn off all the front lights. "No trauma?" I asked.

She shook her head. "Not tonight." She nodded slowly and psychiatrically before continuing up the stairs.

It was amazing, I thought, but Elizabeth had looked happier than all the other women at the table. Certainly more than Fran Bernstein, who hadn't smiled in ten years. Who had seemed to become permanently disheveled due, no doubt, to a combination of serving Frank and her uncontrollable twelve-year-old twin boys.

I finished turning off the lights and checked the air-conditioning. It was going to cost us over three hundred a month in electric bills, but when it was eighty-three degrees at eleven in the evening you didn't have much choice. So I made my way up to bed. I missed the girls. But still, life was as it was supposed to be. Summer was for camp. Winter for school. Christmas was visiting my parents in Palm Springs. Spring for a driving vacation to Florida or Arizona or Canada. Things were orderly. Which made me content.

I thought of watching television, but I had office hours the next morning. Summer was incredibly busy. As it should be.

It still seemed strange not hearing the girls waking up and screaming for the clothes that were at the cleaner or still unwashed. Berta the Polish cleaning woman was there when I left in the morning. Berta, who had arrived in America nine months earlier, had a key for the back door and let herself in three days a week at six A.M. She only charged us from seven to four, since she spent the first hour making herself mammoth omelets and two pots of coffee. From seven till four she used the six eggs, half a pound of cheese and six cups of caffeine to destroy any dust that dared enter our house. Berta Swaboda viewed our house in much the same way Hitler approached Warsaw.

"Missy no home?" Berta smiled at me as I walked out the door. Barbara was still sleeping. But that made no difference to Berta, who had proudly learned those three words of English to be used not merely at the front door and on the phone, but to serve as "hello," "good-bye" and "how's the family?" I smiled as she cracked a couple more eggs into the bowl.

Frank Bernstein was driving out of his driveway when I pulled out of my garage. Frank drove a big Audi. Black. With GRT ACCT on the license plates.

Frank didn't bother to wave. He was already on the car phone. He seemed to be mad at someone, or something.

I thought of stopping off for breakfast on my way to the office, but then figured that it was going to be a busy Monday. The pollen season hadn't started, but between the molds and the trees, I was inundated with old patients getting their weekly shots and new patients who arrived with red eyes and swollen noses, holding woefully onto a piece of crumpled-up tissue.

I liked Lake View, and not because it had provided me with a practice that let me send my daughters to camp and my wife to graduate school. It was a pretty suburb that was far enough from Chicago to make you feel you were in the semi-country. It felt like a town to me. A nice place to raise kids and make a good living.

I had grown up in Chicago, a place I couldn't wait to get out of. It wasn't that I hated cities. I hated apartments and the smells of other people's food in the hallways. I was a very neat child, partly, I suppose, to make sure my world was separate and distinct from the noise and disorder of the city. Barbara had once told me that I was rebelling against the chaos of my family. The laissez-faire attitude of my messy parents and sister. All of whom viewed order as evil and corrupting. She referred to my obsession with neatness as only "mildly neurotic." I didn't go into fits when confronted with chaos. I just cleaned it up. According to Barbara's second graduate school, that was healthy.

Barbara, of course, wasn't as organized as I was. She wasn't a messer-upper but she also wasn't a straightener-upper. So I bore the inconvenience of a sock drawer that had to be rearranged once a week into browns and blacks.

My youngest daughter, Mandy, was like me. While Martha, the fifteen-year-old, resembled her mother. She never knew where things were. It was always her voice in the morning echoing through the house, searching for skirts and hair clips and colored rubber bands she had mislaid. Mandy usually found them for her, just like I always knew where Barbara's watch was. I tried to be patient with Martha and Barbara about their messer-upper qualities. I always had Mandy to nudge when one of them ran around searching for the watch Mandy and I knew was next to the bed. Or under it.

My life had been orderly for years. Not that my parents had helped make it neat. They were too busy teaching school to worry about whether or not the beds had hospital corners. It wasn't important to them that the dishes weren't done after dinner. They would be there tomorrow. My sister Carol cared even less than my parents. She believed in paper plates. When they came out with plastic coated rewashable ones she was in heaven. So even though I was the youngest in the house, excluding my pet fish Hamster, which Carol murdered the night I spent at Al Benjamin's house, it was my duty to keep things reasonably orderly. I always felt that I became a doctor not because of any parental influence but because it was basically a clean, neat, well-organized profession. Things happened that were supposed to happen. Especially in allergy. Summer, even with all the kids between ten and sixteen away at camp, was always my busiest time of year. I knew how much serum I would use to build up my patients' resistance to the allergens that caused them to sneeze and wheeze from May to September. I knew how many prescriptions I'd write and how many patients would have asthma attacks that would require hospitalization. Allergy was a reasonable, rational specialty. Very little blood and death. I was not comfortable with death. It was never neat. Never orderly. So I had become an allergist. I knew my patients would recover.

My office was almost in the middle of town. I had been making plans for the past year to move into a new building that I was planning to build with a number of other doctors just outside town. But construction hadn't begun yet, so, for now, I was still on the second floor at 234 Middlewood.

Mrs. Robins was waiting for me when I got to the office. She got the first shot on Monday morning. She was as orderly as my sock drawer. Mrs. Robins had been coming to allergists for years. She was a typical Hay Feverite and sometime asthmatic: ragweed, trees, and dust. I think she had long ago given up being cured and now considered a visit to her allergist in much the same way she viewed dropping in on a neighbor. It was a duty. A routine. When you're seventy-eight and alone, even a visit to the allergist is exciting.

"Good morning, Mrs. Robins," I smiled as I walked into the waiting room.

"You're late, Klein."

I smiled and looked over at my receptionist Shari Herman. Shari was making up the appointment schedule. Concentrating on writing out a list of who was expected. She hadn't seemed to notice Mrs. R. or me. I turned back to Mrs. Robins.

"How are you today?"

She gave me an exaggerated sniff to show me exactly how she was doing. "Terrible. That pill you gave me last week was the worst. Not only didn't it work, but it didn't even put me to sleep like the other stuff that didn't work." She held up her used torn Kleenex as evidence. "Know what this is?" She didn't pause long enough for me to answer. "Phlegm. That's what I've got, phlegm. I must have blown out a ton of the stuff in my life."

She stood up and tossed down a three-month-old copy of U.S. News.

"These magazines are not only old, Klein, they're filthy." She glared at me, waiting for an argument. I smiled and followed her mumbles into the office.

The rest of the morning was typical, usual, as regular and normal as the tan suits I wore on Monday and Wednesday and the seersuckers on Friday and Tuesday. As predictable as the blue blazer and gray lightweight slacks I put on every Thursday. Shots and more shots. Some new patients who needed tests to determine exactly what kind of shots they should be getting. Then, of course, I had to feel the bumps the shots made. Just how much reaction there was to the serum. So that next time I would know how much to add, and how much to take away. The kind of morning I like best. Same patients, same injections.

Lunch was a lot like my morning. At 12:35 I took off my white smock and put on my tan summer weight suit jacket and walked the block over to The Lunch Box. I knew that the round table for eight would have two other men sitting around it, Dave Redfield, my neighbor and banker, and Harold Goldberg, who ran one of the two men's stores down the street and who sold me my summer cottons and winter wools.

The round table was the only one where men sat. The rest of The Lunch Box crowd was female. Women of all ages. Mothers and daughters. Friends. Sisters. Cousins. Deep in conversation. Relentlessly commenting on everything in Lake View. From the state of education to the lack of a decent Chinese restaurant. Food was an afterthought at The Lunch Box. Both for the customers and the proprietor. You could get the same greasy hamburgers and equally overcooked omelets at four or five other places in town. But The Lunch Box had style and tradition going for it, which in Lake View was a lot more important than the quality of your french fries and the fizziness of your soft drinks. In the early morning and late afternoon, you would see a few men, but not at noon from Monday through Friday. Occasionally, husbands on vacation would show up, but you could tell by their body language just how uncomfortable the place was for them. Often they'd drift over to our table.

Our table had been in existence for years. Dave Redfield's late father, who owned the bank, had started it, and it had just kept on going. Of course back then, men had occupied a lot of tables. Because there were a lot of men working and owning stores in Lake View. But now it was a bedroom community. A place for male commuters to leave from, and arrive at.

These days the round table at The Lunch Box was Lake View's only "Men's Club." A place to find out what was going on in town. Who was retiring and who was going out of business. The makeup of the table was predictable, although during the summer months quite a few regulars were out of town. But Camille Grasso, the owner of The Lunch Box, still kept all eight seats open for us. Once in a while a group of women who didn't know the rules would plop themselves down at our table. But Camille would refuse to serve them and finally, after all their threats to boycott The Lunch Box failed, they would take their furs and flounce off into the afternoon. They'd be back, of course. The Lunch Box was the only place in Lake View where you could be sure to see who was wearing what new clothes and what hairdo had replaced the hairdo of the day before.

Dave was gulping down his cheeseburger, fries, and vanilla milkshake when I sat down. Harold Goldberg, the haberdasher, was mournfully chewing a piece of cantaloupe. He was trying to wait as long as possible before swallowing. Normally a jolly fat man, Harold had recently been told by his doctor to take off fifty pounds. Harold hated every one of those pounds and resented me because of my profession. He mumbled hello as I sat down next to Dave. Arlene, our usual waitress, brought me my iced Sanka before I could unfold the napkin and place it in my lap. She didn't even bother taking my order. The tuna plate was a given during the summer. I tended toward soup and tuna salad on whole wheat toast after Labor Day.

"You look great, Harold," I said.

He speared another hunk of cantaloupe and angrily shoved it into his mouth. Dave quickly ate a french fry, trying to swallow before Harold could notice and resent him.

"I think Harold looks terrific too," Dave said earnestly.

Harold held his knife in the air. It pointed in our direction. "I do not look terrific," he whispered angrily. "I am a fat person. I have always been a fat person. People know me as a fat person. They buy suits from me as a fat person . . ."

"Here ya' go, doc" the waitress said, placing the tuna down in front of me. The cucumber slice looked fresher than normal. The lettuce leaves were more wilted than usual.

Harold pointed to the cucumber I was putting into my mouth. "See, that's thin food. I hate thin food. Jack, you are a natural thin person."

I nodded. Dave seemed to think about it, and made a decision by finishing off his burger.

"I," Harold said firmly, "am not. I will not be happy, nice, or sell a lot of suits as a thin . . ." he shivered as he mentioned the word, "suit seller. People will take one look at me and say, 'poor Harold Goldberg, I'm getting depressed looking at him, let's go to Mort's store and buy a suit.' "

"C'mon, Harold," I said in my best happy-doc voice, "you're still Harold Goldberg. Even at 180 pounds."

He shook his head, and shoved the remaining cantaloupe aside. "At 245 I'm Harold Goldberg. At 180 I'm 'whatdoyathink's wrong with Goldberg?' " He looked down at the empty packet of sugar substitute in front of his coffee cup. "I swear, this is no way for a fifty-year-old man to live." He picked up the pink packet and crumpled it into a ball before throwing it across the table at an empty seat.

"You're not happy, Harold," Dave said seriously, having devoured everything on the plate but the soggy pickle.

Harold looked at Dave Redfield as if he had suggested a pair of white socks with a tux. "No joke, Dave. Two years ago I gave up smoking. Now I give up food. And do you really think I'll live any longer?" He shook his head. "Depression is going to do me in."

"Hello, Harold," a sweet voice said. We all looked up. A woman about Harold's age and weight looked down at him. "Are you all right?"

Harold gave her his best grin. "Terrific, Millie. Feeling wonderful."

She looked worried. "We were going to come in for some summer things for Eddie . . ." Her voice trailed off.

Harold kept on smiling. "I'll be there. Just ask for old Harold. Any time Mil, Eddie could use some new stuff." He lowered his voice. "I've got a worsted, gray," he paused meaningfully . . . "it's Eddie."

Millie leaned back, happy to hear Harold speak. "Saturday, Harold, we'll see you Saturday."

Harold agreed. "All day, any time. I'll be the guy in glen plaid."

Everybody laughed. Millie found her table, and Harold's face sagged even further. "I told you. I told you." He looked up at me as I finished the last of my vegetables. "All you doctors are crazy. I am a fat person." He looked around the table for some fat food. Dave's plate was empty, mine was too depressing for him to consider. "Maybe it's an allergy," he said to me hopefully.

"Sorry, Harold. Maybe I'll buy a new blazer."

He nodded. He at least knew I wouldn't take my business over to his competitor, Mort Drewby, or, as he cynically referred to Lake View's "other" men's store owner, "Mort the Anorexic." The battle of the thirty-seven portly versus the thirty-nine long was of long standing in Lake View. The Morts and the Harolds were two distinct camps. Mort and Harold were friends, and also vicious competitors. Mort usually came to lunch at the same time as Harold but ever since Harold had to go on the diet he had tried to avoid Mort, who could down three cheeseburgers without gaining a pound. I tried to tell Harold that he had much more hair than Mort, but it was no use. These days Harold looked out the window of his store, across from The Lunch Box, and, when he saw his friend and enemy Mort leave with his giant Snickers bar, he would stamp his foot and go over for lunch.

I was about to order some fresh fruit for desert when my neighbor, Fran Bernstein, walked into the resetaurant.

"There's Fran," Dave pointed out. Fran was as timid as her husband Frank was loud. A short, shy woman who might have been pretty if she held her head up. Camille Grasso was leading Fran to a table with two other women. Fran took the chair that let her look directly into a wall.

"Who's Fran?" Harold asked, his business instincts overcoming his depression.

"Fran Bernstein," Dave explained, looking at his watch.

I saw Arlene walking toward me with a dish of fruit, and then turned back to Harold. "You know Frank Bernstein, the accountant?"

Harold nodded. "Thirty-six short, but I can't tell him that."

"Why?" I asked, smiling at the dish of melon, oranges, and bananas Arlene placed in front of me.

"Jerk says he's a thirty-six regular, but we know he's not." Harold looked at me for agreement. I agreed. Harold went on, happy now not to be thinking about himself. "So I put a thirty-six on him and the bottom of the jacket is below his knees. He tells me it's a long." Harold sighed. "So now I just scratch out the word 'short' on the tag. Makes him happy."

Dave shook his head. "What a crazy block."

I nodded. "This summer it is."

Harold glanced at my bowl of fruit, and then looked away without interest. "Yeah, that guy Siegal wasn't a customer, but even so . . ." Harold shook his head slowly to indicate grief.

"Terrible." Dave shook his head respectfully. "A terrible thing."

I drew my knees together. Tightly.

Harold seemed to find the whole subject fastinating. It appeared to make him happy for a change. "I hear the wife got off. She found him in bed with another guy."

"Mother," I said, swallowing a mushy slice of banana.

"Another guy's mother?" Harold asked incredulously.

"Her mother," I said softly. Even though most of the women paid no attention to our table, I didn't want to spread too much gossip. Although Harold would probably give this bit of news away free with each pair of pants.

"She found him in bed with her own mother? Her personal mother?"

Dave nodded. "Elizabeth was upset."

"No kidding," Harold agreed, his eyes still falling out of their sockets. "That's worse than dieting."

Dave nodded. "The whole block is upset."

"How about her mother?" Harold asked. "Was she at least good looking?"

Dave and I shook our heads almost in unison. "A prune," I said.

"Old," Dave added.

"I figured she was old, David," Harold said sarcastically. "But there's old and there's old."

"This one," I explained, finishing the last piece of apple before it turned brown, "was old old. Not dead old, just old old."

Harold nodded. "It's very sick. Extremely sick."

Dave nodded. "The man was . . ."

Harold ignored him. "It is a very sick thing to shoot your husband, I don't care what the excuse. It is totally unnatural."

I sat back and checked my watch, I had five minutes till my next appointment. I started afternoon injections at one. I looked back at Harold, who seemed upset about the whole conversation. Dave just sat there looking as interested as if he were about to get 14½ percent for a mortgage.

"I think there was a reason here, Harold. And besides, she wasn't trying to kill him."

Harold looked at me. "She was maybe aiming for his knees?"

"A little higher," I explained. I knew I was about to cause Harold pain. "She was trying to shoot him in the groin when he fell to his knees and she got him in the chest instead."

"Oooh" was all Harold could get out. Dave nodded through Harold's moan.

I reached for my check. "Stings, doesn't it." I got up and started to leave. Harold was still shaken. In spite of the fact that he hated doctors, Harold was deathly afraid of them. Which is why he did whatever they told him to do, including losing weight. I nodded good-bye and walked out to make my one o'clock injection.

June

S	M	T	W	T	F	S
					~~1~~	~~2~~
~~3~~	~~4~~	~~5~~	~~6~~	~~7~~	~~8~~	~~9~~
~~10~~	~~11~~	~~12~~	~~13~~	~~14~~	~~15~~	~~16~~
~~17~~	~~18~~	19	20	21	22	23
24	25	26	27	28	29	30

July

S	M	T	W	T	F	S
1	2	3	4	5	6	7
8	9	10	11	12	13	14
15	16	17	18	19	20	21
22	23	24	25	26	27	28
29	30	31				

August

S	M	T	W	T	F	S
			1	2	3	4
5	6	7	8	9	10	11
12	13	14	15	16	17	18
19	20	21	22	23	24	25
26	27	28	29	30	31	

Chapter Two

IT HAD gotten hotter in the half hour I spent inside. The temperature was close to ninety. And it was only the eighteenth of June. Convertible tops were down, and most of the teenagers who were staying home for summer school were tooling around in them. I don't usually sweat a lot, but even I noticed the mid-August-like heat as I walked back to the office to inject about twenty more people in the next few hours.

I enjoyed the rest of the day. It was exactly like a Monday in June. Summer was a little different because my teen patients didn't wait until Saturday to come in, but basically the symptoms of my existence remained as predictable as the ragweed that provided for my family.

I got a couple new patients. Children who had been driving their parents crazy with sneezing and sniffling. Mothers dragging in red-eyed seven-year-olds who looked at this office full of needles and started screaming before we were even introduced. Eventually I calmed most of them down. Promising them a visit to Dr. Jack's treasure chest of toys on each visit. Rings, balloons, finger puppets, and rubber godzillas awaited them if they bit their tongue when the needles descended toward their arm.

It was a very ordinary day. At five I finished up, headed out into the oven that was now well beyond ninety degrees, and went home.

Barbara had a class that night. Usually that meant the girls and I would cook something together. Or, rather, Mandy and I would cook something together. Something stir-fried, or perhaps, broiled fish. But now that I was by myself I decided to settle for a simple sandwich. Tuna. In water. On rye. Just a dab of mayo. My diet was even starting to bore me. But the cholesterol news assailed me from every angle of my existence. Doctors' newsletters, the Chicago *Tribune* and the evening news had a weekly story that caused me to abandon even that teeny, tiny mini-dab of mayonnaise for a couple days.

I changed to a pair of shorts and a T-shirt and went outside to eat. The gusts from the air-conditioning vents were driving me crazy. I can only take air-conditioning at home so long. I usually start sneezing. So I headed out into the thick, early evening air. Sat down on the patio and watched the trees stand still. It was as if it was too hot for them to move.

I ate the sandwich and drank my diet soda very, very slowly. I tried not to move a lot. Every time I would shift, the sweat would cause another part of my back to stick to the chair.

"Hey, Jack."

I looked up. Elizabeth Siegal was waving at me and walking over from her house, a can of soda in hand. She took her itsy-bitsy little steps through the grass and quickly arrived at my patio. She plopped down next to me, putting her soda next to my empty plate.

"Mind if I join you?"

I shook my head and finished off the last bite. The sandwich was much warmer than when I had started it.

"Have dinner?"

She shook her head. "Nah, I'm trying to lose weight. Anyhow, it's too hot to eat." She rubbed the can of diet soda across her forehead. Not that her clothes were heating her up. She had on a bikini top and a pair of shorts. I tried to keep looking at the reddish curls that clung wetly to her scalp. Only her breasts seemed to be excited and up.

I pointed to her house. "Are you going to stay?"

"Maybe. I don't know. The insurance guys are still telling my lawyers what they aren't going to give me, and Marty's accountants are telling me all the things he owned. So depending on how much I got left . . ." she paused for breath, "I'll decide whether or not to stay."

"I imagine it gets kind of lonely. It's a big place for just one person."

She slumped down into the chair and checked out the now bright red toes peeking out from her sandsals. "Yeah, but it's kind of nice. Know what I mean?"

I nodded, remembering the loudness of Marty's voice. "Eventually I would think you'd like some company."

Elizabeth slumped down even further. Remarkably, her breasts, which I glanced at briefly, stayed elevated. "Who knows, right now it's nice to be so friendly with all the girls." She leaned over and whispered to me. She didn't seem to notice that her right breast touched my arm briefly. Maybe they weren't real. "You see all this has brought us much closer."

I edged away. She took a sip of her drink and glanced down at her toenails.

"I didn't realize that you and the other women . . ."

She nodded. "Absolutely. It surprised me too. But Fran Bernstein and Jane and your Barbara have been terrific to me. It's sort of like a sisterhood. Barbara said it would make a wonderful seminar subject. Murder as therapy, she said she would call it. She tell you 'bout it?"

I shook my head. "Barbara gets into new therapies all the time."

"Yeah, remember last year when she was going around hollering?"

"Primal therapy."

"And then before that when she arranged Fran Bernstein's refrigerator to help her lose weight?"

"Behavior modification."

"And didn't she—?"

I stopped her before she could go on. "We've been through all of them. That's why it's taken her so long to get her Ph.D. Every time she meets a new professor she starts all over again. She's been in five graduate programs in the last ten years."

"Well"—Elizabeth sat up straighter—"all I know is that I like this murder-therapy stuff. Barbara has this idea that if we all sit around a few times a week and talk about who we'd like to kill, it would make everybody feel better. Get out all our hostility, like. Sort of neat, huh?"

I was getting that uncomfortable tingling in my crotch that I had when I first heard where Elizabeth shot Marty. "Was this Barbara's idea?"

Elizabeth drained off the last of her drink. "Guess so. Anyhow, Fran and Jane think it's great, and who am I to argue? Barbara says that in one shot I got rid of my guilt toward my mother and my husband. Pretty neat, huh?"

"Unless you're the murderee." I was starting to get nervous. I was squirming on my chair. Not noticing the sweat dripping down my back now. Marty's death had been much further away than next door. But it was getting closer. And less of a joke . . .

She waved away my fears. "Oh, we're not really killing anybody. Just talking about it. Actually, I probably shouldn't even qualify for the group because I did it. I mean everybody else is acting out all their murdering instincts, but I did it. Shot the son-of-a-bitch."

I could almost feel it. Feel the pain I forgot about the heat. Thought about Marty really dying. "Did Barbara ever . . ."

Elizabeth wasn't dumb. "No, no, no we haven't talked about people we know. It's just people in our past, you know, mothers and fathers and big brothers who'd surprise you in the shower, and geeks who'd try to feel you up on the dance floor. Stuff like that."

I relaxed. It was another one of Barbara's moods. Something new to try. I smiled to myself. Forget about it, Jack. Think about Elizabeth's breasts. Anything else. I looked up at the sky. And then quickly glanced down at Elizabeth's chest. But only for a brief moment. She didn't even notice. I looked down at my plate.

"Of course," Elizabeth went on, "Fran Bernstein hasn't really talked about her problems yet. She seems to be just listening. But I got a feeling I know the guy she's after. And it ain't Colonel Mustard in the library." She nudged me to see if I got it. I smiled at her to show I had. Thankfully, she wanted to move onto something else. "So why you eating alone?"

"Barbara's got a class." I was grateful to move on. To forget Marty and death and murder-therapy. To put my primal fears on cruise control.

"She sure has a lot of education."

"Credits, Elizabeth, Barbara has lots of credits." I was good talking about Barbara.

"Maybe I should go back to school. I was a great typist."

"Why do you want to go back to school?"

"I don't know, isn't that's what women my age do. Open stores or go back to school, or sell real estate?"

"So open a store." The sun was almost down and still the heat was thick and oppressive.

"No way, stores are too much work. I used to work at Marshall Field's."

"And school?"

"I always hated school. Except for typing."

"How about just getting a job."

"Maybe." Elizabeth stirred, looked around as if she was getting bored. The sound of a car door slamming stopped her. We both turned toward the rear of the garage. We could see the light in it going off. I waited for Barbara.

She walked out the back door dressed like a suburban woman in graduate school. Linen pants and some kind of designer denim shirt. She had aged well. Tall, thin and lanky. If we had had a son he would have been a great basketball player. Barbara always had an elegance about her that allowed her to wear white pants and work shirts and still look chic. She appeared so neat, orderly. Only I knew she could never remember where she put her watch.

"What are you guys doing out here? It's an oven."

"Staying warm." I looked up for my kiss. She gave me a quick peck and sat down on the edge of the chaise lounge.

"Why don't we go into the house?" Barbara asked, looking up at the trees.

"It's not so bad out here," Elizabeth answered before Barbara could move. "Anyway, I hate air conditioning. Marty used to love it. Had the place turned down to fifty-five degrees all the time. That's why I wore so much cashmere around the house."

"Okay"—Barbara wiped her forehead with her sleeve—"but I got to get inside soon. If you two heat freaks want to stay that's fine with me." She took a deep breath and let it out slowly, "It must be a hundred and ten out here. I'd swear we're in Palm Springs visiting Jack's parents."

Elizabeth nodded. "Yeah, I know what you mean, actually I was thinkin' Palm Springs might not be a bad place to settle in, if, of course, I get the money from the insurance."

"Lots of rich widowers in Palm Springs," I suggested with a grin. Now that Barbara was nearby I kept my eyes firmly fixed on the top of Elizabeth's head.

"Elizabeth isn't looking for rich old men," Barbara said sternly.

"Oh, I don't know," Elizabeth said, "depends how old he is. I mean if he's real, real, real old then I might get something out of it. Without giving up anything. Know what I mean?" I could feel the wink.

"You're only reacting to the accident," Barbara explained

grimly. "An emotional overreaction to everybody's accusations."

"I don't think so," Elizabeth answered softly.

"We'll talk about it next time we get together," Barbara said in her finest therapeutic tone.

"Okay, but I still think a rich widower, I mean a very, very old rich widower, is my best bet. Jack and I were talking about my options before, and this one seems the best."

Barbara stood up. "We'll discuss it. Later." It sounded like an order.

I stood up too. I could feel the straps on the chair ping away from my soaked polo shirt. Elizabeth got up gradually.

"Well . . ." Elizabeth tried to shake her curls. They were unshakably damp. "I'll see you around. Thanks for the talk, Jack. See you tomorrow, Barb. Nine?"

I looked over at Barb, who nodded significantly.

Elizabeth took her teeny-weeny steps across the grass, and Barb and I started into the house. Barbara looked at me. "I don't think it's productive to encourage Elizabeth to adopt a traditional dumb widow's role. Especially a male version of a traditional dumb woman's role."

"Wait a second." I opened the back door for Barb, who walked in ahead of me. I took my plate and glass over to the sink. Our kitchen had been remodeled the year before and I still got confused over where everything was. But now I got it right. I didn't take the dishes over to the stove. "How was class?"

Barbara opened the refrigerator, and when she didn't find anything she liked, turned back to me. "Boring, very boring, Jack. Not the best seminar I've taken."

I rinsed the plate and stuck it into the dishwasher. "Are you tired of Reichian analysis already?"

"Orgasm. Orgasm. Orgasm." She threw her hands up in the air. "That's all they talk about."

"I thought that's why you liked it."

Barbara grabbed her book bag and threw it over her shoulder. "I did. But this stuff is really boring."

I followed her out of the kitchen. I turned off the lights as we left the room. There weren't any other lights on in the house, but we made our way through the living room with all its chrome and glass without a bump. I turned the lights on in the hallway and followed Barbara up the stairs. "You ready to drop out?"

"Maybe."

"I hear the University of Chicago has an interesting program. I was talking to Arnie Melton about it, you know the psychiatrist next door to me, I think he was trained there."

"I don't know." We were at the top of the stairs. I followed Barbara and her book bag down the long hallway, past the empty bedrooms into our bedroom. It was so quiet up here with the girls away. I missed them every night.

"Well, I mean, are you going to stay in school?"

She shrugged and turned on the lights. The room, so very white, shone.

We each headed for the first phase of our go-to-bed ritual. I went to my closet to hang up my clothes and put on a pair of pajamas. Barbara went to our bathroom to brush her teeth and wash her face in her sink. We raised our voices to hear one another. "I don't know what I'm going to do. I'm really thinking of dropping out completely."

"You're kidding?"

"I'm not."

I threw my shirts and shorts into the hamper in my closet. "Maybe you could open up a practice. You have a masters in social work."

"Maybe." And, a few seconds later, "I don't know."

I found a clean pair of pajamas. Beige. "Well, I don't think you're going to be happy sitting around the house."

I heard the water shut off. A few moments later Barbara came out and headed toward her side of the bed. She kept her pajamas underneath her pillow. Her clothes usually wound up across the dresser. Like tonight. All the while she seemed intent on something, maybe her answer.

"Well?" I asked, as I tied the string around my waist. I started into the bathroom.

"I'm really not sure. Yet. But I think I've taken enough courses to last a lifetime."

"Two," I said, and walked into the bathroom.

A second later Barbara yelled out, "Two what?"

I tried to remember what I was thinking of. I finished brushing my teeth, and rinsing the brush, before I was able to rewind my memory to the spot. "Two lifetimes."

"Two lifetimes of what?" she yelled back.

I decided to finish washing my face before any further explanations. By the time I got back to the bedroom Barbara was already in bed reading her latest psychological tome.

"I said you've taken enough courses for two lifetimes."

She looked up from her book, over her granny glasses, and followed me as I got into bed and under the covers. It was cold enough for a blanket or two. Barbara should have been married to Marty. They both liked the wind-chill factor to be somewhere in the forties. "So you think I should drop out?"

"I didn't say that. I just think it's understandable that you're getting itchy to do something besides school."

"You're right."

"So do something else."

"Maybe I will." She put the book down, bending the spine. "Groups," she said significantly.

"What about them?" I asked, reaching for the Allergy Quarterly.

"Maybe I ought to be doing groups."

"Didn't you do groups five years ago?"

She looked at me like I was crazy. "That was encounter groups. I'm talking more classic group therapy." She picked up the book. I could hear the crack as the spine of the book gave up the ghost.

"You going to open an office?"

She returned to her reading. "No, I thought I'd start small. Around the block. Jane, Fran, Elizabeth . . ."

A very small group. The words "murder therapy" came back to me. But I didn't say them loud. Why upset her? But I did begin to feel uncomfortable.

"It's just an experiment." She turned on her side. "Good night, Jack."

I didn't say anything. I had always thought of myself as a fairly decent husband. I wasn't a pig like Frank Bernstein or a mouse like Dave Redfield. And I certainly wasn't as aggressive as Marty Siegal. I was a nice guy. Maybe slightly boring. But good. Real good to my wife and my children. I wanted them to be happy. Oh, come on, Jack. You're getting paranoid. Besides, you never once hankered after Barb's mother. But it took a long time for me to get to sleep. The house was too damn quiet. And I was cold.

We had dinner with the Bernsteins the next night. When I got home, I was greeted by a note in the kitchen to meet Barb over there. I washed up, changed into a short-sleeved shirt and girded myself for one of Fran's meat and potatoes dinners. Two-inch-thick pork chops. Sixteen-ounce T-bones. Real food. Stuff for Frank to chew on.

You could see the smoke all the way from my house. When I walked into his backyard, Frank Bernstein was standing at the grill, tongs and fork in hand, stabbing and flipping two enormous cuts of beef. The sweat was pouring off his face, fogging up his glasses. He was entranced by his art.

"Looks good, Frank."

"Yeah." He leered at the meat. A few seconds later he looked up. "Want a drink, Jack?"

"Sure."

He pointed to his house. "Fran's in there. She'll make you one. And tell her to bring me out a gin and tonic. Six ice cubes. The small ones." He turned back to his poking. The flames shot up around the beef.

Fran and Barbara were in the kitchen. Fran was making the salad. Barb was sitting at the kitchen table drinking a glass of wine. The conversation ended in mid-sentence as I walked into the room. They both behaved as if they had never seen me before. Or maybe it was as if they had seen me before and didn't much like what they saw. Or maybe they were just deep in conversation.

I smiled. Raised my hand tentatively in greeting and stood there waiting for someone to greet me back. It wasn't to be my wife.

"Hi, Jack."

"Hi, Fran." I walked over and kissed Barbara on the top of her head. She didn't look up. "Am I interrupting . . ."

Fran, so shy, started getting flustered. "Oh, no, no, no . . . we were just talking . . ." she turned toward the sink and rinsed off the spinach leaves. ". . . girl talk . . ." The words reassured her, because her energy level went up a notch, ". . . your wife, Jack . . ." she tried to come up with something to say . . . "is really . . . really . . . terrific . . . great . . ."

"The best," I said.

Fran, squeezing out a bunch of spinach leaves, turned and beamed at Barbara. "She's doing me a world of good."

Frank's scream broke through the hum of the air-conditioning. The word "drink" came through loud and clear.

"Oh, sorry, Fran, but Frank wanted his drink." She didn't say anything. Didn't even move. I pressed on. "Said something about the small ice cubes . . ." Still nothing. It was me getting flustered. ". . . I think he wanted six . . . yeah, it was six of them."

With a sigh, and very slowly, Fran wiped her hands on the towel hanging over the sink and reached up into the cabinet for a glass. I didn't look at Barbara but you could feel the disapproval in the room as Fran, hunching her shoulders, filled the glass with ice, poured in the gin precisely and then, opening a fresh bottle of tonic, filled it to the rim. She had just finished cutting the lime into a paper-thin slice when Frank yelled again.

* * *

Dinner was the same. The usual. Fran scurried around the table, making sure our plates were filled with meat and potatoes. And being very certain that Frank's meat was cut up. "A man can't waste his time cutting up his meat," he once explained to me. "He's got important things to do. Anyway, Fran likes to do it. She's a housewife. Takes care of the house. She's good at it."

All the way home, Barbara just kept repeating one word. "Asshole." Said with total conviction. Beyond a reasonable doubt. Like a judgment.

June

S	M	T	W	T	F	S
					~~1~~	~~2~~
~~3~~	~~4~~	~~5~~	~~6~~	~~7~~	~~8~~	~~9~~
~~10~~	~~11~~	~~12~~	~~13~~	~~14~~	~~15~~	~~16~~
~~17~~	~~18~~	~~19~~	20	21	22	23
24	25	26	27	28	29	30

July

S	M	T	W	T	F	S
1	2	3	4	5	6	7
8	9	10	11	12	13	14
15	16	17	18	19	20	21
22	23	24	25	26	27	28
29	30	31				

August

S	M	T	W	T	F	S
			1	2	3	4
5	6	7	8	9	10	11
12	13	14	15	16	17	18
19	20	21	22	23	24	25
26	27	28	29	30	31	

Chapter Three

FRANK BERNSTEIN was a big ball of sweat. I figured he was losing a pound a minute there in his driveway at seven in the morning cursing his wife Fran for all she was worth. In Frank's eyes, at that moment, Fran wasn't worth very much.

"She left the radio on," he kept screaming over and over. "The damn fucking car radio was on all night." His white shirt was soaked through. I don't know how long he had been standing there, but I had just opened our garage door, ready to leave for work. And Frank went on hollering. "Doesn't she know it drains the battery? Doesn't that damn woman know anything?" He looked at me. Before I could think of something to say he pointed to his ranch house. "And now she won't let me back into the house. Do you believe it? She left the dishes last night, Klein. Left me alone with the dishes because she wanted to go for a *ride*. Why the fuck does she have to go for a ride at eleven at night, Klein. Got any ideas?"

He started toward me, finger trembling. I thought the man

was going to have a heart attack. From the way his shirt clung to his pudgy body he had been out here a while. The noise of the neighborhood's air conditioners had kept his screams unheard.

"Calm down, Frank. I'll take you to the train."

"It's your wife's fault, Klein. It's all your wife's doing. She has taken a sweet gentle obedient woman like Fran and turned her into . . . into . . ." His face was turning redder as he tried to come up with a word awful enough to describe what Fran Bernstein had become. Finally, he found it. ". . . a terrorist. That's it. She's a terrorist. Your wife's lousy group has done that to one of the gentlest women ever. Do you know she wants to change her *name?"*

I tried to stay calm and position myself between my house and Frank Bernstein in case he wanted to charge. "What was Fran's maiden name?"

He looked away, back at his house, but it still was shut tight and his car wasn't moving. He turned back to me, wiping some sweat off his forehead with the back of his soaked sleeve. "Bea," he said.

"Fran Bea? What kind of name is that?"

"You idiot, Bea was her first name."

"So why did she change it?"

He stood there shaking his head at my stupidity. "Because it was cute," he said. "Frank and Fran. Get it?"

"Why not Bea and Bernie," I said without thinking. It only riled him.

"Frank and Fran is cute. Bea and Bernie is dumb. Frank and Bea is dumber."

I walked toward him. It was like wading through a pizza oven. I didn't think the temperature had gone down a single degree overnight. "Listen Frank, why don't you let me drive you to the station. You can make the seven thirty-five. Have a nice relaxing ride. Read the paper. And when you come home, everything will be fine with you and Fran."

He looked up at me. "*Bea*. You forgot. Her name is *Bea*. Two weeks with your wife and her fuckin' group therapy and she changes her name. Great psychologist. Gets patients to change their names. Not to mention locking their husbands out of the house." He was getting worked up again. "The woman doesn't even have a license. And she's allowed to run around getting women to leave their car radios on all night. Can you believe it? Can you *believe* it?"

I tried putting my arm around his shoulders but Frank shook me off and started back toward his driveway. I followed him. When he got to his car he kicked it in the front tire and turned back to me. He seemed surprised to find me so close to him. "She bolted the doors," he said quietly. "I suppose I could kick in one of the windows, but that would be expensive." The CPA in him tried to get out. "Glass isn't cheap you know," he explained.

"Look," I said, as if talking to one of my patients having problems catching their breath. I was calm, reasonable, everything Frank was not. "Why don't I take you to the station?"

"No, no, no,"—he shook his head many times—"I'm going to walk. I'll show her. I'll have cardiac arrest. Make her happy." He reached in the car and grabbed his briefcase and coat. He slammed the door shut with a vengeance.

"Damn Germans." He gave his Audi a fresh kick. "Trying to punish us for the war. Teach a Jew to buy a German car." He walked out the driveway. As he passed my house he directed his finger to my bedroom window. I could hear him cursing as he headed down the street.

I walked slowly back to my car in the garage. Before I could get there the front door opened and Barbara stuck her head out. She was still in her nightgown, but she didn't look sleepy.

"What was that all about?" she asked.

"Frank was upset."

"I heard."

"Blames you. And your group."

"It's not a real group. We just sit around and talk."

"I know. I know." I didn't want to start anything.

"One week we've done it. Maybe three times. That's it.

They're more like coffee breaks than group therapy."

"Well whatever they are, Frank isn't too thrilled."

Barbara stuck her head a little further out the door. "Tough noogies." She shut the door, and I went to get in my car. I wondered where this so-called therapy was going. I turned the key in the ignition. Hot as it was, I felt a chill.

At lunch I got the second complaint about my wife. Dave paused between gulps of chili to tell me his problems. Harold Goldberg had already left the table, cursing his cantaloupe. Dave and I were alone. He seemed shyer, more uncomfortable than usual. Finally, just before I was ready to pick up my check, he cleared his throat meaningfully.

"Uh, Jack, I wonder if you have a few minutes."

I put down the check and waited while Dave got up the nerve to talk to me. Dave, as I've said, was as shy as his father was aggressive. His father had made the bank successful, and his son had come along for the ride. Dave never forgot that, and his father never let him. Even his death, three years before, hadn't changed Dave's fearfulness or his unremitting hatred of the old man.

He coughed a couple times before getting out the words. "It's about . . . Jane."

Here it comes. First Frank, now Dave.

He fumbled with his oyster crackers, tossing them back and forth in his hand. In a few seconds they were crumbs. Finally I grabbed the bag in midair, "What is it, Dave? I've got an appointment."

He licked his lips and then, folding his hands in front of him, looked at the saltshaker and began talking to it. "Well, you see . . . Jane . . . she just is different." He paused. I sat there and noticed I had five minutes to my next appointment. A friend of one of my daughters walked by the window of The Lunch Box in a pair of shorts about four inches long. I remembered she was only twelve, and then turned back to Dave, who was trying to talk and study his chili at the same time. He looked as if he was counting beans. I glanced at my watch again and announced my impatience with a couple discreet coughs. At last, he looked up. "She's acting like"—his voice rose—"my father."

Dave's face turned red. I remembered how Dave would try to avoid the old man all day long. He never ate at the round table until the day after his father's funeral. So I kept quiet.

Dave went on. "She's picking on me, Jack."

"Maybe it's the heat?"

He shook his head. "No, no, it's not like that. She keeps berating me. I mean, if I closed my eyes I could almost imagine . . . him . . . there."

"We all go through . . ."

He was paying no attention. "You know how snide he used to be, how petty and mean and vindictive he was to me? Always picking. Always trying to find something to make fun of me . . ."

I put my hand on his sleeve. "Dave, listen . . ."

But he wasn't hearing. "And now, Jane. Sweet, dear Jane is acting like that." He shook his head. And paused. Finally, he looked at me. "It's Barbara's fault." He said it quietly.

"Wait till it cools off. The weather is doing strange things." I reached for my check. I didn't want to hear any more. I didn't want to think about any more of it. "I have a patient, Dave, I'm sorry."

Dave nodded slowly and stared down into his greasy chili. I noticed that he had gotten some of it on the lapel of his seersucker suit jacket.

"Maybe you should talk to Barbara about it?"

He shook his head "no" a couple times.

"She probably would be happy to talk to you."

Dave Redfield looked up at me. It was not a pleasant look. "I don't have anything to say to her."

I nodded and got out of there fast. I threw my seventy-five-cent tip on the table. I couldn't wait to get back to the office.

* * *

"You're late, doctor." My nurse Mary said it with a "tsk" in her voice. Mary seemed always about to shake her head at some affront to the medical profession. Fifty and virginal, Mary was a great shot-giver and the only person neater than my daughter Mandy or me. She straightened out the suit coat I had hung up in the closet, making sure that the lapels weren't too curled from the heat outside.

"I'm sorry, Mary, but I was delayed."

She checked the flaps on my pocket to make sure they weren't creased, before helping me into my long white smock.

I looked at my watch, it was only four minutes after one. "I'm sure little Cynthia won't mind that she's not getting her shots on time."

Mary went out to get little Cynthia Markowitz.

The afternoon was, for the most part, uneventful. The usual. The same. Normally, it would all make me feel good. Safe. Settled. But now it gave me so much time to think. About Frank. About Dave. Even about Marty. But especially about Barbara.

When my four-thirty appointment cancelled I decided to see if Arnie Melton, the shrink next door, was free. Summer in Lake View was filled with cancelled appointments. Tennis matches and golf games ran late. Or, on days like this one, the burning temperatures kept people from making the trip from air-conditioned housing to air-conditioned cars to air-conditioned offices.

He had been cancelled out too.

"In winter, they'd never miss a session," Arnie said as he sat back on his couch. I was sitting in the chair that was his. A big black leather swivel job, right next to the couch.

Arnie had moved in next door to me a couple of years before, but we hadn't really started talking until we discovered we were using the same billing service. For some reason, doctors feel closer to people who use their accounts receivable collection agency than colleagues who share the same specialty.

"Actually," I leaned back in the chair, "I'm surprised that Mr.

Oksner missed his appointment. He always wants me to give him his shots, so he makes these special appointments."

"You don't always give shots?" Arnie asked as he put his feet up underneath him.

"No, not usually." Damn, it was a nice office. Warm, woody, it made you want to talk about your problems. If you had any, of course. And I loved the chair. I sank into it.

"Your nurse gives them?"

I settled back into the coolness of the leather. Maybe I should have become a shrink. It seemed so comforting. Then I remembered the question. I sat back up. "Yes, usually. You see I don't make regular appointments for the majority of my patients. They come in once a week to get their shots. They can do it whenever they want. I talk to them if they're having any problems. Otherwise, Mary gives them their injections."

"Is Mary the one who never smiles?"

I nodded. "She takes things seriously. Dedicated to medicine."

Arnie sighed. "Nurses have that tendency."

I scrunched deeper into the soft chair. I wondered how he could remember to listen to patients' problems. I would be sleeping within five minutes.

"Jack. Jack."

I snapped to attention. "I'm sorry. It's just that this heat . . ."

"Don't apologize. It's a comfortable chair."

"No, no, I really think it's the heat. It wears you out. Also the air-conditioning doesn't help."

"Why'd you come in?"

He was sitting there all calm and psychiatric. A nice rumpled look. Wire-rimmed glasses, curly hair, baggy suits. Very psychiatric. More urban than suburban. Right now, he looked serious. "I had a cancellation. That's all."

"Oh, come on, Jack, you could have gone home or given a couple shots yourself. What is it? Impotence? Bestiality? Depression?"

I tried to wave away his options. "No, no, it's nothing. With me, that is."

He sat up. Interested. He straightened his glasses. Got a smile on his face like, I'm sure, hunters get when they spot big game. "A friend?" he asked. "A good friend," he went on, "who has this unique problem but doesn't want to see a shrink? Come on, Jack. I know the scenario. Nobody drops in on a shrink."

I tried to sit all the way forward on the chair. My seat was barely on the edge. "Well . . . see . . . it's . . . not . . . like me . . . exactly."

He held his hands up. "Don't tell me. I got it. Your wife. You think she's seeing another man?"

"Don't be ridiculous."

"You want her to see another man?"

"Come on, Arnie."

"Woman? She's seeing another woman?"

I was starting to get angry. "I told you it's not anything like that. Sex has nothing to do with this."

He nodded his head. "Of course not. This has to do with whether or not you're getting enough bran. Come on, Jack."

I almost jumped up, but thought better of it. That would be much too dramatic. "Listen, I'm telling you, this has nothing to do with me."

He looked at me. He seemed very short, sitting there with that smirk on his face. Actually it wasn't a smirk so much as a tight grin. "Or your wife."

I noticed the geometric prints on the wall. They seemed out of character with the rest of the room. Maybe he hadn't redecorated from the last shrink. I wondered what part of the room was his? The wood or the pictures? I turned to him. "Well, actually. . ."

"Ah, ha, I knew it. Am I right?"

I just nodded.

"Thank you." He seemed to relax. "Shrinks need victories too, you know. A large part of my practice is making good guesses. Your problem is probably that you're going through a mid-life crisis. How about it?"

"How about murder."

He didn't act shocked. "In the past or future?"

"Symbolic."

"That's all right. Murder is good. Revenge in any form tends to motivate."

"What would you think of something called murder therapy?"

Once again, he appeared to take it calmly. I guess shrinks have heard everything. "You still talking about symbolic murders?"

"Yeah." I sat back. "I mean nobody is out there killing anyone. Just talking about it."

"Who is the shrink involved?"

"No shrink. My wife's doing it."

"Some kind of graduate thesis?"

"I don't think so. It's just something she decided to do with our neighbors. I guess these women get together and talk about who they wanted to kill in the past."

"Sounds like one of those encounter sessions. You don't hear too much about them these days."

"I don't think it's the same thing, Arnie."

"Similar. Of a kind." He smiled at me with a look that I knew should make me want to change subjects.

"No, you see, someone actually did kill someone. Her husband . . ."

He looked up. Interested. "Before or after these groups?"

"Before." All of a sudden a buzzer went off outside his office. I turned to look, he just kept staring at me. I figured he wanted me to go on. "Apparently it's had quite an effect on the other women on the block. Two husbands have complained to me about their wives."

"And how they're asserting themselves?"

"Something like that. One wants to change her name, the other one's acting like the husband's late, hated father."

"How old are these people? The women."

"Early forties."

"I wouldn't worry about it." He smiled distractedly. As if he weren't interested.

"The other husbands . . ."

Arnie started to get up. "Tell them to relax. It all sounds normal. I wouldn't get worked up. Tell the husbands it'll calm down. People tend to get infatuated with initial sessions. You know the way people taking writing classes figure after the first session that they're going to write the story of Civilization before the next class? It's the same with therapy. Give it a couple weeks, boredom will soon set in. Anyway, it's summer. Heat does strange things to people, and therapists. Especially women, and men, who find out that they're not thirty-five any more."

"So you're not concerned . . ." We both stood up.

"Yeah, that Mrs. Kaplan will break the couch again."

"Fat?"

He shook his head. "A bouncer. Tends to visualize her sexual fantasies. Not great for the springs."

"Thanks anyway."

He walked toward the door to the reception room. "Don't be silly, it was nice making a good guess."

I started following him to the door. He pointed to another exit. "That leads out to the hallway. I'm sure Mrs. Kaplan doesn't want to see her allergist."

I tried to think of all the Kaplans I had as patients. I gave up after nine. I opened the door to the hallway. "Thanks again."

"Sure. Call me if someone else gets killed."

I opened the unmarked door and told myself that the whole thing was silly. Temporary. Nothing to get concerned over.

June

S	M	T	W	T	F	S
					~~1~~	~~2~~
~~3~~	~~4~~	~~5~~	~~6~~	~~7~~	~~8~~	~~9~~
~~10~~	~~11~~	~~12~~	~~13~~	~~14~~	~~15~~	~~16~~
~~17~~	~~18~~	~~19~~	~~20~~	21	22	23
24	25	26	27	28	29	30

July

S	M	T	W	T	F	S
1	2	3	4	5	6	7
8	9	10	11	12	13	14
15	16	17	18	19	20	21
22	23	24	25	26	27	28
29	30	31				

August

S	M	T	W	T	F	S
			1	2	3	4
5	6	7	8	9	10	11
12	13	14	15	16	17	18
19	20	21	22	23	24	25
26	27	28	29	30	31	

Chapter Four

"WELL?" BARBARA asked as I poured us each a glass of wine before dinner.

"Well, what?" I sat down. Across from her in the living room. She was on the big leather couch. I got one of those contraptions with steel and strips of leather.

I knew I was going to get a backache tonight. The air-conditioning was hitting me in the shoulders. But I didn't want to move. We always sat in those seats. Always had a glass of wine before dinner. To change the routine would invite questions.

"Well, what did Frank Bernstein have to say this morning?"

I took a sip. And put the glass down on a coaster. I reached over to put one under Barbara's glass. "You know what he said. He was pissed about Fran locking him out."

Barbara smiled. "Good. It's time. The man has treated her like dog food for years."

I nodded.

"And what about Dave Redfield?"

That got my attention. "What about Dave Redfield?"

"I hear he's almost as upset as Frank. And since the two of you have lunch together . . ."

"At the same table, Barb."

"Whatever you call it. I just thought he might be talking to you about things."

"Things like him and Jane?"

She reached for her glass and nodded.

"He did mention something."

"And what did he mention?"

"I think the word 'mean' was in there somewhere."

Barbara reached for her glass and took a big gulp. She seemed satisfied. "Good."

I tried to remain calm. "Good?"

"I think it's good that these women are finally doing something about their situations."

"You mean you're doing something about their situations."

Barbara and I seldom argued. But the way her face was set made me think it was time for a confrontation. I wanted to avoid it.

"They," she said, as she leaned forward to look directly at me, "had to do something about it. Can't you understand that?"

"This is beginning to sound like a return to the seventies."

Her mouth tightened. Thinned out. "What is that supposed to mean?"

My tush started squirming. I really hated confrontations. "Just . . . that . . ."

Impatient, Barbara tried using her waving hands to push me along. "Get it out already, Jack. C'mon, c'mon . . . talk to me."

I sped up. "That . . . that . . . it all seems like one of those seventies cliches."

"What cliches?" Barbara kept waving me on. "What cliches are you talking about?"

"You know what I mean. Women have already gone through the 'I'm not feeling fulfilled phase . . .' "

She pointed a thin, sharp finger at me. For a moment it

looked like a blade. "It doesn't mean that some of them aren't still married to shits."

"They chose to be married to them." My voice was getting stronger. Or maybe it was my imagination.

"Choices, choices. Who really has choices?"

"People." I said softly.

"That's what you think."

I decided to end this fruitless discussion. "Want to go out for dinner?" I asked. Her stare turned into a furrowed brow.

"What?"

"Dinner," I repeated.

"This is serious, Jack."

"So is my stomach." I got up. She just shook her head slowly. I took the glasses into the kitchen and put them in the dishwasher.

Angelo's was not the best restaurant in Lake View. There was a fancy French place that people from Chicago would come to in droves. But for all those who lived in Lake View, Angelo's was the place to eat. It was safe, secure. Angelo would greet you at the door as if he remembered you, smilingly usher you to the bar where you would wait for half an hour with the rest of Angelo's good friends whose names he didn't know, and then you'd settle down for a meal of average pasta. You wouldn't touch the veal, and the chicken seemed to have grown old rather ungracefully, but the pasta didn't contain anything more au courant than a sprig of broccoli di rape. You would never find a smoked duck breast in a plate of Angelo's spaghetti.

"How ya doin'. Lookin' great." With a slap on the shoulder and a kiss on Barbara's cheek, chunky, moon-faced Angelo gave us his standard greeting. "A few minutes wait, that's all. Promise. Promise." Gracefully he led us to the bar in the back of the room, past tables filled with people I either knew socially or medically. I smiled and nodded as Angelo paraded us by the tables laden with garlic bread and red-sauced pastas. "Great to see you," Angelo kept saying, as we found our way to the high-backed red leather stools. "Soon. Soon." He waved, and left us there.

"What I like about the guy is his sincerity," I said to Barbara, as we took our seats.

She had calmed down on the ride over. She wasn't smiling but at least she was talking. "One of these years, he might even know you." She swiveled a little in her chair to case the bar. Everyone looked familiar, including the bartender.

Angelo's son Jimmy, whom I had treated for an allergy to wool, came over to take our orders. "Dr. Klein. Mrs. Klein. What can I get you?" "A couple white wines, Jimmy," I said with my first sincere smile of the night.

Barbara said, "One white wine. I'll have a dry martini. On the rocks. Olives. Two."

Jimmy smiled and went off to get our drinks.

I looked at Barbara, who had swiveled around to look at the restaurant. "Since when are you drinking martinis?"

"I felt like a martini."

It wasn't worth talking about. "Tough day?"

She shook her head. "Not really, although Bea was upset this morning."

Bea? Bea? I thought of all the people we knew. No Beas. "Who's Bea?"

Jimmy brought over our drinks. Barbara took a sip before letting me in on the secret. "Bea is Fran."

"Yes, yes . . . Frank told me this morning. That's right, he thought Frank and Bea wasn't cute enough."

"The man is an asshole." Barbara took a larger swallow of her drink.

"A shmuck maybe." I tried to sound warm. "But not an asshole."

She took a bigger swallow. "Asshole. Asshole. Asshole."

No more nice guy. "Shmuck. Shmuck. Shmuck."

She stuck her tongue out at me.

"Mature. Very mature."

"Cute, real cute," the female voice said. "I never stuck my tongue out at Marty. You never knew what the guy would do with it."

"Shmuck," I said as I turned around to see Angelo deposit Elizabeth Siegal at the bar.

"That, too," she said, as Angelo guided her to a seat next to Barbara.

"Great to see you." He smiled at her as he backed away. "Won't be long now. Promise."

"Now that's a shmuck," Elizabeth said as she straightened her pink-and-white checked blouse and ran her fingers through her red ringlets. "Hi, guys."

"What are you doing here?" I asked.

Barbara drained her glass and looked at Elizabeth kindly, putting a hand on hers. "I'm glad you're getting out. We should have called you. It was thoughtless of me."

"Don't be silly, Barb." Elizabeth dismissed her sweetness with a toss of her head. "I just figured if no one was going to ask me out to dinner—a guy, I'm talking about—then I might as well go by myself."

Barbara patted Elizabeth's hand. "Anytime. We're always here for you." She looked at me. I nodded.

"Anytime, Elizabeth. In fact, why not have dinner with us tonight?" I said cheerfully.

The merry widow agreed. We all drank to it.

By the time we were finishing our coffee, Elizabeth had managed to make us forget Bea and Frank as well as Fran and Frank.

"So all of a sudden," she explained, "the insurance comes through and I got enough money to do what I want. And my mother thinks she should get a piece of it."

"Did Marty leave her money?" Barbara asked. She was ignoring her tea. She was still sipping her second martini, which didn't look as easy to swallow as the first one.

"Nah, but he said, in the will, that I should watch out for her." Elizabeth leaned across the table. "I'll watch out for her. The horny bitch."

Angelo walked by the table and smiled. "How is everything?"

Elizabeth smiled back. "Awful."

He patted her shoulder and turned to greet a newly arrived couple. "Wonderful. Great to see you . . ."

"Marty must have taken sincere lessons from that creep." Elizabeth shook her head and took the last sip of her vodka stinger. "The two of 'em . . ." Elizabeth wove a bit in her seat. She grabbed her stinger for support.

Barbara reached over to pat her hand. "I know it's tough. But try to focus your hate."

Elizabeth did some more weaving. At last she took a small sip of her drink. It brought her back. "That's just it, there's nobody left to hate. I can't hate Marty anymore. My mother is still my mother."

"What about your first husband?" Barbara said.

I was about to ask who that was when I decided that the less I talked the more I'd find out.

Elizabeth shook her head sadly when she started to think about her first ex. "He was a kid. He isn't worth hating."

"Yes he was, yes he was." Barbara was holding onto Elizabeth's glass. "He left you."

"Well, yeah, but I had been screwing around with Marty." She tried to lift the glass. Barbara wasn't letting go of it.

"But only because he wasn't satisfying your needs. Remember, they were your needs." Barbara underlined the word "your." I was trying to figure out exactly what her needs were.

"Yeah, but that's only because he was so little. I mean, I didn't know. The guy was six three, I figured his shlong had to be at least . . . average." I nodded. Elizabeth smiled at me. Barbara kept looking into Elizabeth's eyes.

"How ya doin'?" Angelo passed by the table in his gray-and-white paisley sports coat with the open-necked cream-colored shirt, the long pointed collar and the humongous chain his wife had given him for Christmas. He passed on before we could say anything back. His 'great t' see you's" followed him like a gigolo's empty promises.

"Maybe if he had had one of those penile implants," Elizabeth said, shaking her head sadly over her stinger.

"I don't think it makes it any longer," I explained, placing a couple of twenties over the check.

Elizabeth kept shaking her head. "Poor guy."

Barbara reached over to pat Elizabeth's hand. "You. You have to think of you. Not him, them. You."

I slid out of the booth before I heard any more.

June

S	M	T	W	T	F	S
					1	2
3	4	5	6	7	8	9
10	11	12	13	14	15	16
17	18	19	20	21	22	23
24	25	26	27	28	29	30

July

S	M	T	W	T	F	S
1	2	3	4	5	6	7
8	9	10	11	12	13	14
15	16	17	18	19	20	21
22	23	24	25	26	27	28
29	30	31				

August

S	M	T	W	T	F	S
			1	2	3	4
5	6	7	8	9	10	11
12	13	14	15	16	17	18
19	20	21	22	23	24	25
26	27	28	29	30	31	

Chapter Five

ARNIE MELTON walked into The Lunch Box about five minutes after I did. Harold Goldberg was threatening to throw his cottage cheese at Dave Redfield if Dave slurped another bite of chili, when Arnie walked in and looked around for a place to sit amidst the sea of womanhood. I waved and he walked over to our table.

"I had another cancellation," he explained as he came walking up to me. He was wearing a soggy looking seersucker suit with a white shirt and red tie. Harold Goldberg checked out the goods. I could hear him mumble as he shoved a strawberry into his mouth, "thirty-nine short."

"Eat with us." I gestured to the empty chair between Harold and Dave.

"Thanks." He took the seat and nodded to both of them. "I don't think I've had lunch since I've been in town."

"Arnie Melton this is Harold Goldberg . . ." I began the introductions.

Harold reached out a pudgy hand. "Goldberg's Men's Store. Down the street." Leaning toward Arnie he whispered loudly, "Great deal on seersuckers. One left in your size."

". . . and this is Dave Redfield. From the bank."

Dave smiled and nodded. Arnie smiled back.

"We all eat here. Every day," I explained.

"I nibble." Harold grimaced at a piece of honeydew. "They eat. I used to eat."

"Diet?" Arnie asked, looking at Harold's depressing fruit plate.

"Yeah, my skinny doctor told me it was this or this." He made a motion as if drawing a knife across his multifolded neck.

"Arnie's a doctor," I explained.

"Yeah,"—suddenly Harold was interested—"you got any better diet than this? Maybe one that includes onion rings? I'd settle for a couple eggs with home fries. Crispy on the edges."

"It's fine with me." Arnie reached for a menu that was in the center of the table. "I'm a psychiatrist. Whatever makes you happy."

Harold let go of his forkful of melon and looked curiously at Arnie. "I think something in a darker color would be better. Seersucker is too frivolous." He looked over at me and my khaki suit. "Seersucker is okay for allergists. Casual-like. But shrinks need to be serious."

"Sneezing is serious to some people, Harold," I said as Arlene gave me my tuna plate.

Harold paid no attention to me, but concentrated his salesmanship techniques on Arnie. "Perhaps a nice pinstripe."

"How about a beard and a pipe," Arnie said with a smile, as Arlene hovered over him.

"Whatcha gonna have?" she asked between chomps on her Juicy Fruit.

"A turkey sandwich . . ."

Before he could go on, the three of us, almost in unison, started to shake our head "no."

"Turkey roll," Arlene explained.

Arnie looked up and down the menu. "Then chicken salad."

Another tripartite shake of the heads. Dave explained "Old turkey roll goes into the chicken salad."

"Stick to your essentials," Arlene said. "Eggs ain't bad."

Arnie put down his menu. "How about french toast?"

We all looked at each other. Finally I looked up at Arlene. "Anybody ever have french toast?"

She thought about it for a few seconds. "Yeah, couple kids. Looks alright. Want bacon, sausage or ham with it?"

Arnie shook his head. "Just an iced tea."

Arlene seemed satisfied. She went away to the sounds from surrounding tables of "More Sanka!"

"Arnie started working here about a year ago," I explained to Harold and Dave. "He's in the office next to mine."

"Are you originally from Lake View?" Dave asked tentatively, starting out with the first question on the list of "things to ask a new acquaintance" he got from Dale Carnegie.

"New York."

"You married?" Harold asked, shoving the remains of his blueberries under a wilted lettuce leaf. He hated for Arlene to scream at him.

"No. Divorced."

Everybody waited for him to go on. Obviously, he wasn't planning to say more. Finally, Arlene brought over the french toast. Harold examined it.

"It looks okay. Want me to taste it for you?"

Arnie smiled at the fat man. "That won't be necessary."

I noticed Shari Herman, my receptionist, walking through the restaurant on her way back from her daily lunchtime shopping excursion. She was carrying three shoe boxes and a take-out cup of yogurt. She stopped at a table to show off her shoes to various women her age and older. I could hear a lot of ooohing and aaahing across the room.

"Isn't that your receptionist?" Arnie asked as he started in on his french toast.

"Yeah, Shari."

"Attractive," Arnie said.

"A fellow divorcée, Arn." Harold gave him a wink.

"Cute," he said with a nod.

I looked over at her. I had never thought of Shari Herman as anything more than a former patient who happened to grow up. I had first met her as a teenager. Then lost track of her when she went off to college and got married. But, three months ago, she appeared with a rash on her arm. I diagnosed it as nervousness due to the anxiety of her divorce. She recovered and took on the rapidly rotating job of being my receptionist. A position that had been filled for the past five years by women who were "in between" things. Marriages, schools, children, retirement. Nobody thought of it as a career. They quickly became bored with the routine, and as soon as something better came along, left.

So, when Arnie mentioned that she was cute, it surprised me. She was a patient and a receptionist. Two reasons not to notice how attractive she was.

"Not what I figured your type is, Arn," Harold said joshingly. He was starting his jolly fat man routine. When he was trying to convince a customer that the suit really did fit.

"What's my type, Harold?" Arnie asked.

"You know, intellectual."

"Long hair? Sandals? Carries around a book by some South American writer, in the original language?"

Harold nodded. "Yeah, a hippie type. Real smart. No sense of clothes."

"That was my first wife."

"So, now you're going for . . ." I didn't finish.

"Style." Arnie looked around the room. At the thousands of dollars in fashion. "I want to meet a woman who doesn't think makeup is a dirty word." He gestured towards Shari, who was taking out a pair of white shoes from an expensive looking box.

"Look at her. She's good-looking. Dresses well. I'm sure she's almost as bright as Clarissa . . ."

"Your wife?" I asked.

"Yeah," and then, shaking his head to get rid of Clarissa, "so why shouldn't I go out with someone who'd rather see a Bill Murray movie than a concert of baroque Christmas music."

"Someone who likes Palm Springs for the winter," Harold added.

"Aspen for Christmas." Arnie smiled.

I jumped in. "Country clubs."

"Houses with glass coffee tables and big chandeliers." Harold was starting to get worked up.

Arnie nodded. "Right. I'm tired of furniture that looks like graduate school."

"And women who look like graduate students?" I was getting into it as enthusiastically as Harold.

Arnie was nodding even faster. "Yes. Yes. That's the point. I just want to be in love and be happy. With someone who's nice to look at. Who cares about how she looks. Who thinks it's important."

"It is important." Harold pounded the table with a chubby fist. "How we look is how we are."

Dave seemed confused. But then, as usual, nobody was paying much attention to him. Harold didn't even appear jealous of his greasy plate.

"Shari probably is fairly bright. She does a decent job at the office," I said, looking over at her. She seemed thrilled to be showing off her purchases. And the women she was showing them to seemed equally as thrilled by them. "She just wants to be . . ." I tried to figure out exactly what it was she did want to be.

Arnie guessed first. ". . . happy. That's the point. Shari, and everybody else around her, wants to be happy. They want to suffer as little as possible. And I don't think that's so terrible to want to be smiling all the time. You don't have to have shock treatment to think that life is good . . ."

Dave jumped in. Leaped feet first into the conversation.

"You're right, you're right. That's the problem today. Women aren't being women. Everybody's too . . . too . . . uppity."

We all looked at him as if he were slightly mad. Arnie spoke to him softly. "I don't think . . . uppity . . . is exactly the right word, Dave."

"Yes it is. Yes it is. Women aren't happy being women anymore. They just want to be different. Different." He was repeating almost everything he said.

Arnie was settling into a professional pose. He leaned forward. Sincerity oozed from him. "I hope you didn't misunderstand what I said. I didn't mean that women shouldn't work or go to school or be independent. That's not necessarily wrong . . ."

"Yes, yes. It is wrong." The voice was rising. Becoming shriller. "People have roles. They should, should, do them."

"People change, you know, like me." Arnie was speaking softer now. "That's inevitable."

But Dave wasn't buying it. "It doesn't have to be," he said, pulling his check off the table.

"More Sanka?" Arlene was hovering over him with the pot, but Dave wasn't paying attention. Shoving the chair back from the table, he jumped up and pushed Arlene away. But her coffee didn't move away very gracefully. With a big splash, it poured down the front of Dave's suit. Arlene looked at him and shook her head sadly. Finally, she reached in her pocket and grabbed a towel and started to wipe up his jacket. Dave just stood there, looking forlorn.

"You see what happens when you get excited?" Harold said, as if talking to a child. "Now you're all messy."

"It'll dry, Dave," I said reassuringly as Arlene wiped as much liquid as she could off his suit. One of the busboys ran over to mop up the floor. Dave just stood there, looking sadly at his coat and pants.

"It'll be okay," Arnie said reassuringly.

The busboy and Arlene both left, leaving Dave still standing there. Only his check was dry.

"You got nobody to blame but yourself, Redfield," Harold told him, joylessly shoving a blackberry into his mouth.

"Why don't you go home and change?" I suggested.

"I'd rather not," he said firmly, and then hurried out.

"Guy is acting weirder than usual," Harold announced before he was two feet away.

"He seems to be under some stress," Arnie said.

Harold looked amused. "What does he have to be stressed about? He finally got what he wanted." Harold turned to Arnie. "His father dies a couple years ago. Which, I gotta tell you, is what the jerk always hoped would happen. He was so afraid of the old man, he couldn't lift his head off his chest. So Poppa goes, and you figure maybe the idiot son would all of a sudden get happy. The old geezer left him a sackful of money. What more does he want? But no, he still acts like a jerk. Me, I got to fight every day to sell a suit. Him, he just sits there like a shmuck and takes in the money. Major psychiataric problems, right, Arnie?"

Arnie shrugged in a noncommittal way.

I tried to defend my neighbor. "He may have other problems, Harold."

"Go on. Does his wife fool around? No way. Does he?" The notion gave Harold a good laugh.

Arnie just sat there eating his french toast. "I think Dave's going through some tough times," was all he said between bites.

"And I'm not?" Harold said, in a voice that was starting to turn shrill. "My suit sales are down 20 percent and I eat Kibbles and Bits twice a day. And that long shmuck is going through hard times?" He pointed to the doorway. Dave was walking past the window, his hands trying to cover the brown stain on his crotch. Two twelve-year-old girls were looking at him and covering their mouths to keep the giggles in.

"Harold, c'mon already," I said.

He looked over at Arnie who was concentrating on his french

toast. He seemed to remember that he had a potential customer as he directed his words to the top of Arnie's bowed head. "I tend to get excited," Harold smoothed. "It's natural. Extremely natural." He looked over at me for support. I drank my Sanka without a nod. Harold turned back to Arnie, who was finally looking up from his plate. It was a noncommittal expression. Harold kept on going, trying to coax a smile from a member of the medical establishment. "Actually I read where people who get excited live longer." There was the hint of a question mark at the end of his sentence. He looked at me for agreement. And then, when no nods were forthcoming, turned back to Arnie, who was reaching for his check. As Arnie stood up, he smiled down at Harold.

"Nice to meet you." He left some change on the table and started walking toward the cashier. I stood up and grabbed my check. Harold looked at me with concern on his face.

"You sure that guy's a medical doctor? Not just some psychologist or a social worker? I mean, those people don't really know medicine. Right?"

"He's a real live doctor, Harold. Even went to medical school."

"You actually see his diploma, Jack?"

I nodded. "On the wall of his office. Big one."

Harold shook his head sadly. "I read somewhere about being excited. It's okay, I'm tellin' you. It doesn't hurt anybody. Helps the heart get going."

I smiled and started walking away. I could hear Harold sighing behind me. He would stay calm, and worried, for the rest of the day.

Arnie and I walked back to our building together. We were the only ones on the street in coats and ties. Everybody else was trying to wear as few clothes as possible.

"You think we'd be less dignified in shorts and T-shirts?" I asked Arnie as we passed three women in tennis outfits. They seemed a lot cooler than us.

"Probably not to us. But I think our patients wouldn't feel as good about paying us all that money."

I nodded. "You're right. Although allergists generally have it easier than psychiatrists."

"In what way?"

"People don't take us seriously. We're at the tail end of the medical profession. Along with dermatologists."

"You really believe that?"

We stopped at the corner to let some convertibles zoom past. Two were driven by teenage patients of mine. The third, by another lady tennis player.

"See those kids." I pointed to the red BMW convertible. "They see me once a week. But it's like going to the barber's. No big deal. When they go away to college, they'll stop coming back to me for shots. Sneezing doesn't seem too traumatic to them after a while. Especially after they're not around to annoy their parents with the sniffling."

We crossed the street. I noticed there weren't a lot of other people walking. We slowed down as we got to the other side. The ninety-five degree temperature was accompanied by humidity borrowed from the rain forests of Central America.

Arnie wiped the top layer of sweat off his forehehad. "What about asthma?"

"Asthma's different. Although a lot of people don't take that seriously either. They come to me, get a prescription for inhalators and just use that."

"Isn't that dangerous?"

"Could be. But I get a lot more sneezers than wheezers in the office. For some reason, people with hay fever think that shots do more good than people with asthma."

"Are they right?"

I shook my head. "No, but running noses are more annoying to people than bad breathing. It's not socially acceptable. For the same reason pimples aren't. It's not so much that it's fatal as unattractive."

We were approaching our building. Arnie shook his head in agreement. "It's not that different in psychiatry. People don't figure that mental illness will kill you. Anyway, psychiatry isn't chic anymore."

"But you like it, don't you?"

Brett Mandel, an obnoxious fourteen-year-old patient, pushed ahead of us into the building. He didn't even notice who we were, just that we were in the way. He didn't try to keep the door open. Arnie grabbed it before it could close completely. He let me in ahead of him. The air-conditioned corridor was like Paradise.

Arnie hurried after me. "Sure, I like psychiatry. It's the patients I can't stand."

I looked at him. He looked back at me. "Just joking, Jack. Professional humor."

I nodded. We didn't say much as we followed Brett Mandel in his white T-shirt and bright purple bermudas down the dark, cool corridor.

I got to my door before Arnie. I gave him a wave. "See you around."

He waved back. "Tell Harold he's perfectly normal." He waited and then smiled before turning away. "Tomorrow. Tell him tomorrow."

Shari was a few steps behind me. Rushing into the office with her shoe boxes balanced precariously in front of her.

"I'm really sorry, Dr. Klein, I got sort of stalled."

"That's okay."

She tried pushing past me, to get to her post.

"Shari?"

She stopped and turned back to me. She really was fairly attractive. Short blonde hair, a good figure, and a face that was made up to look as pretty as possible. "Yes, Doctor?"

"Uh . . . uh . . ." I tried to think of something to say. "Just wanted you to know . . ."

"Yes?"

I looked at her feet. ". . . nice shoes."

She looked down and then back at me. She seemed pleased. "Anne Klein," she said proudly.

We both smiled.

June

S	M	T	W	T	F	S
					~~1~~	~~2~~
~~3~~	~~4~~	~~5~~	~~6~~	~~7~~	~~8~~	~~9~~
~~10~~	~~11~~	~~12~~	~~13~~	~~14~~	~~15~~	~~16~~
~~17~~	~~18~~	~~19~~	~~20~~	~~21~~	22	23
24	25	26	27	28	29	30

July

S	M	T	W	T	F	S
1	2	3	4	5	6	7
8	9	10	11	12	13	14
15	16	17	18	19	20	21
22	23	24	25	26	27	28
29	30	31				

August

S	M	T	W	T	F	S
			1	2	3	4
5	6	7	8	9	10	11
12	13	14	15	16	17	18
19	20	21	22	23	24	25
26	27	28	29	30	31	

Chapter Six

DINNER WASN'T a big deal in the summer. With the kids away, neither Barbara nor I felt much like cooking.

Of course, when I was growing up, we used to have *meals*. Not just a piece of meat and a vegetable, but meals. Appetizers, starches, bread, salad, dessert. Summer and winter my mother, father, sister, and me sat down at the dining room table and really ate. Everything. From tomato juice to jello, with stops at potatoes, roast beef, peas, and lettuce along the way. Seven days a week. Fifty-two weeks a year, we would *eat* dinner.

Nowadays we just pick. Even when the kids are home, dinner is never more than a piece of chicken and some rice. Or a large salad in hot weather. Perhaps a Sunday roast and a baked potato in winter. But rarely a first course. Never a piece of bread. And dessert is something we each sneak separately after we think everybody else has gone upstairs. But, with the kids away, Barbara and I just nibble.

"Want some of my carrots?" I asked as I picked through the

vegetable plate I had made myself. Along with a glass of iced Sanka, it was enough to eat after slogging home through the heat. I had showered and changed into a pair of shorts and a polo shirt. Barbara was dressed almost identically.

"I'm fine," she said, digging into some chicken salad.

Neither one of us spoke much. Instead, we concentrated on our plates. Finally, when we were almost through, she reached over on the counter behind her and handed me a postcard.

"I almost forgot, we got a card from Martha."

I looked at the front. It was one of those self-addressed ones we had given her before she left. I turned it over and noticed that all the boxes were checked in correctly. "Having good time." "Sister is fine." "Like camp." And finally, "Miss You." In the space reserved for comments she had written, "Mandy is thinking of cutting all her hair off."

I looked up at Barbara. "You really think she will?"

Barbara didn't look up, but picked out the celery from her salad. "No, not really." She stopped her fork in mid-spear. "But you never know."

I nodded and went back to my cauliflower.

Barbara was still eating when I finished. I put my plate and dish in the dishwasher while she removed all the vegetables from her chicken salad.

"You really don't like vegetables anymore?" I asked as I stood over her, leaning against the dishwasher.

She shoved a sliver of carrot over to the side. "No, nothing permanent. Just a phase."

"I didn't think shrinks went through them."

"I'm not a shrink and what's them?"

"Phases is them. And, by me, you're a shrink."

She looked up at me with a smile. We had been married twenty years but still I got turned on by Barbara's smile. Maybe "turned on" isn't exactly the right combination of words. My crotch didn't itch and my hormones didn't start pouring through my body, but still there was a warmth that went through me that was more than just ordinary. It wasn't the same kind of thing as watching Mandy do her gymnastics or seeing the girls asleep at night. No, this was sexual. And while it might not have been the kind of sexual feeling men found in Penthouse or Playboy, still it was pleasurable. All thoughts of "murder therapy" were banished. Permanently. This was my wife, who looked so sexy on this ridiculously hot night. She made me feel good. Why shouldn't I do the same for her?

"I mean it, you really are a shrink," I said, still glowing with the warmth of her smile. She moved the hair back from her forehead ever so slightly. It made her seem younger. Vulnerable in a way she hadn't been in a long time. "You've taken as many courses as any shrink I know."

She sat back in her chair and looked at me. "I hope you're not disappointed that I haven't gotten my degree." She paused. "Yet."

"I'm not," I answered quickly. "Not at all."

"It's not because I didn't want to . . ." she said seriously.

"I know that," I answered hurriedly. "I know that."

"I could have."

"I know," I said even more quickly.

"Good."

Then the pounding began.

"Jack. Jack." The screams, a woman's screams, came from outside the kitchen door. The pounding shook the glass in the door. The windows rattled. Even over the roar of the air conditioner you could hear the screams.

I ran to the door. It was Fran. Fran Bernstein. Pounding on the glass panes of the door. Screaming my name.

She was pushing at the door with her shoulder. So that when I unlocked it, she came hurtling into the room. She bumped straight into me, still screaming my name.

"Fran. Fran." I held onto her. Trying to soothe her, help her make some sense out of the panic.

"Jack." She took a deep breath. Shook her head as if waking up and then looked at me in panic. "It's Frank. It's Frank."

Heart attack. It had to be. Maybe a stroke. I started to reach for the phone when Fran took my hand and pulled it away.

"No, no. He's choking." She gasped it out. "On food. Please, Jack, please . . ."

I pushed her away and started to run out the door. Through the heat, across the lawn, cursing the fact I had planted bushes the year before between our yards.

I pushed my way through the bushes, sticking my knees, my arms, on thorns. I remembered my medical bag as I burst through the branches. But I wasn't going to go back. Behind me I could hear Fran crying. I didn't know how far behind she was, but I knew there was no one else out there. Nobody walking. Nobody whose windows were open. Barbara and I were the only ones hearing Fran's screams.

Then I was there. The kitchen door was open. I hurtled through it, ran into the room. I was going to help, I was going to save Frank Bernstein's life. It was what I had been trained for. Saving lives.

And then I saw him. I pretended it wasn't too late. Ran to Frank Bernstein lying on the floor, blue-faced, tongue sticking out, hands around his throat as if he were trying to rip out whatever thing was keeping his breath from coming out. I hit his stomach. WHAM! Nothing happened. I hit it again. Harder. That big bloated belly. Still nothing. Then, with both hands, one on top of the other, I punched down on Frank Bernstein with every bit of strength I possessed. WHOOSH! It was out. A giant clump of brownness came flying straight up in the air. Like a rocket ship it zoomed up toward the ceiling and then slowly descended to the gray-and-white tiled floor. It landed without a sound. And I was leaning over that swollen face, breathing into his mouth. Pushing my breath into his body. Trying to breathe for him. Forcing my air down into his lungs. Again. Again. And again.

I heard Fran in the background. Crying softly. And still I kept breathing into Frank's mouth. Puffing, puffing, and nothing came back. The only time Frank moved was when I moved him.

Picked up his head. Pushed down on his chest. Grabbed his wrist to feel for a pulse. And there was nothing.

I didn't want to turn around and look at Fran. I knew she was there. I could hear Barbara talking to her, whispering to her. And then the crying seemed to stop.

Death, while at the top of my list of fears, was not part of my existence. I never had to see it. My patients usually died of something else. Even when they were at their worst, asthmatics clutching desperately for breath, a shot of cortisone would bring them back to life almost instantly. Not since my internship had I been confronted by death. And so I waited, pretended to be doing something to this body that had died ten, fifteen minutes ago. Trying to forget that this really had been Frank Bernstein. And then, finally, I had to turn around.

Fran was cuddled into my wife. Her body still shook as Barbara looked at me. Stared sadly at me. She shook her head slowly from side to side. I nodded.

"He's gone," Barbara said, squeezing Fran's shoulders.

And then there was silence.

It took at least two hours for it to be over. Two hours for the paramedics to get Frank's body out of the house. For the police to finish asking their questions. For Barbara to get Fran upstairs. I called the drugstore and had them send over some sleeping pills. Talked to the funeral parlor and arranged to pick up the body after the autopsy. Called the director of the camp the Bernstein twins were at and made plans to meet the boys at the airport the next morning.

I decided that the calls to the rest of the family and to Frank's office could wait till morning. I had had enough death for one night.

By nine I was alone in the kitchen. Barbara was upstairs. She was planning to spend the night. Nobody had cleaned up. The only thing that had been put away was Frank's body. Fran's usually spotless kitchen was a mess. This sleek, modern, almost white-on-white kitchen looked like it had died too. There was a half-eaten salad on Fran's plate. And a glass of water. But in front of Frank's place there were enough bowls of food to feed the rest of the block. A platter with half a cut-up steak still on it. A bowl of little new potatoes. A basket of rolls. And a half-drunk beer. The plate Frank had eaten from lay broken in two parts on the floor. Next to it, spread among the pieces of the green-and-red floral patterned dishes, were the remains of Frank's dinner. A chewed roll, a couple potatoes, and about four pieces of well-done meat. Great big chunks of charred, barbecued sirloin. I looked over at the piece of meat I had pushed out of Frank's windpipe. No wonder the man had choked on it. Even half-chewed it was the same size as those on the platter. It would have gotten stuck in an elephant's throat.

I went over to the counter to pick up a roll of paper towels. So why had Frank Bernstein tried to swallow the meat? Why didn't he cut it up? Even a child would know that a piece that size would wind up being stuck in his throat. Anger. That had to be it. The same anger I had seen the other day, when Fran (or was it Bea now?) had locked him out of the house. The same apoplectic, vessel-bursting rage must have made him grab one of those chunks of meat and bite into it as if it were his wife's throat.

I took a few paper towels and walked back to the half-chewed meat. Trying not to look too closely at the cause of asphyxiation, I wiped it off the floor, picked it up very gingerly and, holding it as far away from my body as possible, carried it over to the sink without looking at it. I shoved the whole mess down the garbage disposal and then turned back to cleaning up the rest of the chaos that lay on the floor near Frank's seat.

I got the food out of the way first. The remnants of his final meal. Then I turned to the crockery. There weren't too many little chips from the plate. What was there, I managed to clean up with Fran's mini vacuum cleaner. I cleared Fran's place setting, and threw away all the leftover food. I even wiped the white formica table with a damp sponge. I stepped back and gazed at my work. I never minded cleaning up. Especially at times like this, when it was almost therapy.

Ooops! Silverware. Under the table. Two forks, a butter knife and a dessert spoon. I walked over and leaned down to pick them up. I looked around for the other knife. For Frank's steak knife. For what he had forgotten to use to cut up his steak into manageable bites. But the knife wasn't here. Fran had had one. It was different than the regular utensils. White bone-handled. I remembered not putting it into the dishwasher, but washing it off and placing it in the dishrack. There had to be another knife around somewhere. I checked the floor. Maybe somebody had kicked it away. But it wasn't anywhere. Not under the counters, in the wastebasket, or even in the magazine rack. It wasn't there. No steak knives were there.

And then I remembered. Frank didn't need a knife. The only time he used one was when Fran wasn't around. She cut up all his meat. Spooned the food onto his plate, poured him his beverage, and always, wherever we were, whether it was a restaurant or somebody else's house, took her knife and cut up Frank's steak or lamb chop or chicken into perfectly appropriate, precisely even, little pieces. Frank would continue talking while Fran would be bustling about getting his food. He would talk while she spooned, talk while she cut, and talk while he ate. No doubt he was talking while he died.

I didn't want to think about those oversized pieces of meat. It was stupid of me to consider it.

Fran wouldn't do anything like that. After all, she was Fran. Even if she were called Bea, she was the same person who got Frank his drink with the little ice cubes. Who slunk around the house, shoulders hunched, looking at the floor. Mindful of her role. But maybe the new Fran/Bea cut up the meat. Made the chunks too big to swallow. Frank wouldn't notice. Frank made assumptions about his life. He knew when he sat down, the chair would be there. But, of course, he also assumed that his car would start in the morning. And that his meat . . .

I shook all the thoughts out of my head. I stopped looking for the knife. Turned off the lights. And tried to forget about those things. They didn't happen to me. On my street. With my friends. But now two of my neighbors, two men on either side of my house, were gone. Dave and I were now the only men on this short block of Apple Tree Lane. There were four of them. And two of us. With all the kids gone for the summer, there were just six people living in four houses on Apple Tree Lane. It was now Dave Redfield and I standing outside after dinners and Sunday barbecues. The two of us looking into the kitchen window at the four women talking around the kitchen table. I couldn't wait for fall. For the children to come back. We needed them now. And they weren't here.

I started to leave and thought about Fran. Maybe now I'd have to start thinking of her as Bea. With her new old name perhaps she'd be less hesitant. Stronger. Stand straighter. Maybe now that she didn't have to make heavy meals for her family, she would lose weight. Maybe now that she didn't have to cut up her husband's food for him, she would become somebody who wasn't always flinching from the onslaught of Frank Bernstein's bile.

I closed the door. Left the air-conditioned comfort of that now uncomfortable kitchen for the late evening heat. I looked at my watch. A cheap digital I wore in spite of Barbara's attempts to get me into something European and over five hundred dollars. It was only nine o'clock. I thought of taking a walk. Just down the block. It was too hot to go much farther. I started down the side path of Frank's ranch house. Walking carefully on the evenly laid cobblestones, past the peonies, roses, and pansies that Fran/Bea tended to so lovingly. The smell of the flowers cut through the thickness of the humidity.

The street seemed deserted. The leaves on the trees moved slightly, but you couldn't feel any kind of breeze.

I walked to the end of the block. Past Elizabeth Siegal's. I thought of ringing her doorbell and teling her what happened, but then thought better of it. I crossed the street. In the distance I could hear some teenagers yelling. Nobody was giving a party tonight in the neighborhood. There were no lingering barbecue smells. And no doors were open to let out the sounds of summer, television reruns. The world was safely sealed inside and I felt so sad. Frank really was dead. Just like Marty, he had died. And I didn't want to know why.

There were lights on all over Dave Redfield's house. I stopped in front of it. Dave was looking out the window. I could see his face pressed up against the picture window in the living room. I waved. He just kept looking. Pressed his tiny nose against the glass trying to figure, no doubt, what was going on out there. I waved. And then waved again and again. Finally, he saw me.

He ran out the door. His knee-length madras bermudas and pea-green polo shirt glowed in the darkness.

"What's going on?" he puffed, as he came scurrying up to me. I looked in back of him, but I couldn't see Jane.

"It's Frank."

He grabbed my wrist. I could feel how wet his hands were. They almost slipped off until he grabbed me once again. "Tell me," he whispered, as if it were a secret. "I was in the basement, in my workshop. I thought I heard an ambulance. Is he all right? What is it, Jack? Is it serious? Really serious?"

"He's dead, Dave."

Dave looked at me wonderingly. "Dead?"

I nodded. His hand dropped away from my wrist. All the air seemed to have left his body.

"Are you sure?"

"Uh-huh. I was there."

He inhaled. Trying, no doubt, to suck some air back in. "Heart attack?"

"Asphyxiation."

He looked at me strangely.

"He choked, Dave. On a piece of meat."

He nodded. And then shook his head from side to side. "He always ate too fast. You know how fast Frank ate, don't you, Jack?"

"Yeah. The talking didn't help, either."

Dave took a deep breath. He wiped the new beads of sweat off his forehead. He just kept on shaking his head as if trying to remember something. Trying to figure out exactly why Frank died. "I always tell Jane, we eat too fast. That's our problem. We eat much too fast. Much too fast."

"Yeah," I agreed. "Everybody does everything too fast."

"I can't believe it, Jack." Dave turned away from me. He looked up the street. The headlights of a car were coming towards us. "It's probably Jane," he said. As it got closer, he moved towards me, until he was hovering in my shadow. The car turned into the driveway with a screech. It stopped at the sidewalk and the window came down. Jane peered out.

"What are you guys doing out?" The only part of her I could really make out in the darkness was her teeth. Bright straight teeth that dominated Jane's angular face. Jane Redfield was a plain person. Only her teeth shone.

"Jack has bad news," Dave said, bowing his head.

"Barbara?" Jane said quickly. "Is she alright?"

"Frank," I said sadly. "Frank Bernstein died. Tonight. A couple hours ago."

Jane's mouth opened in shock. "You're kidding."

Dave and I shook our heads almost in unison. He looked at me to explain. "He choked on a piece of meat."

"Ate too fast." Dave said.

Jane opened the door and stepped out. She was wearing a white skirt and a blue short-sleeved blouse. She always looked like she was ready to play some kind of sport. She was tall like Dave, but far more athletic looking. Now she just leaned against the car, running her strong hands through her short straight pale blonde hair. "Unbelievable, unbelievable." She looked up at me. "How's Bea?"

Dave and I turned toward each other. I figured out first who the Bea in question was.

"Barbara's with her." I pointed across the street. To the Bernstein house, which, I noticed now, was completely dark. "I'm not sure she's realized what's happened. Still in shock."

"A shocking thing," Dave said sadly.

"You think I should go over?" Jane said to me.

"No, I got Fran . . . er . . . Bea . . . some sleeping pills. They should knock her out. Why not wait till the morning? I think that would be better. The morning."

"The morning," Dave echoed. "Much better."

Jane looked across the street. Past our house toward Elizabeth's place at the end of the block. "Does Elizabeth know?"

"I don't think so."

Out of the corner of my eye I could see Dave shaking his head in agreement.

"I guess she must be out," Jane added, ignoring Dave.

"Yeah."

We all stood there for a second. I'm not sure any one of us would have mentioned Frank Bernstein as a close friend. But he was "there". He was part of our lives. We all saw him practically every day. Whether it was going out to the end of his driveway to curse the delivery boy for throwing his paper on the street. Or putting up with his insistence on our telling him exactly which brand of scotch we wanted for our drink. Or which kind of white wine. "Drinks" he would always say, "are my specialty."

Finally, Jane started to get back in the car.

I moved away from Dave. "I'll see you in the morning."

"Do you have any . . . any . . . ideas about the funeral?" Dave asked hesitantly.

"I thought I'd talk to Fran . . ."

"Bea," Jane said firmly.

I kept on talking. "Tomorrow. I'll talk to . . . Bea . . . tomorrow."

Quietly, we waved good-bye. Jane started the car again and

parked it in the turnaround next to the garage. Dave began walking back into the house. And I just went home. I didn't look back. Just thought about why Fran Bernstein didn't cut up her husband's meat into smaller pieces. And wondered what next.

June

S	M	T	W	T	F	S
					~~1~~	~~2~~
~~3~~	~~4~~	~~5~~	~~6~~	~~7~~	~~8~~	~~9~~
~~10~~	~~11~~	~~12~~	~~13~~	~~14~~	~~15~~	~~16~~
~~17~~	~~18~~	~~19~~	~~20~~	~~21~~	~~22~~	~~23~~
~~24~~	~~25~~	~~26~~	~~27~~	~~28~~	~~29~~	~~30~~

July

S	M	T	W	T	F	S
~~1~~	~~2~~	~~3~~	~~4~~	5	6	7
8	9	10	11	12	13	14
15	16	17	18	19	20	21
22	23	24	25	26	27	28
29	30	31				

August

S	M	T	W	T	F	S
			1	2	3	4
5	6	7	8	9	10	11
12	13	14	15	16	17	18
19	20	21	22	23	24	25
26	27	28	29	30	31	

Chapter Seven

FRANK BERNSTEIN'S funeral was not exactly memorable. It was so quick, so hurried, as if everybody wanted to get it out of the way and get back into their air-conditioned cars.

I don't mean to suggest that there wasn't a crowd. Frank had a big family, a couple sisters and lots of nieces, nephews and cousins. His accounting firm had recently merged, so that all told there must have been a few hundred people assembled in the chapel. I hesitate to call them mourners, because basically the tone was set by the Rabbi, who seemed to be delivering Eulogy Number *3*.

The boys were more anxious to get back to camp than to display public grief. They had always been closer to each other than to their parents.

The main source of comfort for Fran were the women on her block: Barbara, Jane and Elizabeth. The first two, especially, fluttered around her constantly. Barbara appeared to have moved into Bea's house permanently. Jane could be seen making casseroled pilgrimages over to Bea's at least three times a day. Elizabeth went there a bit less often. But they were all together at the service. Bea, Barbara, and Jane in black. Elizabeth in a light gray. I sat with Dave Redfield, who was the only person crying. Even though I had made most of the funeral arrangements, I felt somewhat out of the whole thing. Arnie Melton, and probably even Barbara, would call it "denial." I just kept thinking of allergy injections and pollen counts. Death was too close to consider.

It took another five days for the funereal aspects of the occasion to disappear completely. Five days in which the heat gave up some of its anger. It was now the first day of July, and the weather was comfortably nestled in the low eighties. The callers at the Bernsteins had stopped calling. Apple Tree Lane was once again without cars lining the streets. The boys had gone back to camp. I drove them and Bea to the airport. It was the first time I had seen her cry since the night her husband died.

As we came back from O'Hare Airport, as we turned off the expressway and started down the shaded Lake View streets, I noticed that Bea had put away her Kleenex. She was staring out the window looking at the Sunday strollers. Men and women in shorts pushing buggies. Older couples in white trousers and straw hats. It was the kind of summer Sunday that made it appear reasonable to have chosen the Midwest as a home. The heat of the past month was forgotten. The approaching heat of July and August was not even contemplated.

I couldn't think of anything to say, but I felt that I had to say something. No wonder I became an allergist, I was good with life. It was death I had trouble with.

I kept my eyes on the road while I spoke. "How you doin' . . . Bea." I was getting better at calling her by her new name.

A sigh. Bea was a major sigher when Frank was alive. An unsmiling sigh that punctuated many of Frank's demands. She seemed to be still sighing out of habit. "Better, Jack." She turned and looked at me. I glanced over quickly at her. Her face was more relaxed than it had been in days. Thinner too. Apparently she hadn't eaten much in the past week. She looked like she had been to a spa. Barbara had even taken her out to get her hair cut the day before. All the curls were cut off and what was left made Bea Bernstein chicer, less harried looking.

"Do you have any plans?" I asked, trying to think of all my questions before she came up with the answers. I had never really spent any time alone with Bea Bernstein. In spite of living next door for almost fifteen years, this was probably the first time we had been alone, without spouses or neighbors to push along the conversation.

"I . . . I . . . I . . . I don't really know." I came to a stop sign and waited while a Mercedes whizzed past. It glowed in the sun. Blinding me with the shine of its paint job.

"You'll stay?"

"Yes, of course."

I checked the cross street each way for any zooming convertibles. There were just a couple joggers far away. I started going again. "It must be . . . difficult." Now that was the all-time dumbest remark of the year. Barbara would have said, "No, actually it's easy."

Bea was much nicer. "It is, but . . ." she turned to me and I could see her smile. "Friends, good friends, make it better."

"I'm glad you have them."

She nodded. We drove the rest of the way without saying anything more than "nicer weather." I didn't want to ask her why she didn't cut Frank's steak into smaller pieces that night.

Mrs. Robins was waiting for me the next morning.

"Klein, you're out of uniform," she cackled with joy. "You should have been in that dumb white coat of yours already." She looked around the office. "A mess. A fine mess." She pointed to the tattered magazines. "I wouldn't touch one of those magazines for all the tea in China."

I gestured for her to follow me into the office. She wasn't

budging. "I hear you've had a couple accidents on your block this summer, Klein."

I could see Shari buttoning the pink and gray Versace smock she had purchased herself. She looked up as Mrs. Robins spoke. "Anybody get hurt, Dr. Klein?" she asked sweetly.

Mrs. Robins looked fiercely at Shari, who was selecting a sharp pencil to chew on. "Dead, Miss. They're both dead. Right, Klein?"

"Right, Mrs. Robins, now it's time for your shot." I tried moving her. For a woman who couldn't have weighed more than a hundred pounds she was immovable. She seemed to enjoy conversing with Shari, who she once told me was only slightly less of an airhead than my usual receptionist.

"Seems pretty strange to me, young lady. One block, and a short one at that, with two accidents." Mrs. Robins inclined her head toward the receptionist's window. ". . . very suspicious accidents if you ask me."

Shari nodded in agreement.

"How many houses you got on that street, Klein?"

"Four. Now why don't we get our shot, Mrs. Robins?"

I knew the "our" word would make her shift gears. "Our shot? Who do you think you're talking to, Klein? Some senile idiot?" She looked at Shari for support. "I've been sneezing a lot longer than he's been sticking needles in people. Trust me . . . what's your name, little girl?"

"Shari."

"With an 'i'?"

Shari nodded.

"Figured." She started walking ahead of me. Mumbling all the way. "Hate names that end in vowels. Shari, Debbie, Teri. Consonants. In my day names ended in consonants. Susan, Margaret, those were names."

I followed her into the office. Obviously, Apple Tree Lane, or at least the 100 block of Apple Tree Lane, was going to be big news in town this summer.

* * *

Arnie Melton walked over to The Lunch Box with me. His five-day-a-week twelve o'clock appointment was on vacation for the summer. "Anorexia camp," he explained as we walked down the block. "They fatten 'em up for a couple months and then send them back to me."

I didn't say much. Just grunted and nodded. I had already spent the morning telling three of my patients that, "Yes, it was amazing that two men have died by accident this summer on one block."

"Jack, Jack, you all right?"

Arnie had stopped in front of Harold Goldberg's store. I didn't realize it until I had gone a few feet past him. Past the resort outfit, and in front of the madras shirt and matching golf cap.

"What?"

"You okay?"

I gave him a big smile. "Sure. I'm fine. Fine."

"Worried about something?"

"No. No." I smiled some more.

"Because I heard about that guy . . ."

"Frank Bernstein?"

"Yeah, friend of yours?"

I shrugged. "Sort of."

He looked at me with a worried expression. "I know that I didn't take you seriously last time . . ."

I shook my head a few times. "No, no, that's all right. Really. I promise. It's all a coincidence."

"So your wife . . ."

I shook my head some more. Even faster now. "No, it was just one of those things. Frank ate too fast. Much too fast. Much too fast."

Arnie still seemed concerned. "You sure that everything's okay."

I nodded. And smiled. "Coincidence." I thought about saying something and then decided not to. "Just an awful coincidence."

Arnie let go of my arm and started to walk again. I followed alongside him. Trying to pay attention. For the first time in weeks the streets were crowded with people.

"Women," Arnie said, surveying the groups of twos and threes that walked up and down the block. "They're all around us." He seemed to have forgotten his concern. It made me relax a little. "We're just guests here." His outspread arm took in most of the street.

I looked. We were the only two men in sight. "We live here, Arnie."

He shook his head. "No, they live here." He pointed to two women. They were excited to see each other, laughing and gesturing at something: new clothes or a new hairdo.

"This is their home. This suburb is their domain. Men drop in for dinner and weekends."

"I live here. This is my home, Arnie."

He shook his head. "Wrong. Let me ask you, did you ever go into the supermarket in the daytime?" He went on before I could answer. "Well, I did. Last week. You know how I felt?"

"No."

He didn't stop to listen. "Like a Zulu in South Africa. The women looked at me like I was going to put poison in the luncheon meat." We were at the corner. He turned to me and went on, gesturing with his hands as he got more and more worked up. "I expected to move to the suburbs and find a nice, simple small town. It's much more complicated than that."

"It's the eighties. Feminism . . ."

He grabbed my shoulder. "You don't understand, Jack, this isn't feminism, this is womanism. Feminism, I can deal with. It makes sense. Women should be able to do what they want and men should share the responsibilities. I can deal with that. But this has nothing to do with feminism. This is more like Amazonism . . . Lysistrataism. Them. Us."

A couple tennis players swinging oversized rackets walked past and looked suspiciously at us.

"See those two?" He lowered his voice when the two tanned

women with pink-and-green headbands, respectively, turned our way. "They aren't interested in a career or their husbands doing the cleaning up. Their career is being with each other. They've got take-out stores and pizzerias and fried chicken places and Chinese joints and some cleaning lady to wash the paper plates. They don't need us, Jack. Don't you get it?"

Before he could go on, I started across the street. Arnie followed. Head down, shuffling across. We waited for an Audi and a Volvo to zoom past and then made the curb. The Lunch Box was just a few stores away. A lot of women seemed to be heading there. A couple of them were dragging little kids too young to be sent to camp.

"Remember what you said the other day, Arn? These are the kind of women you want to settle down with, have a couple kids . . ."

". . . I know, I know. It is what I want. It's just that lately . . ." He hesitated, watching a phalanx of women hurrying toward us. They made a sharp turn into The Lunch Box, but you had the feeling they weren't going to let us by if we had run into them. We would have stopped. They would have kept going.

Quickly I turned him into The Lunch Box.

The Fourth of July was part of the permanent fabric of my life. Just like giving an injection to Mrs. Robins every Monday morning at 9:01. It was the tuna platter I ate each summer, the pancakes I cooked on winter Saturdays.

Fourth of July was the Elm Wood Country Club party. I joined the club when I first set up my practice. It was business. A chance for the new allergist in town to pick up some clients. The problem was that I wasn't very athletic. I hated golf, played tennis like a beginner, and got winded after one lap of swimming. Barbara got into tennis for a few years, but lately her enthusiasm for the game had dwindled. This summer I don't think she had been to the club at all. But still, it was the Fourth. And so we went.

Elm Wood wasn't the prettiest club in town. It was surrounded on three sides by middle-income developments. The ten-minute drive there took you past quarter-acre plots of colonials and ranch houses that differed only by the color of the bicycle lying in the front yard.

So Elm Wood tried to separate itself from the surrounding blandness. A shrub-lined driveway, and a limestone clubhouse, gave it the outward pretense of history. But inside you were surrounded by people who really wanted to be someplace else. By people who wanted to get into Fern Dale Country Club on the lake. Instead they settled for Elm Wood. For a golf course that still had to plant trees. For a swimming pool that wasn't quite Olympic sized. A dining room that lost its chef every August to alcohol or the half-frozen turbot served to the club president.

But still, every Fourth, dressed in my white bermudas and a brightly colored polo shirt, pink this year, I went for the afternoon barbecue and fireworks.

"Can this please be the last year?" Barbara asked as we walked around the side of the clubhouse toward the pool area where the barbecue took place. I could already smell the gasoline fumes wafting across the putting green. The giant grills were being fired up.

"I didn't know you disliked it that much," I said, as we passed by a few golfers teeing off I looked closely, but I didn't know anyone. Not even a patient.

"I don't, it's just that I don't have the time to drive here. I'm much too busy to be bothered with this place. Besides"—we came around to the pool, there were a hundred people in summer frocks—"I don't know anybody anymore." A waiter carrying a tray of gin and tonics and vodka and tonics approached us. The gin and tonics had swizzle sticks with little British flags stuck in them. The vodkas had Russian Hammers and Sickles stuck into their red straws. I grabbed a vodka. Barbara shook her head "no" to the waiter, who shrugged and went on his rounds.

"Let's mingle," I said.

We kept walking toward the crowds. Men at the deep end. Women toward the middle, near the five-foot marker on the side of the pool. The college kids huddled together, ignoring sexual distinctions, near the diving board. The little ones stayed near the shallow end, under the watchful gazes of five or six grandmothers.

I looked for a familiar face. I realized, as I got closer, that most of them were women. Patients. Mothers of patients. People whom I had seen at The Lunch Box.

"It looks like a Ralph Lauren convention," Barbara whispered to me as we went past the giggling teenagers.

"There are a couple crocodiles."

"On the kids," she pointed out. "Grandmother clothes. Anyway Ralph doesn't make stuff for the real little guys."

A wave. From the women. I wasn't sure who it was directed at. But then I recognized Elizabeth Siegal's curls. She bounced out of the crowd. Holding onto a glass of beer, she Betty Booped her way along the side of the pool to us.

"Hi, guys!" Elizabeth was in one of her more demure outfits. No symbols of Ralph or Calvin or Giorgio. Just a loose red-and-white checked shirt and a white skirt. The lighter-than-air breasts were merely soft bumps under the voluminous shirt. She gave each of us a kiss. On the cheek.

Marty Siegal had joined the club a few years before. He liked the poker games on Wednesday nights. But this was the first time I had seen Elizabeth here.

"We could have driven you over," Barbara said in a tone of voice with a reprimand.

"No, no, no," Elizabeth said with a giggle. Her voice reminded me of her chest. Big but light. "You never know who I'd meet." Barbara got an elbow nudge.

"Here?" I said incredulously, looking around at the collection of pot-bellied forty-year-olds and jogger-thin fifty-year-olds sipping their Union Jacks and Hammers and Sickles.

"Ya never know." She smiled, and, grabbing us both by the

arms, led us to the women's division of Elm Wood. "Some shmuck might get caught screwing around in a sandtrap . . ." she paused to stop the giggles—"with me."

"I don't think you're ready to meet anybody, yet, Elizabeth," Barbara said in the same stern tone of voice.

"Who knows. Who the hell knows," Elizabeth said happily as we arrived at the crowd of Hammers and Sickles.

The various greetings took a couple minutes. I seemed to know more of the women than Elizabeth, although about half of them called me "Dr. Klein." After the hellos and the howareya's there didn't appear to be a lot of interest in me. Barbara had been sucked into a group. They were surrounding her, and she seemed to be lecturing on something. They were all fascinated.

Elizabeth and I were alone. On the edge of the crowd. Looking over the swimming pool.

"Strange place, Jack," she said as we walked away from the pack. We were alone. Midway between the male and female segments of the Elm Wood Country Club. "It's like when we had parties in Junior High School. The girls in one room, the guys in the other. We'd talk about boys and they'd talk about"—she looked quizzically at me "—what did you guys talk about?"

"I don't know, the usual stuff."

"What's the usual stuff?"

Irwin Levy waved from the band of men. The wave came before the big wink when he saw Elizabeth. I didn't wink back.

"Girls. I guess we talked about girls. And sports. We must have talked about sports."

She pointed to where Irwin Levy was trying to sneakily point us out to a guy who seemed to be in the midst of telling a joke. The guy took the time to look our way and nod approvingly. He whispered something to Irwin, who laughed and whispered it to the guy next to him, a sunburned Buddy Friedman.

"Dirty jokes," she said sweetly, innocently, "bet you guys told lots of dirty jokes."

"Guess so. I never remembered them."

She looked away from the male pack and straight at me.

"That's why I like you Jack. You don't remember dirty jokes." I felt myself blushing. I looked up toward the setting sun, trying to make the heat turn my face red. It didn't fool Elizabeth. She pinched my arm. "You are cute, Jack, you really are cute."

"Do you want to meet some people?" I said hurriedly.

She looked at the circle, expanded now by some sweaty tennis players. "Nah," she waved the whole group away. Dismissed them completely. "I met these guys before. I even married one of them. Go ahead," she pushed me toward the guys. "You're entitled. I'll go do the girls." She gave my ass a pinch. I jumped. She giggled. "You are cute, Jack. If I didn't like Barbara so much . . ." I walked quickly to the crowd of masculinity.

Nudges. Lots and lots of elbows shoved into my ribs. A couple "ey . . . ey . . . eys." I felt like I was in a fifties sitcom. All the guys waiting for me in the Frat House after my date with the "loose" woman. Except that all the winks, all the innuendoes, were being carried out by successful middle-aged men. Men in madras slacks and brightly colored golf socks. Men who led prominent law firms, put miles of wire on buckteeth. Surgeons, owners of small businesses, medium-sized businesses, guys who got to work every day at seven and worked constantly until five. Now they were thrilled to be acting like they had just jerked off to the newest issue of Penthouse.

Irwin Levy lifted his eyebrows about three feet into the air. He was a commodity broker who alternated between driving a Mercedes and a Dodge. Between being two months late with his dues and giving clambakes at the club for the entire commodities exchange.

"Nice little piece, huh Jack?" He gave me his white-on-white grin. It had been bought, and not paid for, until a year later. His dentist was a floor below me.

"She's my neighbor, Irwin. Elizabeth Siegal. Marty's wife. Widow, to be exact."

That got a wince out of him. "Not the one who shot Marty . . ." He didn't have to describe the events of that historic night. The aim for the crotch and the hit in the heart had been broadcast all over the phone lines in Lake View.

I nodded and sipped the rest of my gin and tonic. I was down to the ice cubes.

"Ohhh" He let out a long, slow, almost painful, breath.

"Want to meet her?" I asked with a little grin.

He waved away the idea. "No, no, no. That's fine. That's fine."

With Irwin spreading the word about the identity of the girl with the hennaed curls, the interest in raising masturbatory fantasies about her seemed to disappear and we were left with the usual things to talk about. I couldn't wait till dinner. My burnt hamburger was something to anticipate eagerly.

The problem, I realized as I tried to come up with a joke to share with the "boys," was that I had never been really comfortable with the "boys." I could play sports well enough so that, while I wasn't the first one chosen, I wasn't an afterthought, either. Sent ignominiously out to right field to await one of the two balls that were hit out there a season. But still, I never could think of something to say when there were a bunch of people present. I didn't know how to pick up the conversation, build on a joke. With a small party I was fine, making my contribution like everyone else. But when you added people, my brain slowed down. Liquor didn't help. It didn't release inhibitions. Turn me into a stand-up comic. It made me tired.

Age hadn't changed my natural reticence. It was no different now that I had money and some social success. Barbara was always more at ease than I was, which is why I hated to be without her.

Saved by the beeper. A loud "eeeee" stopped the conversation around me for a second. Two other doctors reached for their belts and their pagers. But I knew my sound. I picked it off and looked at the number listed on it. My answering service. With a disappointed look, trying to make it appear as if I were upset to be leaving this convivial group of guys, I headed for the clubhouse. Barbara didn't notice me leaving. She was still surrounded by that same group of women. Only Elizabeth waved. I waved back and pointed to my beeper.

It was Mrs. Robins. Her yearly asthma attack. She had checked herself into the hospital. By the time I got there, after arranging for Barbara to go home with Elizabeth, Mrs. Robins was safely ensconced in her room. The steroids the emergency room physician had injected her with seemed to have done the trick. She was sitting up in bed. Dressed in one of her frilly high-necked gowns, looking at least ten years older than her seventy-eight years. A nurse was bustling about, fluffing up her pillows, drawing the drapes, when I walked in.

"Not exactly hospital dress, Klein."

I walked over, and taking a stethoscope out of the emergency kit I had grabbed out of the trunk, leaned over to listen to her breathing. "How you feeling, Mrs. Robins?"

She took a shallow breath. I leaned over and listened to her. By now, after fifteen years, we had the routine down. She breathed. I heard the slight wheeze that was left from the violence of the attack.

"You sound pretty good, Mrs. Robins." I stepped back and smiled down at her. The nurse, whom I didn't recognize, was busy arranging Mrs. Robins' clothes. She always kept an overnight bag packed, figuring she was going to spend a couple nights in the hospital each year. The nurse was putting her house slippers by the side of the bed.

"Modern medicine is wonderful, Klein... Now that I'm on steroids, I can expect to stay up two hours more each night, have swollen feet, a moon-shaped face, and be more irritable than usual. I am thrilled, Klein."

I took a paperback of *The Women's Room* from her case and placed it on the nightstand. "You don't have a choice, Mrs. Robins. If you don't take the steroids, you won't breathe."

She looked at me with pursed lips. "No kidding." The only defiance was in her voice. She seemed much smaller.

I reached for the chart that was next to her bed. When she was admitted, her breathing rate was 190, about 110 below normal. Ten minutes after the steroid injection it was up to 275. "I think you can get out tomorrow," I said, and then took her hand. Ostensibly I was feeling her pulse, but she seemed so weak, so alone, that I just wanted to hold it for a second.

After about thirty seconds she looked over at me with a sort of smile. "Horny, Klein?"

I didn't let go. "Incredibly, Mrs. Robins."

"Haven't had sex in thirty-five years," she said with the same wry smile.

"Bout time then."

She turned away and let go of my hand. It just lay there, lifeless on the beige cover. "Too tired now, Klein. Too tired." She closed her eyes. I patted her hand. She looked over at me. "Stop acting like I'm an old lady, Klein."

"I'm acting like you haven't had sex in thirty-five years, Mrs. R."

She nodded. "That's better. Much better."

I pulled into my driveway about seven-thirty. I had to do some paperwork at the hospital, plus take care of two more people who came to the emergency room with asthma attacks. They were young enough, and seemed to respond quickly enough to the medication, so that after a short rest I could send them home. That was one of the nicer parts of being an allergist. Usually the medications for asthma emergencies worked so quickly that a physician could actually see the results of his prescription. I was feeling good about my choice of profession. Whistling as the sun started to go down.

The street was deserted. Bea didn't seem to be home and Elizabeth and Barbara were apparently still at the club. I parked the car in the garage and, instead of going into the house, stepped outside; walked to the curb. It was such a pretty night. Somewhere in the seventies. The smell of fresh grass was in the air. I could hear sounds of baseball in neighborhood yards. A couple firecracker pops sounded from far away. Only our block seemed quiet. Without celebration. I remembered before all the kids went to camp, before they reached the magic age of ten, how we would sit out there on a summer night, watching them play baseball in the street. All the parents sitting on the curb, trying to umpire, trying to make sure that the youngest still got his turn at bat, watching them race into the woods for lost balls, and kissing scraped knees and bruised egos. Now we'd have to wait for our grandchildren to come over and play the games of summer. When I was growing up in Chicago, playing baseball between parked cars and red lights, I used to dream of empty streets and hot summers spent outdoors. And for a few years that's what I had. Until the kids left. Until they spent their Julys and Augusts away from their parents. And now there was no one to watch from the curb. Just the sounds of other children. Far away.

June

S	M	T	W	T	F	S
					~~1~~	~~2~~
~~3~~	~~4~~	~~5~~	~~6~~	~~7~~	~~8~~	~~9~~
~~10~~	~~11~~	~~12~~	~~13~~	~~14~~	~~15~~	~~16~~
~~17~~	~~18~~	~~19~~	~~20~~	~~21~~	~~22~~	~~23~~
~~24~~	~~25~~	~~26~~	~~27~~	~~28~~	~~29~~	~~30~~

July

S	M	T	W	T	F	S
~~1~~	~~2~~	~~3~~	~~4~~	~~5~~	6	7
8	9	10	11	12	13	14
15	16	17	18	19	20	21
22	23	24	25	26	27	28
29	30	31				

August

S	M	T	W	T	F	S
			1	2	3	4
5	6	7	8	9	10	11
12	13	14	15	16	17	18
19	20	21	22	23	24	25
26	27	28	29	30	31	

Chapter Eight

I GOT UP early the next day. For some reason I couldn't sleep all night long. By the time Barbara got home, around ten, I was already in bed. But even though she fell asleep quickly, I tossed and turned throughout the night. By six I was taking a shower. I listened to the radio while I shaved. The temperature was on the rise again, but, according to the radio we had at least two more days before we hit the nineties for the second time that summer.

"Missy, no home," Berta the cleaning lady informed me as I came downstairs at six-forty-five. She was just washing the remains of her six-egg omelet and was about to attack the house.

"Good morning, Berta."

She smiled at me and pointed to the coffee pot.

"No thanks."

She nodded happily and poured me a cup.

I took it and tried to sip with a smile. Berta smiled back.

I pointed to my watch. "Have to run."

Berta nodded again. The smile was even bigger. She pointed to the cup. "Berta make."

I blew on the coffee and tried to drink as much as I could without causing too many blisters on my tongue. "Wonderful."

After a few more sips and nods I managed to get out of the kitchen. I figured I'd stop at The Lunch Box to get my English muffin and orange juice.

For once, The Lunch Box contained more than a sprinkling of men. In fact, of the twenty or so people in the place, half of them were wearing suits and ties. The women also appeared to be workers and not tennis players. I didn't recognize anybody until I saw Dave Redfield turn around from a table of bankerish-looking men. He gave me one of his shy waves and turned back to his group.

I picked a small table in the corner for my muffin and juice and was reading the *Tribune* comics when an "excuse me" Dave Redfield cough caused me to look up.

"Morning, Jack," he said softly, holding onto the back of the chair across from me.

"Hi, Dave." He was waiting for the invitation. "Why don't you join me."

He nodded and folded himself into the chair. A waitress came by to offer him some coffee, but he turned her down. He was into one of his shy moods. I could tell by the way he held his head. On his chest.

"How was your Fourth?" I asked, reluctantly laying Doonesbury down. I tried to glance at it, but I had turned the paper upside down.

"All right." He nodded. "All right."

He started moving his neck around, always a bad sign with Dave. It meant that something really was bothering him. I didn't want to ask.

"Mrs. Robins had to go into the hospital yesterday. Asthma."

I knew she banked with Dave, but he didn't seem concerned. Obviously he had his own problems. "Yes, well, I didn't have too great a day either."

I settled back and drank some water. "What happened?"

Dave turned to look around the room. Nobody was looking at us. "Jane," he said. That was it. I waited for the rest, but that was all he said.

"What about Jane?" I finally asked impatiently. I liked Dave, felt sorry for him all those years his father humiliated him, but sometimes he was a pain in the butt.

"She's trying to drive me crazy."

"Are we talking *Gaslight?*"

He nodded furiously.

"And you're Ingrid Bergman."

"Sort of." He did some more neck twisting. Then he straightened the lapels on his blue blazer.

"What is she doing, Dave?" I talked very, very slowly.

"I keep losing things."

"Like what?"

"Cuff links, belts, papers."

"And . . .?"

"I know she's been hiding them."

"How do you know?"

"I know."

"But how do you know?"

He set his mouth. "I just know."

"Did you catch her doing it?"

He shook his head. "No."

"Well then . . ."

He was unyielding. "I'm telling you, Jane is trying to make me think I've lost my marbles."

"Why would she want to do that?"

"Because she hates me."

I thought of Frank Bernstein and the giant chunk of sirloin and then wiped it from my mind. I didn't want to think about Bea and Frank and why the meat wasn't cut up. If I said anything to Dave Redfield, he'd start sweating through his shirt. I tried reasoning with him. "Dave, listen, every marriage has its ups and downs. Like any relationship . . ."

"You talking about me and my father?" The voice got pinched. "Because that's what she talks about. Talks about that man all the time."

"Dave, listen."

He didn't. "He's dead. Do you understand that?" Dave's face started turning red. If I didn't know that he was in good shape, I would have started worrying about his blood pressure. "It's me now. And I know what I'm doing." He started to get up from the chair. I reached out to hold him back. He stepped away before I could get to him. "I'm a grown man, Jack. I can do what I want to do."

"Sit down, Dave."

"No." He rose to his full six-foot-six inches. "I don't think I will. It's time I ran my own life." He pointed to his chest, actually to the polka-dotted bow tie his father had worn for at least twenty years, it seemed. Dave Redfield's dad was always in blue-and-white polka-dotted ties. Dave didn't wear his dots until his father died. And he only wore his occasionally. "We should be sticking together, Jack, you know that? We need each other."

"What does that mean?"

He looked around once again. The place was still half-full. Nobody was noticing him. "That now that Frank and Marty are . . . gone, we better stick together."

"Dave, what are you talking about. Maybe Jane is right, and you are crazy."

He got a dumb smile on his purple face. "Uh-huh, yeah, right, you won't think I'm so crazy when your wife starts going after you, like mine. Maybe she'll make you think you're going nuts too." He reached over and messed up my neatly folded paper. "Probably try to convince you that you're sloppy, Jack. That would drive you nuts."

I refolded the paper neatly. "Maybe you should talk to Arnie Melton, Dave. I think you're going through some tough times."

He thumped his chest again. "I'm going through tough times! What do you think you're going through. Your wife has become the Sigmund Freud of Apple Tree Lane. How do you think that's going to work out, Mr. Big Shot?" He looked at me disdainfully and stormed out of the restaurant.

I couldn't even try to read Doonesbury. Not that Dave had upset me that much. But, still, too much was happening on Apple Tree Lane. And nothing ever happened on Apple Tree Lane. Maybe now that the heat wave was breaking, things would get back to normal. And we could have a typical, unthinking, summer.

But the day didn't get any better. Shari called in sick, which meant Mary had to sign in patients and help me with the injections. Mrs. Robins phoned three times from the hospital telling me she wanted to get out. And Barbara left a message she was having dinner with Bea and Jane. The final blow was the news from one of my patients that the two perfect days of eighty degree weather were now but a memory. By eleven-thirty, apparently, the thermometer was up to ninety-four.

I spent my lunch hour checking Mrs. Robins out of the hospital, for which she was not in the least grateful. When I got there, she was already dressed, packed and waiting. I gave her my best bedside smile.

"Don't you dare ask how 'we' are today." She aimed one finger at me. One quivering finger.

"Okay, how are I today?"

She nodded at that. Appreciatively. "Not bad, Klein. Didn't think you had it in you. Not at all unfunny."

I checked her breathing, and made sure she wasn't about to have another attack. The signs looked good.

"I told you I was fine. I could have been home two hours ago."

"Paperwork, Mrs. R. If you dropped dead, your relatives could have sued us for millions."

She stood up, gripping the sides of the chair. "Forget it, I would have come back to haunt them. They know it." She reached for her overnight case. I got it first.

"You'll need a wheelchair to take you out."

"Like hell I will." She tried to pull the case away from me. I won. She just stood there glaring while I called the nurse and got her settled. Defiantly she placed the case on her lap. She rolled down the corridor, scolding the nurse for going too slow.

I drove almost as slowly back to the office. I kept the windows down and tried to time my route through the back streets, along the lake, past the nicest homes in town. I was going to pretend it wasn't an oven out there. That it was beautiful summer day.

I parked along the lake. Not in the beach parking lot. It was full already. This was where the fishermen went. But now, in the middle of the day, there weren't any fishermen out. So I could look in peace at the gently breaking water of Lake Michigan. I walked out and sat on the hood of my car. Didn't pay any attention when I heard a car pull up behind me. It must have been a convertible, because I could hear the radio blaring and a girl's giggles before it came to a stop. I took a quick glance around.

The car never stopped. Tires screeching, it made a U-turn and started out of the lot at fifty miles an hour. I recognized Shari Herman's convertible. That didn't surprise me. I figured on my receptionist falling ill on nice summer days. I didn't figure on Arnie Melton driving the car.

He came into the office about five-thirty. After my patients and nurse had left. I was picking through the old magazines, trying to get rid of the ones that were too badly torn, when the door opened and Arnie Melton skulked in. Maybe I was imagining the skulking part, but he didn't seem quite as sure as usual. Not quite so bold.

"Hi, Jack." A shy smile. I noticed that the top of his forehead was freckled and sunburnt. A convertible, sun-beating-down-on-top-of-your-head burn. About to peel. It didn't seem to make him uncomfortable.

"Hey, Arnie." False macho bonhomie.

"Listen, Jack . . . I was wondering. Maybe you'd like a drink. Just for an hour or so. How about it?"

I stood up with all the remnants of my New Republics and New Yorkers that were out of date, and out of covers. "Sure," I smiled graciously, "why not. My wife's out with the girls."

He beamed. Just a couple guys out for a night on the town.

The Cozy Tea Parlor had started serving drinks about a year ago. So now, amidst the chintz and early American furniture, you could get a martini along with sticky buns and chicken pot pie.

Arnie and I sat in the bar, formerly the Aunt Pitty Pat Room. It was filled with *Gone With The Wind* memorabilia, with an emphasis on crockery that resembled black servants. When the first black families had come to town, the Uncle Tom salt and pepper shakers and the Aunt Jemima flour tins were removed from the shelves, but the local name of the room still hadn't changed. It would always be the Aunt Pitty Pat Room.

It wasn't very crowded. A couple of elderly matrons sipped wine while waiting for their tables. Arnie and I were the only men in the place. Even the bartender, in ruffles and crinolines, was a woman. But the martinis were strong and the mixed nuts were dry roasted. It was a pleasant place to drink. A small chintz filled room with little tables and big chairs.

Arnie was on his second martini. I was still sipping my first. We talked about the usual doctor stuff: billing, conventions. Finally, the Bombay gin seemed to work its magic on Arnie Melton. He was melting into the chair. He looked at me over the rim of his martini glass.

"About Shari . . ." he began.

I nodded.

He put the glass down and settled back, hands clasped in his lap, more a patient than a doctor. "I'm sorry about her not coming in today."

"That's alright, it was a nice day." I smiled to show I wasn't upset.

Another sip of the martini. He couldn't look me directly in the eye. His gaze hit my Adam's apple. "You see, I didn't want to make a big deal of me and . . ."

"Shari?"

A big sip. "Yeah, see we wanted to sort of keep it . . ."

"Quiet?" I suggested.

"Yeah," he put the glass back down again and started to play with the nut bowl. It was in the shape of a teapot. He took off the top and took out a filbert. "You know how these things get around . . ."

"Has it been long?"

He shook his head. "A few days, maybe a week. Last week, actually."

"You went and asked her out?"

He put the filbert in the ashtray and picked up the martini glass instead. He was almost thorough with his second one. "I'm not sure, we sort of bumped into each other that night. We both left the office at the same time . . ." He shrugged and then took the last sip. "You know how those things happen. Don't you?"

"It's been too long for me to remember."

"Yeah, well, it's been a while for me too."

"So it was just . . . one of those things?"

He nodded and looked around the room for a waitress. She was laying out the cocktail napkins for an elderly couple. The waitress, who was even older than the people she was serving, laid her napkins out very, very neatly.

"You going to have another one?" I asked, I hoped, lightly.

"I thought so." He looked a bit guilty. He pointed to my almost empty glass. "What about you?"

The waitress was slowly making her way toward us. I had nothing to go home to. No patients in the hospital to see. "Sure."

He waited until the waitress was almost upon us to raise our hands like little boys having to go to the bathroom. "Can we please . . .?" Arnie pointed to the empty glasses. Without missing a step she nodded briefly and continued on with her empty tray toward the bar. Arnie went on, "So, anyway, Shari and I have just started going out."

"A fling, huh?"

"Who knows, Jack. I'm having a good time."

"Is it what you wanted?"

"I think so. Certainly different than Clarissa."

"Better?"

The waitress came sliding slowly over. You could hear the cracking in her back as she placed our martinis down on the shiny table. She lifted the empties slowly onto her tray and without uttering a word slid back toward the bar.

Arnie waited until she had left. "Yeah, it's better, Jack."

"What does Shari think about it?"

He got a big grin on his face. "She likes me, Jack. Isn't that amazing? The wimp gets the cheerleader. Can you believe it?"

I shook my head "no."

"Me too. I'm as shocked as you. I mean, I moved out here so I'd meet somebody different than Clarissa. But I never expected . . . Shari." His grin quadrupled in size.

"I'm glad for you."

"She makes me very happy, Jack." He got a big smile on his face. "All my dreams . . ."

". . . have come true?"

". . . have changed."

I raised my martini glass in a toast. "To a great summer."

He raised his glass. "Let's hope it lasts a lot longer."

I wondered if they had turned up the air-conditioning. I was starting to get cold.

June

S	M	T	W	T	F	S
					1	2
3	4	5	6	7	8	9
10	11	12	13	14	15	16
17	18	19	20	21	22	23
24	25	26	27	28	29	30

July

S	M	T	W	T	F	S
1	2	3	4	5	6	7
8	9	10	11	12	13	14
15	16	17	18	19	20	21
22	23	24	25	26	27	28
29	30	31				

August

S	M	T	W	T	F	S
			1	2	3	4
5	6	7	8	9	10	11
12	13	14	15	16	17	18
19	20	21	22	23	24	25
26	27	28	29	30	31	

Chapter Nine

MY MOTHER told me I took things too seriously. Dumb things. Things I had no control over. I worried about people on television shows. Cried at dumb movies. My parents said that they stopped arguing when I was three, because I would go into the bathroom and throw up. And they were crazy about each other. Friendships, too, were serious business to me. Girl friends were the worst. I could never just "go out" with somebody casually. I had to be crazy about them. Mad about them. Relationships had to be perfect. My older sister, Bernice, once fixed me up with a girl who was everything I should have wanted in a human being. Pretty. Bright. Kind. Except there was this piece of spinach between her back teeth that I would see every time she laughed. That was the other problem with her. She laughed a lot. Which wouldn't have been such a big problem if it weren't for the spinach between her teeth. It made the laugh less attractive. Instead of gay and madcap it became loud and crazy. The evening that had started out so promisingly (at least in my fantasies in the shower) ended with a sense of uncomfortableness on both our parts. I didn't try explaining why it didn't work out to my sister Bernice. She just kept berating me for a week for screwing up my last chance at female companionship. Two weeks later, it was the middle of August, I met Barbara. Everybody else at the barbecue was sweating bullets. She was crisp and starched. It wasn't until after we had started going out, and I had fallen madly in love with her, that I found out she was a secret slob. By then it was too late. I was committed. I was in love.

But now, as I drove home from my drinks with Arnie, I reminded myself just how much of a burden I had always placed on myself. Of how seriously I took just about everything that wasn't really that serious. Except Frank Bernstein's death, which I seemed to have forgotten about. Every once in a while I thought about not seeing Frank anymore. It didn't bother me all that much. What I was frightened of, I was so sure, was the closeness, the proximity to me, of death itself.

The world was tilting. It was all askew. Frank and Marty were too young to die. And Arnie couldn't date Shari. Arnies stayed married to Clarissas.

Our street was dark. The only lights on were at the Redfield's. My house, Bea Bernstein's, and Elizabeth's were all black. Obviously the girls were still at dinner. A flash of fireflies lit up the cloudy night. The clouds seemed to be keeping the heat in. Letting it build up for another uncomfortable day. The first, I feared, of many. Years from now I would remember this summer for the enervating heat of its days. It would probably be referred to by one and all as that "unbelievably hot summer" and not "the summer when Frank and Marty died." Death is a given. Heat is less predictable.

I put the car away and closed the garage door. I looked across the street at Dave Redfield's. The only light was upstairs. Probably in his bedroom. I tried to imagine him as Ingrid Bergman trying to discover the source of the bumping and thumping above. Telling Jane that she was driving him mad.

I walked toward the house. Missing my family. My children at camp. My wife away. My parents in Palm Springs. My sister and brother-in-law in Los Angeles. It was still a neat life. An orderly one in spite of the events. It would right itself. Soon. It had to.

Barbara got home after I fell asleep. At least she was sleeping when I woke up in the morning. I had only Berta to say good morning to. So I left the house feeling, for some reason, for some unknown cause, sad. Almost tearful. Feeling, maybe, the way I should have at Frank's funeral. It was all getting to me. That was what was happening. Nobody to talk to. Too much to think of.

At the office I kept staring at Shari whenever I had a chance, but she seemed the same. She did her job as efficiently as ever. Making appointments, calling in the patients. She smiled when she saw me. But gave no evidence that I knew anything about her relationship. Or maybe she didn't care. Didn't think anything of it. After all, marrying a doctor was probably what she was expected to do. So maybe she saw Arnie Melton as her destiny even if I didn't see it that way. She had made her mistake, but she divorced it, and was now making her life what it was supposed to have been.

Lunch was not much of a help. Harold, grumpy as ever, kept stealing french fries from Dave's plate. The three of us ate in silence until Ben Bracken joined us. Ben was about eighty years old and retired from his stationery store that was torn down a year earlier. He had made enough money from the sale to spend winters in Arizona and three months up north.

"How's Hilda Robins' allergies?" was the first thing he asked as he sat down. He was in his usual suit and tie. His summer blue seersucker with a white shirt and a bright red bow tie. Ben was a dandy. Tall. Thin. A few strands of white hair laying across his freckled scalp. He said he had once won a Ramon Novarro lookalike contest. Nobody disputed him.

"Who's Hilda Robins?" Harold asked, getting so brazen with

his potato stealing he even dipped it into Dave's ketchup.

"Max Robins' widow," Dave said, pushing his hamburger special plate a couple inches further away from Harold and his steamed vegetable platter. It was a new addition to The Lunch Box menu.

"Dandy woman," Ben said, and gave the table a big wink.

"Yeah, yeah." Harold bit into a piece of carrot and then looked at it as if he were checking it for botulism. "I know her. Not bad looking. For an old dame, of course." He made it clear to us he wasn't interested.

"The woman's a looker," Ben answered with a grin.

"Howyadoin, Benny?" Arlene the waitress, leaned over and kissed Ben on the top of his head. She smoothed the strands back into place. Ben looked up at her.

"Great, just great, m'dear. You're looking younger than ever."

"You too, Ben. Still eating egg salad on white?"

"With lettuce and tomato, darlin'."

"You got it, Benny." She looked over at Dave guarding his plate from the encroachments of the wild Harold. "You two could take some lessons in how to treat a lady from this man."

"What the hell was that all about," Harold asked as he contemplated the boring array of overly steamed vegetables.

"The lady appreciates old-fashioned virtues, my boys," Ben announced proudly, taking the paper napkin and placing it across his lap. "Now tell me about the adorable Hilda."

"She's fine, Ben," I said

"Charming woman."

"She had a little problem with her asthma the other day. . ."

"I told her last year to come back with me to Arizona . . ."

"But she's fine now. Home. Ornery as ever." I smiled when I made the last remark, not wanting Ben to feel I was disparaging his Hilda.

"Good, good," he said, taking a sip of water. "She didn't answer her phone on the Fourth, so I thought she might be out of town. Visiting her family."

"She's home, Ben."

"I'll stop by after lunch." He looked across the table at Dave and Harold, who were warily eyeing each other. Dave was on the alert for any attempt on his dwindling stack of fries. "We refer to that as calling on a lady."

Ben's attempt at gallantry got two harumphs.

"I'm sure she'll be glad to see you, Ben," I said, looking at the two grumps staring at me as if I had somehow betrayed the male sex.

Harold jumped in before Ben could say anything. "I'm sorry, I can't see it."

"Can't see what, Harold?" Ben asked kindly.

"Can't see getting married at your age. I mean, why do you want to get tangled up again. What's the point?"

Dave jumped in quickly. "Once is enough. Maybe too much." He bit into his hamburger with such a vengeance that the tomato squirted onto his plate.

Ben looked at the two of them and then shook his head sadly. "You certainly haven't changed, Harold. But I'm shocked at you, David."

Dave Redfield picked up the last of the french fries, five of them, and shoved them all into his mouth. Harold looked like he might go for the soggy tomato covered in mayo. But he held back. It was an effort.

"It's been a difficult time, Ben," Dave said. "I haven't had an easy summer."

"Jane and the kids okay?"

"The kids are fine," Dave said with finality. The missing name was hanging over the table.

Ben wasn't dumb. He looked at me. I shrugged.

Ben's lunch saved us from any further conversation.

Dave and I walked out together. He turned in my direction rather than going to his bank. I didn't ask him about it, but just watched him sweat his way alongside me.

"We're supposed to have dinner tonight, you know, Jack."

I hadn't remembered anything. I glanced up at him.

"Jane's birthday," he said. "Bea's having everybody over."

"The block?" I asked trying to pick up the pace. Dave, who was in much better shape than me, was still sweating in the ninety-two degree heat. I could see that his white shirt had big sweat stains on it even after a half-block walk. We crossed the street. Dave didn't bother to check both ways for traffic. It was quite unlike him. I checked for both of us.

"Yeah, the whole damn block. What's left of us."

"We'll get drunk together, okay, Dave? Just the guys." I touched his elbow to remind him that we had reached the curb. He tripped over it anyway. I caught him by the elbow before he could fall.

"Thanks, thanks." He stood there. On the curb. Running his hand through his hair. "I'm not myself, Jack."

He was. Only a little more so. But the normal state of nervousness seemed to be replaced by fear. "It's been rough for all of us, Dave."

"Not for you yet, Jack. It's Jane who's driving me nuts." I could see Shari's Mustang hurtling down the street at seventy miles an hour. Tires squealing, it pulled into Arnie Melton's parking space in front of our building.

"You're driving yourself nuts, Dave. Give Jane some time. We all go through these . . . crises."

He stood there trying to button his tan suitcoat. After he closed it, he seemed to pull himself together. "I know. I know."

"Good. Just remember that these things happen." I noticed that Shari and Arnie had closed the top of the convertible and seemed to be headed into the building. Arnie was carrying a stack of boxes. Shari was whistling. I started walking, slowly.

Like a depressed puppy Dave followed me. "Just wait till your wife turns on you." We reached the entrance to my building. I stopped. Dave kept on walking, talking, gesturing.

"David!" I yelled.

He walked on for a few more steps until he realized that I wasn't next to him. Quickly he turned around. He ran back to me. "I'm not myself, Jack. I got to do something about all this."

"Maybe you should go away?"

He looked at me. "And give her the satisfaction . . ." With a stomp of his feet he was off down the street.

I thought about Arnie and Shari skipping down the hallway. And then David running down the street. Then I tried to figure out where I fit. I finally decided I was in a holding pattern. But was something coming?

It wasn't much of a birthday celebration. Just the neighbors and a couple friends of Jane's. Her parents made a brief appearance. An older quiet couple who had to go home to bed before eight.

I spent most of the time getting drinks for everyone. Bea, even though she had only been a widow for ten days, was happily feeding the dozen guests. It was too hot for a barbecue, so she had made lots of cold dishes and spread them all out on the dining room table. The guests ate off their laps in Bea's living room. Bea sat in the big red winged chair that had always been reserved for Frank. She sat there, eating her Thai chicken salad, drinking her diet soda, feet perched on the ottoman that Frank wouldn't allow even his children to touch.

By ten, the only people left to clean up were from our block of Apple Tree Lane. The women were in the kitchen, and I was hiding out in the den, watching the White Sox game on TV, when Dave skulked in. I realized I couldn't even tell him the score in case he asked. I had no idea who the Sox were playing.

"Did you notice?" he asked, sliding into the room and sitting across from me on one of the two leather couches. I was on the other one. A burgundy leather number that Frank had picked out for "his room," as he liked to call it.

"Notice what, Dave?"

He leaned forward, hands cupped under his chin, looking at me as if I were the chief of police. "What she's doing?"

"Not exactly, David."

He glanced down toward the floor. "Notice the socks?"

I looked at his socks. One was white. The other blue.

"They don't match," I said innocently.

Instantly the forefinger of his left hand was pointed at me. "See! It isn't my imagination. Told you. Told you."

I nodded. "Right. Right, Dave. They are two different colors. You are perfectly correct."

"And you know why they are two different colors?"

I thought of some silly answer, but figured shaking my head "no" was my safest choice.

"Because my . . . wife . . . rolled . . . them . . . up . . . that . . . way."

I nodded.

He went on. A man possessed. "She did it on purpose."

I pursed my lips to look as if I were semi-agreeing with him.

"She's doing that a lot these days. Jane used to do perfect laundry. But no more. No more."

"It's summer, Dave."

He slammed a fist into the palm of his hand.

"You don't believe me, do you? You don't believe she's rolling up blue and white socks together, do you?"

"I do, Dave, I just don't think it's part of any . . . conspiracy."

He fell back. Into the leather. "Okay, okay." He held his hand up. "Fine. Fine."

"Dave." I sat forward, in a doctorish sort of way. "Maybe you should talk to somebody about this whole thing?"

"A psychiatrist, right? Isn't that right? Isn't that who you're tellin' me to talk to. Right, am I right, am I right?"

I nodded. "You're right."

He got up off the couch. Looked down at me. His finger was shaking and pointing at the same time. "You laugh now, but wait till it happens to you. Like it happened to Marty and Frank. And now"—he looked around the room. He ignored the sound of the television. "—it's my turn. But it's not going to happen to me. Just you wait. Just you wait." He turned and ran out.

* * *

"Your friend Dave Redfield is driving Jane nuts." Barbara was getting into bed. I was already in it. She had thrown her shorts and shirt on top of the dresser and slipped into the shortie white nightgown she wore in the summer.

"He says she's trying to drive him crazy."

Barbara turned off the light on her side of the bed and climbed in under the quilt. She shmushed up the fluffy pillows until she found a comfortable position. She was looking up at the ceiling while she talked to me. I still had my light on. I was reading a June issue of Time when Barbara started talking. For now I put it aside.

"You know," she said with that Barbara edge of sarcasm, "Dave really is going crazy. Jane says that everything she does sets him off."

"And everything she does . . ."

"He pull the *Gaslight* bit on you?"

I looked over at her, she was smiling. "Yeah."

"The man is crazy, I'm telling you, Jack. He sees this conspiracy of women all around him. He thinks Jane and Bea and Elizabeth and me, can you believe it, the man thinks I care enough about him to drive him crazy. Why, why Jack?"

I reached over to turn off the light. I lay there like Barbara, staring up at the ceiling. I pulled the quilt up to my chin. It felt like fifty degrees in our bedroom. The way Barbara liked it. I was shivering. "It hasn't been a good summer for men on this block."

"What are you talking about?"

I turned on my side. Barbara was now on hers. Still, we weren't touching. "Well, first, Marty. Then Frank. And then Jane goes and declares her independence from Dave. It's like Apple Tree Lane just discovered feminism."

Barbara turned away. On her back again. "It's not feminism. Nobody wants to go downtown and work. Or stay here and open a store. We've discovered each other, Jack."

"What does that mean? Since when did you need to discover each another."

"Since we realized the choice wasn't between staying home or becoming lawyers."

"What is the choice?"

She pushed herself backward. Pushed until she was sitting up looking down at me. "It's a question of our relationships to each other. How we make the best out of our interaction."

My eyes rolled upward, I couldn't help it. "What does that mean, Barbara? Explain that last sentence."

She went on as if the last question hadn't been asked. "We have to accept the fact that we live and work in a community. Together."

"Yeah, so?"

She looked at me and shook her head. "See, see what I mean."

"What do you mean, what do you mean?" I sounded like Dave Redfield, repeating everything.

"I mean your hostility is symptomatic. You're all quite happy to get women into your environment, into your offices where you can control them. But this is our environment."

"What environment, Barbara? The bedroom? The house? What is this all supposed to mean?" I hardly ever get angry, but I could feel myself starting to tense. Calm down. Please, I told myself, don't get upset.

"This is the town we live in. This is what we have to control."

"You already control it. You're responsible for its economy. You run the school board. Most of the men visit on weekends. What more do you want?"

She waited until I stopped gesturing. She was much calmer than me. "I want, excuse me, we want women to be aware of their power, to be aware that they can exercise it. That they have choices."

"What about us?" I was talking so very quietly that I could hardly hear myself. Barbara leaned down. "What should our choices be?" I asked.

"You've always had choices. That's Feminism 101."

"And that's what I'm telling you, you're talking early Gloria Steinem."

She pounded the mattress. "You just don't understand. You just don't get it, Jack."

"What is there to get?" My voice was getting very, very soft.

"Us!"

"What's an Us?"

"Me." Another pounding of the bed. "Jane. Bea. Elizabeth. We're an Us. And you know what . . .?"

"What." I just mouthed the word, didn't even try to project it.

Barbara didn't wait for it. "I'll tell you what, soon there's going to be more like us." She turned on her side. Away from me.

I just lay there. Shaking my head from side to side. But she had fallen asleep by the time I thought of something to say. She even, it seemed, snored louder than usual. And by morning, she had managed to abscond with most of the covers. My toes were practically blue.

We woke up at the same time. Seven. It was one of those awkward mornings that every marriage goes through. When you're not quite sure how to behave, how you should be mad at each other. So we played the silent game. Getting showered in silence, brushing our teeth in silence, putting on our clothes without saying a word.

I got down to breakfast first, so I had to make the coffee. I thought about being petty and making just enough for me. But no, I was too big a person. Too nice a guy. So, I made so many cups we could have had the whole neighborhood over. Actually, after I left for the office she probably was going to have most of the neighborhood over, for whatever it was they did. Rediscovering relationships. Or just cursing out the men in their lives. Past and present. I thought about pouring the coffee out, after giving myself a mug. I thought about it for a while. I had a feeling that this argument was going to last. Although I usually chicken out and make up before it gets too complex. But this time . . .

June

S	M	T	W	T	F	S
					~~1~~	~~2~~
~~3~~	~~4~~	~~5~~	~~6~~	~~7~~	~~8~~	~~9~~
~~10~~	~~11~~	~~12~~	~~13~~	~~14~~	~~15~~	~~16~~
~~17~~	~~18~~	~~19~~	~~20~~	~~21~~	~~22~~	~~23~~
~~24~~	~~25~~	~~26~~	~~27~~	~~28~~	~~29~~	~~30~~

July

S	M	T	W	T	F	S
~~1~~	~~2~~	~~3~~	~~4~~	~~5~~	~~6~~	~~7~~
~~8~~	~~9~~	10	11	12	13	14
15	16	17	18	19	20	21
22	23	24	25	26	27	28
29	30	31				

August

S	M	T	W	T	F	S
			1	2	3	4
5	6	7	8	9	10	11
12	13	14	15	16	17	18
19	20	21	22	23	24	25
26	27	28	29	30	31	

Chapter Ten

AS WEEKENDS go, it was terrible. We didn't even have the children to goad us into making up. There was just us in the house. Trying not to pass each other on the way to and from the kitchen and the bathroom. And if, occasionally, in spite of all precautions, we did pass each other, then we tried very hard to look at the carpeting. To examine it in minute detail. I stayed outside on Sunday. She spent the day with "the girls." I waited for Elizabeth to come out and sun herself, but she never showed up. So I read the *Tribune* slowly, made sure to cover myself with sun block, and went to sleep early. Very early.

Hilda Robins was there before me on Monday morning. Tapping her sensible shoes on the linoleum of my cool hallway. It was going to be a hundred-degree day. It was already in the upper eighties and the hallway felt like a meat locker.

"You're late, Klein." She stopped her tapping as I got to the door with my keys.

"You're early, Mrs. Robins." I smiled.

She coughed slightly and waited while I unlocked the door. Not wishing to get crucified for rudeness, I motioned for her to go in ahead of me.

"It's dark in there, Klein. You think I'm going to get raped by some maniac who's looking for narcotics. Or pollen serum."

I kept on smiling and walked in to turn the lights on. Only when they came on did Mrs. Robins enter the waiting room.

"I suppose I'll have to wait while you do your doctor stuff?"

"No, why don't you come in. I'll do my doctor stuff in front of you."

She followed me in. I motioned to the examining room. Looking both ways, she walked in and sat down in the chair next to the door. I was outside, changing from my lightest summer coat into office whites.

"I suppose you know that Ben Bracken is in town," she said with slightly less disdain in her voice.

"I had lunch with him the other day."

She was nodding as I walked over to the file cabinet to get her chart.

"The old coot came over to see me last Friday."

"He said he might."

I took the file into the office. After putting it down on the table, I walked over to wash my hands.

"Looks good," she said, without quite as much hostility.

"Arizona is good for him, you should go down there sometime. Good for you, too."

"What's that supposed to mean?"

"Just that you might like it. Good for asthma."

"So is death." she said as I dried my hands on one of the brown paper towels.

I walked back to the desk and sat down on the little stool. "I think I'd prefer Arizona."

That got me a "humph." I checked her chart out for the dosages she'd need and started putting the syringe together. I kept talking to her while I made up it up. "He's a sweet man . . ."

"Letch." She rolled up the sleeves of her starched white blouse. She didn't even flinch as I put the needle into her right arm.

"A sweet letch then."

She rolled down her sleeve and buttoned the cuff. "You always surprise me, Klein. Not that you're exactly Henny Youngman, but you're a bit more amusing than you look."

"Thank you, Mrs. Robins." I threw away the needle.

She didn't get up to go off into the waiting room. My patients usually had to sit there for fifteen minutes to see if they had any adverse reaction to the injection. But Mrs. Robins didn't budge. I tried to look like I was cleaning up.

"Klein . . ." A pause. I was surprised. Mrs. Robins rarely paused. "Klein . . . let me ask you something."

I turned to her. I had a feeling if I said anything she would use it as an excuse to make a joke, avoid whatever it was she wanted to say to me. So I waited. Waited while she adjusted her blouse. Straightened her already perfectly set hairdo. Finally, with a nervous cough, she began. "How do you think I would be able to withstand the . . ." she seemed to be combing through her mind for the appropriate word. At last it clicked into place. ". . . rigors of marriage." She gave me a look that demanded I treat the question seriously. One laugh and she would plunge the nearest hypodermic into my jugular.

"I don't see where it would be a problem, Mrs. Robins."

"Then you don't think my asthma will get any worse?"

I shifted on the stool. It was not the best place to spend time. "I can't answer that. Right now it's fairly well under control. One hopes you'll get off the steroids in the next couple weeks. As far as it getting better or worse, well, you've had it for twenty-five years now . . ."

"Twenty-seven."

"Well, then you know how unpredictable it can be. With steroids, however . . ."

". . . I get depressed. Did you know that, Klein?"

"Different people have different reactions to the drugs, Mrs. Robins."

"I'm not interested in different people's reactions. It's mine that matters. And the fact is it depresses me, Klein."

"You'll get off them soon, Mrs. Robins."

"And if I have another episode?"

"You know the answer. . ."

She leaned back with a sigh. "You know how long I've known Ben?"

"I imagine quite a while."

"Be specific, Klein."

"Shall we say, forty years?" I could hear Mary and Shari walking into the office.

"Sixty," she said with feeling. "Ben and I and my late husband used to pal around together when we were all single. Later on, Ben's wife Maude and I were quite friendly."

I heard Shari's giggles float past the door to the office. I tried to listen to the conversation in the hallway, but I feared the wrath of Mrs. Robins if I moved my head in any direction but hers. I stayed fixed to my stool.

"It's not a total surprise that Ben has asked me to move to Arizona with him."

A good opening for me. "As I said, the desert air could be helpful."

She paid no attention. "The point I'm trying to make is I don't want to burden him with another invalid. I don't want him spending the rest of his days taking care of a wheezing asthmatic."

"You're taking a chance too. Ben's at least eighty."

"The man's a lion, Klein." She started to get up from the chair. No creaks. No lower back strain. Mrs. R. got up like a fifteen-year-old. Her back never bent. I'm glad I never had her for an English teacher. "So no guarantees, huh Klein?" she said, as she looked down at me.

"I'm sorry, no. But I don't see why—"

"Yes, yes, I've heard it before, why I can't lead a normal life if I just take care of myself. Same old medical gibberish. This profession is full of cliches."

"They don't teach English in medical school."

She started to leave the office. "Unfortunately not. Literacy can give one more comfort than most of your prescriptions." She stopped and felt the bump on her arm. "No reaction," she snapped, and continued out the office.

I marked down the "no reaction" on her chart and took it out to the file area. Shari was showing a new blouse to Mary, who was admiring it while taking out the day's charts.

I smiled at the two of them. They didn't notice me.

"Folie à deux," Arnie explained as we ate our sticky buns. I licked the cinnamoned sugar off my fingers. We were eating at The Cozy Tea Room. I had suggested it to Arnie when he mentioned we should go over to The Lunch Box. I didn't feel like listening to Dave Redfield's madness, although it was a subject I broached after we had ordered our iced teas and turkey salads. I told Arnie about Dave's fears after the death of Marty Siegal and Frank Bernstein.

"Folie à deux is a pattern of behavior that is seen in more than one person. For instance, if two sisters in the same household are both kleptomaniacs, it could be called a *folie à deux."*

"Is it common?"

He picked up the final crumb of his sticky bun. "Not uncommon. Imitative behavior isn't all that unusual in mental illness. Especially in the same family."

"What about the same block?" I buttered the last piece of my bun.

He looked around for the sticky bun lady. "Possible. It's all based on proximity. Someone rewards the aberrant behavior and others start to duplicate it." He waved to the woman in the frilly jumper who was depositing the little treats on everybody's plates. She finally noticed him. Being one of the only two men in the room helped. He turned back to me. "Then, if someone else imitates the behavior, it's referred to as a *folie à trois*. Four makes a *folie à quatre*."

"Sounds cute."

"It's not." He watched the sticky bun deliverer stop to refill the plates along the way. "Eventually, it can lead to mass hysteria, like in Jonestown. It seems also to build, so that what could originally have been neurotic behavior can become almost psychotic."

"So the person who first exhibited the symptoms . . ."

He finished the thought. ". . . isn't as seriously ill as the last person. It's like chicken pox. The first kid always gets the mildest case." He smiled as the bringer of the sticky buns deposited two on his plate. She noticed his smile and put two more down on top of them. I got two of the littlest ones I'd ever seen. I didn't smile as she walked away.

"Does this sound like a *folie à deux?*"

"You mean *folie à trois*. Dave is telling you that his wife is out to do unto him what the other two did unto their husbands."

I reached for a bun and broke it in half. "I didn't mean that I took it seriously."

He popped one of his stickies into his mouth, uncut. He chewed and swallowed before talking. "Sure you do. You did a few weeks ago. Remember when you came to me about murder therapy? And then, after the next guy was killed, how I tried to get you to admit how worried you were?"

I buttered each half very slowly. "Yeah, but I was more interested from a hypothetical point of view."

"Come on, Jack." Arnie leaned back in his chair. "You were concerned about what your wife was doing with these other women. Nobody talks to a shrink hypothetically. Especially you. You wanted to see if it was dangerous what she was doing."

"And . . .?"

He put his fingers together to make a steeple. "Could be. I hate to use the analogy, but she sounds like a loaded pistol with a hair trigger."

"Come on, Arnie, you don't know Barbara, she's—"

He put a hand up to stop me. "I'm not talking about her. As far as I can tell she has a happy marriage."

I nodded.

"It's the other one I'm talking about. Dave's paranoia may not be so nuts, you know." He pointed to my plate. "You using all your butter?" I shook my head and he reached forward to swipe a couple of pats. He used them to cover the top of one of his three remaining buns. The man was not worried about cholesterol. He took a big bite of the butter-smeared bun and kept on talking. "One of the problems with paranoids is that people don't take them seriously. They really may be persecuted. Take this guy Dave." Arnie finished off his bun. He licked the sugar off his fingers and settled back. "Just from meeting him that one time I would classify him as insecure. The man has always been henpecked. First, his father. Then, his wife."

A waitress gently placed our turkey salads and the melon slices surrounding them, in front of us.

"So here you have the son getting along for a couple years without the father. Still not too sure of himself or his place in life. Then, bam, all of a sudden his meek, supportive wife starts to take on an identity of her own. She becomes his father. Strong-willed, determined. No wonder the guy's gone nuts."

"So you think he really isn't being paranoid?" I took a bite of turkey. It had long ago ceased to be alive.

"I'm not saying that. What I am saying is that the possibility exists that Mrs. Dave can be doing things to drive him nuts. Mean little things, like rolling up a pair of mismatched socks. It would drive the guy crazy, because here he's gone and killed his father . . ."

"Wait a second . . ." I started, but Arnie held up his fork before it plunged into the ersatz turkey.

"No, no, I meant symbolically. He wouldn't have had the guts to kill his father, although he probably would have loved to. So his father is dead and now his wife is doing the same things to him. I ask you, wouldn't you go a little nuts?" He took a bite of his salad and then looked at me. "Hey, what is this stuff?"

"I don't know. . ." I pushed my plate aside. "But do you think it's dangerous, what he's going through?"

Arnie tried to eat around the pieces of turkey. "To whom?"

"To him."

"Probably more so than to anybody else." He threw his fork down on the table. "This stuff is shit. Why are we eating here, Jack?"

"Because you wouldn't believe me about the food." Arnie had insisted any place that made great martinis had to have good food.

"From now on, I'll listen." He took a couple swallows of his iced tea. "Anyhow, the original question is still on the table."

"What's that?"

"How dangerous is Mrs. Dave? That seems to be the more pertinent question. He is really only dangerous to himself. She, on the other hand, in a classic *folie à trois,* could truly present a danger to him." He finished off his iced tea and smiled at me. "How many houses on your block?"

"Four."

He leaned back with a soft smile. "Two to go."

I tried to smile back, but it was impossible. "How's Shari?"

Instantly, he forgot psychiatry. Arnie was too happy with his life to get upset about mine. "Great. Just great. Fabulous."

"Different than your first wife?" I was glad to change the topic.

"Clarissa hated shopping" he explained, his grin growing ever bigger. "Shari loves it."

"I know."

"So do I."

"I'm happy for you." I tried to be sincere.

"Thanks, Jack." He bought it.

June

S	M	T	W	T	F	S
					~~1~~	~~2~~
~~3~~	~~4~~	~~5~~	~~6~~	~~7~~	~~8~~	~~9~~
~~10~~	~~11~~	~~12~~	~~13~~	~~14~~	~~15~~	~~16~~
~~17~~	~~18~~	~~19~~	~~20~~	~~21~~	~~22~~	~~23~~
~~24~~	~~25~~	~~26~~	~~27~~	~~28~~	~~29~~	~~30~~

July

S	M	T	W	T	F	S
~~1~~	~~2~~	~~3~~	~~4~~	~~5~~	~~6~~	~~7~~
~~8~~	~~9~~	~~10~~	~~11~~	~~12~~	13	14
15	16	17	18	19	20	21
22	23	24	25	26	27	28
29	30	31				

August

S	M	T	W	T	F	S
			1	2	3	4
5	6	7	8	9	10	11
12	13	14	15	16	17	18
19	20	21	22	23	24	25
26	27	28	29	30	31	

Chapter Eleven

I THOUGHT OF calling Barbara up. To try and patch things up. But decided to cook instead; chicken teriyaki.

"It's different," she said that night, with a hint of a smile.

"You think so?"

She took another chunk of white meat and chewed it for a second. "Absolutely. Much better."

And that was all there was to it. The fight was over. Forgotten. For now.

We even had sex that night. A little more actively than usual. The absence of children in the house seemed to make it freer, younger. We didn't hide underneath the covers or worry about the kids walking by the closed door and opening it. We even laughed. An occasion for happiness.

Afterward, we snuggled up against each other in the middle of the bed. When the air-conditioned temperature felt like it was going below freezing I pulled the quilt over me. I knew Barbara was still hot.

"Isn't visiting day next week?" I finally asked, brushing the hair away from her forehead and kissing it.

She stretched, raising her arms above her head. "Two weeks. Weekend after next."

"Have you talked to Jane about it?" Traditionally we drove up to Camp Moccasin in Duck Lake, Wisconsin, with Dave and Jane Redfield. Dave hadn't said anything to me so far this year. But then he had other things on his mind.

"Not really." Barbara finished her stretching and curled up in a fetal ball. She turned away from me, grabbing a piece of the cover and then sliding her tush so it fit right above my left hip. I didn't want to move. It felt nice. Nicer than being alone.

"Are the two of them going?"

"I guess so." Barbara yawned. Sex always made her tired. She was usually asleep five minutes later.

"You want to drive with them?"

Another yawn. "Sure, why not?"

"Because . . . because . . ." I was trying to figure out how not to break the mood. ". . . becaue of the way things are . . . between Jane and Dave."

I could hear her starting to breathe through her nose, a sign of impending snoring. "Don't worry," she said quietly. "It'll be fine."

I worried.

Dave Redfield was having breakfast at The Lunch Box. Sitting there eating alone, eyes staring out the window, trying not to drop scrambled eggs on his khaki suit. His eyebrows rose as he saw me walk past. I went in to ask about the camp trip.

"Only if you sit with me in the car," he said, staring unblinkingly at me as I sat down.

"David," I said patiently, "I think you're being a little crazy."

"Sure, sure," he said rapidly, shaking his head up and down.

"I may be crazy, but at least I'm alive. And when we get up there I want us all to share a motel room."

"The four of us?" I waved off the waitress bringing over the coffee pot.

"Sure, why not? Those motels have two double beds. You and I can sleep in one. And our . . . wives . . . can sleep in the other one. That's what they want. Isn't it?" His voice was rising and he was shoveling the eggs in faster and faster.

"I don't think so, Dave. I really don't." I was trying to act normal. Quiet, easy, like a shrink trying to talk somebody out of jumping off the top of Sears Tower.

He gulped down the last of his eggs and looked over at me, fork still poised in mid-air. His watery brown eyes were wide open, looking amazed. In total wonder at a world gone mad. "They want each other, don't you realize that Jack, all they want is each other. No men. I'm surprised they even let us onto the block." He tried to refocus his eyes. For a second they were crossed. "They want Apple Tree Lane, our block, the one where we bought houses, to be without men." He looked at me scornfully. "But you don't believe it do you, Doctor Klein? You know better." He leaned toward me. "I'm telling you, they're going to do it."

"Dave, are you coming to camp with us?" I decided that ignoring his psychoses was the best way to deal with them.

He pursed his lips and stared at me for a second. "Uh-huh. I guess it'll give me protection for a few days. She wouldn't dare do anything in front of you." He looked at me for confirmation. I nodded. "So maybe it's a good idea if we do come with you." He jumped up, grabbed the check and started to walk out. It was as if he had forgotten I was there. I followed him to the cash register. He was finished paying by the time I caught up with him. I held onto his arm, stopping him from going outside.

"Dave, I know I mentioned this before, but don't you think you should talk to somebody?"

He looked at me like I was nuts. "She is not doing my laundry now," he said triumphantly.

"Dave, all she's doing is asserting her independence. It'll work out. Trust me." I moved my hand to his shoulder. He slid out from under it.

"I was a happily married man till six weeks ago." He was trying to control himself, talk reasonably. "And then all this started. I am now a miserable man." He looked like he was going to burst into tears. "I know I sound as if I'm acting crazy, but I think I'm going crazy." I thought he was beginning to cry. "First my father..." He didn't finish the sentence, but walked out of the restaurant. I waited for a few seconds before leaving myself.

Ben Bracken was standing in front of The Lunch Box when I got outside. He was watching the scurrying Dave Redfield rushing toward the comfort of his late father's bank. Ben was *tsking* loudly. He was dressed in a blue and white seersucker suit. His remaining strands of white hair had been plastered by the humidity onto his freckled scalp.

We watched Dave running away. Finally Ben turned to me. "Poor man. It would make his father ill, if he knew."

"He's got a lot of problems, Ben."

"Always had," Ben said softly. "With a father like that it would be hard not to. Dave should have been a teacher. Manual arts. Always good building things. Would have been happy."

"I don't think that would have helped this summer."

"It would have happened sooner or later." He turned to watch Dave go into the building. "You working today, Jack?"

"Busy season, Ben."

"I'll walk you." He started toward my office. Not the speediest of paces but steady. Constant. The man kept himself in terrific shape. Walking every day of his life, he once told me. Nine months a year in Arizona and three in Lake View.

The streets were fairly empty. The stores in Lake View didn't open until ten. Now there were just some receptionists, a couple nurses and a few doctors going to their offices. The usual joggers and strollers seemed to have been kept inside by the heat of the morning. The grass on the median strip in the street was turning brown. It was only July but it felt like the end of August, when you wait for the cooling days of autumn. Watching the weatherman each night for hints of winter storms coming from the west. So Ben and I walked along, looking at the stores selling things to wear.

"Town's pretty quiet these days," he finally said.

"It's early."

"These days it is. In my time, everything was open at nine. "Course back then men owned the stores. Wives wouldn't let 'em hang around the house till ten o'clock. These days, what with women buying all the stores, you gotta wait until the owner puts on her makeup. Takes a lot longer than shaving."

"You should have hung on to your place a few more years, Ben. You would have been unique. The only place open at nine."

"I don't think so, Jack. When I was working here it was a small town. Now. . ." he looked up and down the street. At the windows filled with dresses and jewelry and tennis clothes. ". . . it's a place where the men only come to sleep. Take that table Camille Grasso keeps open for the men at lunch. It's like a ghetto. Back when Camille's father was running the place it was a regular restaurant. You'd go in for lunch and men and women'd be eatin' together. Talkin' to one another. No more. That's one of the reasons I left Lake View. Figured it might be different someplace else."

"Is it?" We had reached the corner. Ben was looking both ways.

"Sort of. Down there, everybody's pretty much retired, so you hang around with whoever isn't in the hospital. Doesn't make much difference what sex they are."

We started walking across the street. A speeding Corvette almost nailed us. I grabbed Ben and held on. It zoomed past. The driver, a woman with long blonde curly hair never flinched. Never looked our way.

"See what I mean, Jack? Don't even notice a man around

here." He chuckled as we made it to the curb. We kept on walking toward my office. "That's what Hilda misses. Having some men in her life. Looks forward to coming to see you each week."

"You're kidding?" I thought of her voice dripping with sarcasm. Looking askance at everything, and everyone, in the office.

"Nope, she likes you. She was crazy about my Maude."

"So I heard."

"Yeah, Hilda and I should get married. Settle down." He looked up at me. "Have a couple kids." He got a big smile on his face.

"She's worried, Ben."

His face turned serious. He looked down at the ground. At my black loafers and his walking shoes. "I know. Figures I'm going to wind up taking care of her." He looked back up at me, questioningly. He didn't have to ask.

"I don't know. She's healthy enough. But I can't predict when she's going to have another asthma attack. Or how bad it's going to be. She would be better off in Arizona, though."

He nodded. We had reached my office building. We both stood in front. Trying to position ourselves in what little shade was left.

"She doesn't want to leave Lake View, she keeps saying. Tells me she was born here, she ought to kick the bucket here. Stubborn old coot." He smiled again when he finished. "But that's why I love her. Miss her when I'm gone."

"So why don't you move back here?" I asked, moving to the door. The sun was creeping toward our tiny patch of shade. Ben Bracken ignored the heat.

"I don't know, it's not the same anymore. Hilda's about the only person I grew up with who's left. All the other friends are gone. Either gone gone or moved away someplace. The only reason I come back each summer is to see her. And if we were shut up inside all winter, we'd probably kill each other. I love the woman, but twenty-four hours a day could drive you bonkers. I'd probably look forward to her asthma attacks."

The two of us looked at each other, smiled and then started laughing.

"You're a very sick man, Ben Bracken."

"That's what the ladies love, doc." He gave me one of his nudges.

"I'll tell her to give in to you, Ben."

"You do that, Jack." He patted my back and with a wave, headed down the street. He was singing as he walked away, doing what looked like a samba step.

Ben made me happy. I wished he did still live in Lake View. But he didn't, and my list of male friends, short enough to begin with, was dwindling.

"Women Without Men," Barbara said almost defiantly. "That's what we're calling it."

"A dating service? You're going to start a dating service?"

She looked at me coldly. Harshly. We were waiting at the bar at Angelo's. Waiting for Elizabeth and Bea to join us. It was Thursday night. Where else were you going to go in town?

"It's just the opposite, Jack. It's to help them get along without men. That's why we call it Women Without Men. It's women who don't need men. But they do need help."

"So do the men," I said with a smile. I tried to sip my martini casually, as if the whole thing didn't worry me. I wasn't like old paranoid Dave Redfield. Was I?

If Barbara had had long hair, she would have tossed it back over her shoulder. "Men don't need the help." She pointed to her chest. "We do. We're the ones who are left alone. Without jobs, without money, without . . ." She tried to think of something else without. I was about to suggest "men" when she came up with it. "Sustenance. Emotional sustenance is what women need."

"And you're going to charge people for that?"

She picked up her martini, it still had the five cocktail onions mixed up with the ice cubes. She avoided them. Saving them for the end. "We're charging them," she said quietly, evenly, "for the services we provide. When their husbands leave them . . ."

"What happens when they leave their husbands?"

"A rare occurrence, if you'll check the figures. What we do is help them cope with the situation. Jane can help them with real estate, get them a new house if they need it, sell the old one . . ."

I tried to catch her eye. It was impossible, she was talking over my shoulder. I jumped in anyway. "Barbara, Jane Redfield is the world's worst real estate person. You know that. The woman can screw up any deal. She is guaranteed to get you the worst price for your house. Or show you a split level when you want a studio apartment."

Barbara lowered her gaze. I got it right between the eyes. I blinked. "Jane is not the same Jane. She NOW understands why she was a failure. She will be a success."

"Fine. Fine." I waved Jane off. "Now, tell me what Bea and Elizabeth and you are going to do? Once Jane has sold their house at a loss."

"Don't be cynical with me, Jack Klein." Another shot in the left eye. I didn't blink this time.

"I mean it, Barbara, what are you guys going to do for the money? You are going to charge something for this, I assume?"

"Not a lot, but enough."

"So what are you going to do?"

"Help them, Jack. Is that so hard to understand? Elizabeth and Bea have already been through this, and I believe I can offer some aid in giving them the tools they need to deal with the emotional side of the situation."

"Bea's going to give them casserole recipes for one?"

"Bea Bernstein is a very strong person, in case you didn't know. And Elizabeth can help with things."

I held my tongue. Literally biting it with my teeth and keeping it from jumping out and saying something that would warrant me getting hit in the face.

"Very funny, Jack. Really funny." She leaned toward me. "You know the problem with you is the problem with men. They can't take anything seriously. Even leaving their wives." She flung her hands up in the air. "No big deal, I'll run off with a twenty-two-year-old and leave her with the house, the kids and three hundred dollars a month. No problem. She can handle it." She moved back a little. Leaned against the bar. "Well, she can handle it a lot better than he could in the same situation. And we're going to make sure she has the people around her to do it for her." She looked at me seriously. "Other women. That's what she's going to get."

"Want another martini?" I pointed to her glass.

She glanced down. Picked up the onions and shook her head.

"I do." I nodded at Jimmy the bartender and turned to Barbara. "Why are you so upset?"

"I'm not upset." She threw the cocktail spear back into the almost empty glass. "I'm just trying to make something clear to you."

"C'mon guys, loosen up." The voice of Elizabeth Siegal cut through the anger. "It's going to be a fun night."

"Where's Bea?" Barbara asked, looking around the restaurant worriedly.

Elizabeth pointed toward the outside. "Parking."

"Nice of her to drop you off," I said kindly.

"Yeah, well, she didn't want me to sweat too much. It's terrible out there. Can you believe it?"

"Bea is thoughtful," Barbara added for my benefit.

Elizabeth looked at me. "Maybe she thinks I'm Frank."

"Elizabeth!" Barbara's tone was reprimanding.

"Well, you know she's been so subservient"—Elizabeth looked at me with pride at the choice of words—"so subservient," she repeated, "that she's gotta do something for whoever she's with. Next thing you know she'll cut up my chicken."

"Hi." Bea's voice, which seemed to have become stronger since Frank's death. "Are you okay, Elizabeth?"

"As okay as I can be. This weather is crazy. I can't do anything with my hair. Nothing."

I turned to greet Bea. She was dabbing her forehead with a

handkerchief. I realized she not only sounded better, less scared, she looked a heck of a lot better since Frank had choked to death. She had lost a lot of weight and seemed, for the first time since I knew her, actually to be standing up straight. She appeared a couple inches taller. Maybe she had slouched all those years to let Frank appear taller than he was. But this Bea Bernstein had a neck. Standing straight, shoulders back, a smile on her face, pudgy Fran was now cute Bea.

"You look swell, Bea."

She nodded. "Thank you, Jack. But it's your wife's doing."

Barbara reached out to pat Bea's arm. "No, no, it's all of us." She looked over at Elizabeth. "Together." Elizabeth gave me a wistful smile. Barbara didn't notice. "That's the way things get done . . ."

"Together." Bea finished the sentence for Barbara.

"Together," I echoed. They all looked at me. Only Elizabeth grinned.

I think if the evening had only been the three of them and me, I could have taken it. Been more comfortable. But the fact that Jane Redfield made an appearance in the middle of the lasagna sort of started things going bad. Angelo placed a chair for her between Barbara and me. I wound up with just enough room to cut my lasagna with a fork. I didn't even try to reach for my glass of wine.

"He's crazy. Nuts. Out of his mind." Jane started talking before she sat down. "The man is bananas. Truly mad."

Nobody had to ask who she was talking about.

"He doesn't want to eat with me now. Says he's going to make his own dinners. I swear they're going to be bringing the straightjacket for him any day now."

"What set him off today?" Barbara asked in her new tone. It sounded significant, important.

Jane got a slight smile on her face. Her narrow face, the Waspiness of her cheekbones, made it perfect for a thin-lipped grin. On Bea, it would have been lost. "He discovered that one of the pilot lights was out on the stove. Accused me of trying to blow up the place, or at least asphyxiate him. I think he went to the hardware store to buy a gas mask."

"So you came over here?" I asked.

"Uh-huh. Bea had mentioned you were all coming for dinner. Lasagna looks decent."

Barbara waved the waitress over. Jane ordered a salad. "I'm three pounds overweight," she said.

"One of my boobs is three pounds overweight," Elizabeth announced to the table. The three other women didn't smile. So Elizabeth turned to me. I grinned. She grinned back and squeezed my thigh. An affectionate squeeze until she lingered a couple seconds too long. I started to feel my face turning red. Since nobody else was noticing me, it didn't really matter. Elizabeth didn't look at me, and a few seconds later her hand moved away.

Barbara stared at me. She didn't seem to have seen what was going on underneath the table. "Talk to Dave," she said firmly.

"About what?"

"About how he's driving his wife crazy."

"She's . . ." I didn't finish the thought, but let Barbara go on. She, Bea and Jane looked at me like the judges at Nuremberg.

"If you don't talk to him, at least find someone who's a professional. Like that friend of yours. The one in your building."

"Arnie Melton?"

Barbara nodded. "Anybody, just get some valium into the man."

Jane jumped in. "He's driving me nuts. I don't know what's going to happen when the kids come back from camp."

"Have you tried . . . talking . . ."

"She's tried," Barbara said in exasperation. "He won't listen, the man is incapable of listening to reason."

"Just like Frank," Bea sighed. "He never listened to anyone."

"I don't know about that, Bea." I didn't know if I was defending Frank or "Men."

"How can you say he ever heard her?" Barbara asked sharply.

"Delicious garlic bread," Elizabeth said sweetly.

"Frank never heard anything I said"—Bea breathed in deeply—"I don't know how typical he was . . ."

"Typical," Jane answered quickly.

Barbara nodded and looked at Elizabeth, who just shrugged. "Marty never listened to anyone. Man, woman, dog . . . he only heard himself."

"That's what I've been trying to tell you, Elizabeth." Barbara was leaning across the table, ignoring her pasta, talking to Elizabeth like a real estate agent trying to explain why this handyman's special was worth half a million dollars. "Marty was typical."

"Of what?" I asked innocently.

Barbara kept on looking at Elizabeth. "The Martys of this world can't relate to anything but their jobs. They don't understand people."

"Especially women?" I said softly.

"Especially women," Barbara said with a firmness that my words lacked. "He could only relate to things. And his needs."

"That's what drives me crazy." Jane jumped into the conversation. "Dave sees everything in his own terms. Marty and Frank die, so he's got to be next. It's like a baby."

"They're all babies," Bea explaained to me, "It's when they're sick that you can really tell. Frank would lie in bed with the covers up to his eyes and moan real, real loud. We'd use the boys' walkie-talkies. You know, the GI Joe kind with all the army stuff painted over them?"

We all nodded.

"He'd use the walkie-talkies to tell me when he wanted something to drink or eat. Frank used to think you could eat a cold to death." She smiled, probably happy she didn't have to feed him any more. Or cut up his meat. "And the pain. It was always amazing how much pain he was in. If he stubbed a toe, he'd holler for an hour."

"Childbirth," Barbara explained to Bea. "Since men never

have to experience childbirth, they figure that everything they feel is the worst thing possible in the world."

"They wouldn't make it through labor," Jane said, picking up a bread stick and taking a big bite.

"Do you really think there would be something like natural childbirth classes if men had children?" Barbara leaned back in her chair. "They'd start with Demerol in the second trimester."

I coughed. A small, unobtrusive cough that got their attention. They looked at me as if they were surprised I was there. "I really think you're exaggerating a bit . . ." I never got a chance to finish.

"Wait a second, wait a second . . ." Jane held her hand up to ward off Barbara and Bea. Reluctantly the two B's returned to their lasagnas. Taking small bites, however, so they wouldn't miss their chance to laugh at anybody with a penis, I thought meanly. Jane looked over at me. "You think Frank Bernstein was bad? Dave makes Frank look like a stoic. Remember that bad back he had a couple years ago? Do you know he still complains about it? Everytime the man has to put on a pair of socks he goes into his moaning act."

"Bad backs really are chronic." I felt like the last marine on Bataan.

"Chronic, shmonic," Barbara got in before Jane could. "Do you know how many women have bad backs from childbirth? Millions. But they still lift grocery bags, carry around infants . . ."

Jane's turn again. ". . . and don't moan in the morning. I still have to tie his shoes."

"Get him loafers," I suggested. Nobody smiled. But Elizabeth gave my thigh a squeeze.

"He won't wear loafers. He says they're not bankerly. They're too flashy. So you know who has to lean over and tie Mr. Banker's shoes every day?"

"Frank wore loafers," Bea said softly. "But I had to tie his bow ties. He never learned."

"He didn't want to learn." Barbara pointed her fork in my direction. It moved up and down, zeroing in. "Why should men learn how to do anything? Why should they when they have us, and their mothers, to do it for them?"

The salad arrived. Along with the side of Italian dressing. It seemed to break up the ferocity of the conversation. Elizabeth was actually the one to calm things down.

"You know, it's our fault too. They act like children because that's the way we treat them."

"No," Barbara said, "that's the way most of them are. I don't know whether its genetic or environmental, but they just aren't capable of acting like grown-ups."

"Dave's problems started with his father," Jane said with a certainty that wasn't usually present in her conversations. "And now I'm his father, mother, wife, and enemy all rolled into one."

"You're damn right you are."

It was Dave's voice. Slurred and sloshed. In back of me. And as I turned around I felt Dave's hand come down on my shoulder and squeeze. Squeeze it to stay upright. I could smell Dave's breath. But all you had to do was look at the bloodshot eyes, the body leaning to one side, to recognize the symptoms of a drunk. Jane turned away. Everybody else stared.

"Go home," she said across the table, still not looking up at her husband, who leaned over her, placing his right hand palm down on the table for support. "Get out of here."

"David," I reached over to pat his hand, "Jane's right. I'll drive you." I started to push my chair back. But he had me penned in. He was leaning over, his bourbon breath spreading out across the table.

"I'm not going anywhere." His words came out weaving. "I'm staying here with the gals." He gave my shoulder another squeeze. "Love bein' with the gals."

Angelo appeared on Dave's right, in back of Barbara. "Great-taseeya. Just a few minutes wait. How 'bout going to the bar?"

Angelo's eyes never really stopped on Dave, or the table. They just kept jumping across the room, trying to make sure that people were eating fast enough.

"My husband is not staying," Jane said to her host.

"I'm so sorry," Angelo said, finally looking up at Dave. Then he got a whiff of the Jack Daniel's breath and drew back in shock.

"I am too staying." Dave's words came toward us in hills and valleys. Each word had its own rise and fall.

"Maybe another night." Angelo smiled. He seemed to be torn between leaving this unstable drunk and trying to keep him from throwing up in the middle of his restaurant.

"Nah." Dave tried to push himself back up and lean on Angelo. Angelo wasn't buying it. As he reached over, Angelo leaned back, Dave lurched forward, stopping himself only by grabbing the top of Barbara's head.

My wife screamed. "Let go of my head, damn you, Redfield."

Dave looked down, aware, for the first time it seemed, he was holding onto someone's head. He seemed amused by the idea. A silly grin came on his face as he looked down at Barbara's angry expression.

"Now you know how I feel, Barbara." Dave's words seemed to be more focused.

"Maybe some other time," Angelo kept saying. "Tomorrow we have delicious veal on the menu. I'll give you a table right away. No waiting." The other tables seemed to be noticing Dave Redfield. Angelo wasn't amused. Barbara even less so.

"Get your paw off me, Dave Redfield." She said it loud enough for the tables near us to start looking.

"David." I stood up and tried to grab Dave's arm. He moved away. But still he held onto my wife's skull.

"Dinner. I want to have dinner with you guys."

"Tomorrow is veal paillard," Angelo said, backing away from Dave. "Delicious, very, very delicious."

"Just wanna drink," Dave slurred.

"Let go of Barbara's head," Jane demanded.

Dave looked wonderingly at his hand. Finally, he let go.

"Thank you, David," Barbara said quietly.

"It's nothing. Men are gentlemen, you know." He seemed to move backward, fall just slightly. I jumped up and held him there. Angelo walked over to grab him by the elbow. But David wasn't moving. He looked at me. "You got your gas mask yet?"

I shook my head. "C'mon, Dave, I'll take you home."

"Better get it, never know what you're going to find when you go home. Lots of accidents happen 'round the house." His body was listing. Angelo shoved Dave back to me.

"Get him out of here." Jane looked up at me. "Just leave him somewhere."

"Sure, sure." Dave's words took a long time to get out. "You want me out of here, permanently." He leaned toward me. "And you're next, Jackie boy." All of a sudden he moved away from me. Toward Angelo.

But Angelo was ready. He held him up as two Mexican busboys came running over. "José, Roberto, why don't you help the gentleman outside? He could use a little air." Angelo leaned over to pat the cheek of the slumping drunk. "You'll be fine, great, terrific."

"Never," said Jane.

I looked down at the table. They were all trying to avoid looking at drunk Dave between the two busboys. Nobody was saying anything. They all looked embarrassed except for Elizabeth, who was calmly finishing her lasagna. Angelo had gone off to greet some new arrivals at the door. If I didn't help, we'd be there another half hour.

"I'm going to take Dave home," I said to the table. Meanwhile I went up behind Dave to prop him up. José and Roberto were able to throw his arms around their shoulders.

Barbara looked up at me. "Get him out of here." She turned back to the table.

"I'll take the car." I groaned, as I tried to push Dave forward.

Elizabeth was the only one to look up. Everybody else didn't want to know us. "See you, Jack. Take care of him." She smiled at me.

It took a few minutes to get him outside. Three minutes of me steering and the busboys pulling. Finally, we managed to prop him up against the side of the restaurant. Couples were scurrying from inside their air-conditioned cars to quickly get inside an air-conditioned restaurant. I thanked the busboys and gave them each five dollars before they ran back inside.

"Wanna rest for a couple of minutes?" I asked patiently.

He slid down the side of building. Slowly, inevitably, falling down, until he reached the sidewalk. He looked like a puppet without a puppeteer; floppy and sad.

I leaned over to try and raise Dave up. Nothing. No movement. I pulled a little harder. Still nothing. He lay there. Head slumped forward. The short-sleeved shirt he was wearing was already stuck to his body. The whiteness of it turned brown. I looked down at his chinos. So far they weren't wet. But I didn't know how much longer they'd stay clean. What now? Dealing with drunks is not part of my life. Drunken men in the suburbs usually had wives to take them home. They'd appear once a year at the end of some party, make a couple passes at neighbors and get carted off by their long-suffering wives. They were mostly happy, childlike. Dave Redfield was a serious drunk.

I kneeled over to pinch his cheek. Hard. On the fourth pinch he opened his eyes slightly. They were puffy. Bloated.

"Jack?" he asked.

"Let's go, Dave." I reached down for his arms and tried pulling him up.

"Where?" he asked.

"Home." It was impossible to get a firm grip on his sweaty shirt.

He nodded slowly. Just once. Then opened his eyes a little more. He glanced around. Gradually seeming to realize where he was. "What's going on, Jack?" It was as if he was coming out of anesthesia.

"You're outside Angelo's."

A few blinks. "Right, right. I went there to see Jane." He looked up at me, waiting for me to tell him whether or not he was inside.

"Get up and I'll tell you about it." He considered the offer, and then, very gradually, he raised himself. I pinned him against the wall. Held him there while he tried to recover his balance. After a minute I let go slowly. He slid down a little, and then stopped, trying to take control of his body. He moved back up the wall, until he was straight.

"Tell . . . me . . . what . . . I . . . did." Each word was separate. Each took minutes to emerge.

"You slobbered all over our table."

His mouth dropped. "You mean I . . ." He stuck his finger in his mouth.

"You didn't throw up, David."

He let out a breath of air.

"You were drunk, Dave."

"Was I"—he wiped his mouth—"obnoxious?"

"A little."

"Was Angelo upset?"

I shrugged. "Who can tell." I indicated my car parked a half a block down the street. "I'll drive you home."

He stopped to think about it for a second. Then, turning around, he looked into the restaurant. The table with the women from our street was visible. They were listening to Barbara. She was pointing at Jane.

"What do you think she's telling Jane?" Dave asked. It was as sane a voice as I had heard come from him in weeks. Hesitant, almost shy. The Dave I had always known.

"It's not important, Dave. You had a bad night. Things will get better in the morning."

He shook his head. "I don't think so." He turned away from the restaurant and looked at me. He was crying. "I'm not very good with women, you know."

I didn't say anything.

"I'm very shy. Women have always frightened me." He started walking toward the car. I stayed next to him. He walked slowly. Righting himself every time he stumbled over a crack in the sidewalk. "The only reason Jane married me was that we were both so shy. We found each other in a bar one night."

I stayed next to him. He kept looking at the sidewalk. Aware of the dangers of tripping.

"We were the only ones not talking."

"So you started a conversation?"

"She started talking to me," he said, as if it were the worst moment of his life. "You know how it is."

I nodded. He didn't pay any attention.

"So we got married. I thought it would be perfect. Both of us were so shy."

I stopped. We were at my car. He leaned against it. Against the hood. I just took out my keys. Waiting for him to decide to get in.

"I thought that once my father died, I would become . . . you know." He looked at me to come up with the right word.

"Confident?"

"Yeah, that once I took over the bank, everything would be fine." He swayed a little, but then righted himself. "But it didn't happen. You know what I mean?"

"I'm not sure, Dave."

"Well, it's like, you know I should have been chairman or at least president."

"Executive vice-president is important, Dave."

He shook his head. "It's not. It's not." I couldn't tell if he was crying. But he looked very sad. "It's not important. But I can't be president. I still don't trust myself. I still don't. And he's dead."

"Let me take you home." I tried to put an arm around him but he turned away.

"And now Jane is . . . what I had always wanted to be. And

it's driving me crazy, Jack." His face was turning colors. His mouth closed, as if holding something in. He breathed through his nose and then slowly opened his mouth. He seemed surprised that nothing came out. "She's trying to . . . be what I always wanted to be." He nodded, as if he were telling himself just how right he was. "She wants me dead. Just like . . ."

And then, blessedly, he passed out.

June

S	M	T	W	T	F	S
					~~1~~	~~2~~
~~3~~	~~4~~	~~5~~	~~6~~	~~7~~	~~8~~	~~9~~
~~10~~	~~11~~	~~12~~	~~13~~	~~14~~	~~15~~	~~16~~
~~17~~	~~18~~	~~19~~	~~20~~	~~21~~	~~22~~	~~23~~
~~24~~	~~25~~	~~26~~	~~27~~	~~28~~	~~29~~	~~30~~

July

S	M	T	W	T	F	S
~~1~~	~~2~~	~~3~~	~~4~~	~~5~~	~~6~~	~~7~~
~~8~~	~~9~~	~~10~~	~~11~~	~~12~~	~~13~~	~~14~~
~~15~~	~~16~~	~~17~~	~~18~~	~~19~~	~~20~~	21
22	23	24	25	26	27	28
29	30	31				

August

S	M	T	W	T	F	S
			1	2	3	4
5	6	7	8	9	10	11
12	13	14	15	16	17	18
19	20	21	22	23	24	25
26	27	28	29	30	31	

Chapter Twelve

THE NEWSPAPER delivery man found Dave on the front lawn. They said there was at the most a pint of blood left in him. Hiding somewhere in his leg. From the waist up, the pathologist told me later, there were over four-hundred cuts. Four-hundred places for blood to pour out on the grass.

He had jumped through the den window. The oversized picture window that looked out on the side of the house. And nobody had heard or seen anything. For six hours no cars had driven down Apple Tree Lane. And all the air conditioners in the neighborhood muffled any noise that Dave and the breaking of the window might have made. So he laid there, turning the grass brown, and dying by himself.

Barbara ran over to comfort Jane, who had slept through the night. The air-conditioning was too loud, she said. So loud that she couldn't hear anything that happened outside the bedroom. Particularly her husband plunging head first through the window. The sirens had awakened her, just as they had sent everybody else on the block out of bed and onto the street.

Barbara, Elizabeth, Bea, they all gathered around Jane. Comforted her, petted her, took her inside to be together. I was left with the cops and Dave's torn up body. It was going to have to be a closed casket. There were so many cuts on his face that the only way he could be identified was by his clothes. By the short-sleeved shirt and pants he had worn when I put him to sleep on the floor in the den. On his side. Sleeping so deeply I thought he wouldn't wake up until dawn. Obviously I was wrong.

"Sometime during the night, Dr. Klein," one of the policemen explained. "He must have been lying here a while before the newspaper guy found him." He pointed to the wide circle of brown grass around the body. "Blood's been dried. Guy's turning stiff. Must of happened early in the morning. Sure you didn't hear anything?"

I shook my head.

"Well, I guess the guy must've woken up drunk." He paused and looked at me. "You sure he was drunk when you left him?"

I kept staring at Dave. Trying to figure out how he had gotten there. Finally, I looked at the policeman, who was patiently waiting for me to answer. "He was very drunk. You can check with Angelo's restaurant. I carried him out."

"Good, good." The policeman closed his spiral notebook and clicked his pen before putting it back into his pocket. "The way I figure it, he was still drunk, and just walked through the window."

I didn't nod. Because it didn't make any sense.

The policeman turned away.

"Suppose he saw somebody outside."

He turned back "What's that, doc?"

I shook my head. "Nothing. Just trying to figure out why it all happened."

The policeman nodded. "Doesn't look like there's any other explanation. I don't think his wife threw him out."

He was waiting for me to agree with him. Eventually I nodded too. No way. No way. Couldn't be. Maybe, just maybe, and I wasn't really sure of it, but just maybe Bea cut up Frank's steak in too big pieces. But Jane couldn't throw Dave out. No way.

So I stood there for another hour. Watching the policeman take measurements and photographs. His partner was in the house talking to the new widow. Finally, they let the paramedics take away the body.

I waited until they had him on the stretcher before I looked at Dave again. Pretended that I was in medical school. That this wasn't a person.

The first time, all I had noticed was the blood. Caked all over his body, making his face unrecognizable. No eyes, a tiny slit of a mouth. The nose practically torn off. Only the clothes and the height told me who was lying there. But now I stared. Watched as the two men lifted him onto the stretcher and then rolled him away. Rolled him past me toward the truck. He was still dressed as I had left him. Except there was something in his hand. Something he was holding onto so tightly that it was still there. From far away it looked like a string. But then as it got closer, I realized that it was too big for that. Too wide. And it had too many polka dots. It was a tie. A blue-and-white polka-dotted bow tie. The kind of bow tie David's father used to wear. The kind of bow tie that David started wearing after his father died. Only he wasn't wearing it when I left him. He didn't have it on him. It wasn't in the den. So where did it come from?

The policeman noticed me staring at the outstretched hand that clutched the tie. "He must have ripped it off before he took off. Or maybe he took it off afterwards. Trying to get some air."

I didn't answer.

"It is his tie, isn't it?"

I nodded. I don't know why I nodded. But I did.

The cop started walking away. "Good. Makes it all very simple."

* * *

I stayed home for the rest of the day. Watching the window people board up the jagged hole. The lawn people clean up the grass. They used a leaf blower to get up the millions of fragments of glass. But there was nothing they could do about the color of the grass. It was a deep, deep brown. As if it had been dyed. After they finshed cleaning, after it looked somewhat respectable, I went inside the Redfield house, into the kitchen where Barbara was making a pot of coffee.

"How is she?" I asked.

"Terrible." Barbara went on measuring the water. She didn't look at me.

"It's a mess."

"I thought you got it cleaned up?" She flicked on the button and turned toward me.

"I meant the situation."

"He was crazy." She started out of the room.

"Not that crazy."

Barbara stopped after a couple steps. "Since when are you going into psychiatry?" She still wasn't looking at me. She started playing with some cannisters on the counter. Rearranging them. I didn't think they needed rearranging.

"I put him to sleep, Barbara. He was sleeping soundly. Why would he get up? And then jump through the window?"

She finished moving the coffee cannister and then glanced briefly at me before starting out of the room again.

"Ask your friend Arnie. It makes sense to me." She was gone before I could mention the tie.

I kept thinking about it. Where it came from. How it got into his hand. Did he go upstairs to get it, then come down to jump out the window? And that was the problem. He didn't walk out the window. He jumped. Head first. If he had walked through the glass, there would have been cuts all over his body. But this was a head first dive. Actually, it was hands first. His hands had been slashed up worst of all. The veins in both wrists severed. By the time his feet came through there was no glass left to cut them. So he dove, arms stretched out. Trying to catch hold of something. Like a blue-and-white polka-dotted tie.

But I had too much to do to try and think about where the tie came from, who was wearing it, and why. I had to do an encore performance of what I had just done for Frank Bernstein. The funeral arrangements, the notification of the bank, calling the camp.

It took at least two hours, and by the time I was finished, I was exhausted. Depressed and exhausted. It was noon. Elizabeth came downstairs.

"You okay, Jack?"

She was still wearing the fluffy housecoat she had come over in six hours ago.

"No, Elizabeth. Not at all."

She walked over and kissed me on the top of the head. "You are sweet."

I shifted my bottom on the seat. Turned it sideways, so that I could look up at her. Without makeup, her smile seemed more real. There was a sweetness about her, almost an innocence, I had never seen before. "This has not been a good summer."

Elizabeth stopped smiling. She walked over to the coffee maker to pour herself a cup. Then came back to the round pine table and sat down next to me. She held onto the cup with both hands as if trying to warm her hands.

"What do you think, Jack?"

"About what?"

"All the stuff that's going on."

"I think it . . ."

"Sucks?"

I tried to smile. She didn't. "Yeah, something strange is happening, Elizabeth."

"It's real hot. People don't do well in hot weather."

"It's a little worse than not doing well, Elizabeth."

She nodded. "I know. I just mean the heat does strange things to people."

"Like makes them swallow big chunks of meat and jump through windows?"

She took her time. She blew on the steaming coffee. "Maybe. Maybe."

Somebody was coming. I could hear the footsteps on the stairs.

It was Barbara, carrying a tray. There were some scraps of the cheese and crackers she had brought up to Jane.

"What's happening?" she asked, walking over to the sink.

Elizabeth and I both said it at the same time. "Nothing."

Barbara nodded and rinsed off the dishes. "Jane's doing better. Bea's going to stay with her. I'll stay tonight."

"I could stay," Elizabeth said. She didn't sound like she really wanted to.

"No, I should." Barbara put the rinsed-off dish and the empty cup into the dishwasher. "It's my duty."

"As head of Women Without Men?"

Barbara slammed the door of the dishwasher. "No, as her friend. That's what I am. Remember? I realize it is a very difficult concept for some men to grasp . . ."

"Especially dead ones."

"What is that supposed to mean?"

I looked at Elizabeth. She was trying to climb into her coffee cup.

"Just that three men have died this summer on this block." I looked over at Elizabeth. "I'm sorry."

She looked back at me, smiled and shrugged.

"What are you trying to say exactly, Jack?"

"That"—I tried figuring what I could say. I needed Elizabeth's coffee mug for support, but she was holding onto it.—"something is going on here."

"Nothing is going on here. Death is normal, Jack."

"Heart attacks and cancer and strokes are normal. This isn't, Barbara. Don't you understand that?"

Eyes rolled up to the ceiling. "You don't understand, Jack. You just don't understand."

"What's there to understand, Barb? Strange things are happening around here. Can't you see it? Can't you figure out that something weird is happening?"

She walked toward the coffee pot, shaking her head all the way. Slowly, precisely, she poured herself a cup of coffee and then turned back toward us. "I'll tell you what I understand, Jack. There are three women on this block who need my help."

"What about the men?"

"They're dead." She walked out the room.

I walked Elizabeth home a few minutes later. She seemed embarrassed and tried to scurry as fast as her pink fluffy mules would allow her.

She got to the front door of her house without anyone seeing us. It was the middle of the day. Another scorcher. Elizabeth must have been dying in her down housecoat.

"I'm sorry, Jack," she said as she opened the door. The cold air poured out. We both stood there for a moment.

"About what?"

"You. You seem so upset."

I tried smiling nonchalantly. It didn't feel quite right. "It's Dave. It's like nobody cares about him."

Elizabeth stood there. I realized there were tears in my eyes. She was blurring up. I kept on going. "Nobody cares about anything around here. Not Frank or Dave . . ."

"Or Marty?"

I nodded. "I'm sorry Elizabeth, but it's like we're the enemy. And each death is a victory for women or womanhood or something—"

She touched my cheek. Held her hand there for a little too long before letting go. "It'll be okay. I promise."

"When?"

"Labor Day. By then, it'll be fine. Kids'll be back from camp. It'll be fine. Really."

"You sure?"

She thought about it. "I hope so."

I left it at that.

"I loved the guy," Harold Goldberg cried into his tuna platter. Big blobby tears that fell into the sliced cucumbers. I had told him about Dave five minutes before.

We were the only two men at the table. I had come over after leaving Elizabeth. I needed to talk to someone, even Harold.

"I picked on him too much." Harold shoved the plate of tuna fish and veggies aside and wiped his eyes. "Maybe if I had been nicer he'd be alive today." He started to shake his head in agreement. "I loved the lug." He blew his nose so loudly that three tables turned and looked at us. Harold didn't care.

"Harold, I don't think it was your fault."

He looked up at me. "You sure? I didn't drive him to it?"

"No, no, it was a lot of things."

"I didn't mean to pick on him, Jack. You know that? It was in fun. Wasn't it?" He looked at me for any sign of support.

"Dave was going through some rough times, Harold. They had nothing to do with you. Promise."

Harold grabbed a melba toast from the bread basket. He ripped open the paper and started crunching the toast as he spoke. "I liked him, you know. Really. I really liked the big guy. I just never . . ."

I waited for him to collect himself. I played with my tuna fish, nibbled it as he tried to regain some semblance of composure. It took a while. Nobody seemed to notice.

"When's the funeral, Jack."

"Monday."

"I'll close the store. It's the least I can do." He coughed a few times.

"I could use a new black tie."

He nodded. "I'll have one sent to the house."

"The other one got dirty at Frank's house. After his funeral. I don't think Barbara sent it to the cleaners."

Harold nodded again. "I've got something in a nice silk. Twenty-five fifty."

"That's fine."

"Can't have too many dark ties."

"Especially nowadays."

He nodded. We both looked at our tuna fish plates.

David's funeral was a lot warmer than Frank's. The minister who performed the service had also buried David's father. So his eulogy was filled with references to the old man. But there were also plenty of descriptions of Dave that showed that the eulogizer actually knew his subject. Dave's and Jane's daughters looked in shock.

I sat with Harold. The women were together. But it wasn't just the four of them. There were others. Women I recognized from around town, from the country club, from neighborhood parties. They sat together. Seeming not to be mourning Dave as much as supporting Jane.

Barbara spent most of the time at Jane's house that next week. I dropped by a few times. Talk seemed to stop when I walked into a room. And the conversation was mainly about the weather. I tried to get into Dave's closet to see if the tie was there, but Barbara had some charity pick up all Dave's clothes the day after the funeral. They even dismantled his workshop in the basement. Within minutes, it was as if Dave had never been there. After a few days, the girls went back to camp.

On Friday I had to call up Martha and Mandy to tell them we wouldn't be coming up for parents' weekend.

"We're needed here," Barbara explained to me as she made one of her infrequent visits to our kitchen. Jane needed Dijon mustard.

"Who's 'we,'" I asked.

"Me is we," she said. "It would upset Jane."

"What's that supposed to mean?" I asked as I steamed a bunch of vegetables.

"Just that Jane is very fragile these days."

"So am I. In case you haven't noticed I'm the only man left around here."

She grabbed the mustard and left.

Arnie Melton took pity on me. Said I was in a daze. So he took me out for a drink.

We went to the fancy French restaurant in Lake View: Chez Pascal. It had been opened a year ago by Eddie Schwartz, asthmatic son of Arthur Schwartz, Lake View's wealthiest lawyer. Arthur had bought his son the restaurant after Eddie graduated from a cooking school in England. Six months of apprenticeship in a Parisian bistro later, Eddie opened Lake View's first, and finest, outpost of semi-nouvelle food. It was a big hit in the area. Reservations had to be made weeks ahead, and most of the time the food was worth it.

The bar was not very large. There were five stools facing a beveled glass wall. You were off in a corner of the room. It was a place to wait rather than drink. Eddie's mother, who served as the proud hostess, led us to the bar. Arnie and I had smiled and nodded as she regaled us with Eddie's exploits. Finally, she let us drink in peace.

But before we could start talking, Eddie Schwartz, with a high, high toque blanche on top of his head, emerged from the kitchen door.

"Hi, Dr. Klein."

I introduced him to Arnie.

"You the doctor going out with Shari Herman?"

Arnie smiled, proudly, I thought.

"She used to babysit for me," Eddie explained.

Arnie smiled.

Eddie nodded and gave me a bemused look. "Excuse me, Dr. Klein," he said, "I gotta get back in the kitchen. Nice to meet you, Dr. Melton."

Eddie scurried back into the kitchen.

"Ever eat here?" I asked Arnie.

"Not yet."

"It's good."

"Shari promised to take me for my birthday."

We both sipped our wines. Arnie tried not to look at his watch. "Listen, Arnie, if you have to go, I understand."

"No, no, no." He pointed to the short French bartender and indicated another drink. "I want to be here. I really do. I want to help." He looked at the clock on the wall, quickly, furtively. I caught him.

"You heard about Dave?" We hadn't seen each other since the "accident."

"Yeah. Terrible. I guess he was crazier than I thought."

"Well, your *folie à deux* is now a *folie à trois*."

He shook his head. "I don't think so. I was just kidding about all that kind of stuff."

"It was a joke?"

"No, no, no. I meant that a *folie à deux* or *trois* isn't necessarily what's happening. It's all just a coincidence . . . probably."

"Three people, three husbands, all dying under strange circumstances in one month. A weird coincidence, Arnie." I was biting my lip between sentences. It was starting to come back. Frank's body. Dave's body.

He patted my hand reassuringly. "Look, if they had all been shot, then I would start worrying. But none of the men has died the same way. Each one is different."

"I still don't know about Dave."

"What's there to know, Jack. I saw the guy, remember? I know how nuts he was. I can believe that in his paranoia he'd try to commit suicide."

"By jumping through a first floor window? I never heard of that."

Arnie shrugged. "So he was drunk too, right?"

"And sleeping, Arnie. He was sound asleep."

Arnie scanned the restaurant. "What was that?" he asked, looking at the sconces on the wall.

"I said that Dave Redfield was sleeping when I left him."

Arnie turned to me. "Yeah, well, I guess he woke up."

". . . and jumped out the window, Arnie." I leaned forward trying to get his attention. I wanted to shake him. Grab him. Wake him up before it was too late.

"Right." He grinned. A man in love. He hadn't heard a thing.

I moved away, reached for my wine glass and gulped it down. After a minute of quiet, Arnie realized something was wrong.

"Is everything okay, Jack?"

"Why do you ask?" What an asshole.

"It's just that you seem upset." He tried looking psychiatric. The brow furrowed.

"I tried to explain . . ."

"Explain again."

"Dave Redfield jumped out . . ."

". . . his window. I know that. What's upsetting you?"

I was going to be patient. "I'll say this again, Arnie. Slowly. Very, very slowly."

He looked.

"I don't understand why he jumped out the window. At twelve at night. After he was asleep. Are you getting all this?"

"I'm paying attention, Jack. I promise."

I decided to believe him. "Then listen."

He brought his hand up to his chin.

"So why did he do it?"

"Jump through the window?"

"Yes."

He leaned against the padding that circled the bar. "Maybe he had a bad dream."

"Okay, but you don't jump through windows after nightmares."

"If he was a true psychotic, he could."

"You saw him, Arnie, the man was not schizoid. He was tense, nervous, but he wasn't certifiable."

Arnie held up his hands for quiet. "Okay, how about this. Suppose he thought somebody was outside the window . . ."

I nodded. "Good."

"What do you mean good?" He lowered his hands.

"I mean that's what I think happened. He thought he saw someone outside the window, someone he hated . . ."

"Like his mother?"

I shook my head. "Father. Remember."

Arnie nodded furiously. "Right, his father. The guy hated his father." He got a big smile on his face. "Solved the whole thing. Right?"

I shook my head. "Nope."

"What do you mean nope?"

"Because it wasn't just a dream."

"A nightmare. Okay, sorry, it was a nightmare. Ready to go?" He stood up and laid some money on the bar. Slowly, the bartender walked over to pick up the bills.

"It was real, Arnie. I don't think it was a nightmare, a bad dream, or a drunken fantasy. I think there really was someone there."

"C'mon, Jack." He gave me a punch on the shoulder, the kind of man-to-man hit that I was used to getting around the country club bar. It was unlike Arnie.

I sat on my stool. Even though he was bouncing from foot to foot trying to get going I was stubbornly waiting to tell him what I knew had happened. "I think someone was dressed like his father."

"Jack, Jack." Arnie smiled down at me. Sweetly. He almost patted me on the head. "Jack, Jack," he kept repeating.

"Okay." I turned sideways on the bar stool. Away from Arnie. "I won't say anything else."

"No, no." He was speaking in soothing tones now. "Tell me everything."

I looked away. "Forget it, Arnie."

"It's been a difficult summer, Jack," he said in the same gentle voice.

I looked at him. His face was so much more relaxed than it had been since I met him. He was happy. So very happy that he wouldn't hear anything I said. Wouldn't care about the bow tie. "I'll finish my drink, Arnie."

"Good. Have a few, Jack." He patted me. "I got to run."

"See you." I waved him off. He waved back and ran out the door.

I turned away from the room and sipped my drink while the bartender stared off. Everybody had someone these days. Arnie and Shari had each other. Barbara had Bea and Jane and, sometimes, Elizabeth. Ben Bracken might get Hilda Robins. And I was alone.

"Would you like something to eat, doctor?"

I looked straight ahead at the mirror over the bar. Eddie Schwartz was leaning over me.

"No. But thanks, Eddie."

"How about some dinner?"

I turned around. The room was staring at us. All those people wanting to get close to the new culinary star of Chicago were observing me with a "Who's that guy with Eddie Schwartz" look. I glanced up at Eddie. "Place seems full."

He pointed to a tiny table against a column. Out of the way. A table that you could see from but required a lot of neck straining to be stared at. "I keep that one open. How about it, doctor."

"Why not?" What was I rushing home to?

I hadn't eaten or drunk so well in a long time. By the time the check arrived I had made my way through four courses and a bottle and a half of wine. The champagne with dessert was complimentary. I was feeling warm, comforted. Eddie's version of chicken-in-the-pot reminded me how real food tasted. After weeks of Angelo's weighty lasagna, The Lunch Box's tinny tuna, and my own boring vegetables and fruit, the taste of food treated respectfully made me forget, for half an hour or so, my problems.

I hadn't been drunk in years. Not really drunk. High, actually. A warmth that made the bad things of my life seem like they had happened in a faraway past. Their connections were not with me, and my life, so much as the town I lived in. They were already part of history, stories to be told years later, part of the descriptions of this hot summer we would all dwell on years from now, on a particularly hot day in October. Or a very cold day in March. Unexpected weather. Out of synch with our normal patterns. The deaths of the three men on Apple Tree Lane were part of the heat of the summer. Part of the summer's events. Each death made some sense. Only taken together were they unexplainable.

I rolled down the windows on my Saab. Opened them all and drove a little faster than the speed limit to get a breeze going. I put one arm outside the window, slapping the side of the car as I hummed along with the radio.

Life wasn't so terrible. It would be okay in the morning. Even if I was alone, I was alive. That was what was important. The chaos of Marty's and Frank's and Dave's lives were of their making. Their deaths, violent and messy, seemed so predictable. Inevitable. It wasn't going to happen to me. The regularity of my life was going to prevent anything like that happening. I was different than they were. As different as could be.

The lights were off on Apple Tree Lane. Just one, in Jane Redfield's bedroom. Otherwise it was dark. The whole street. All four houses were black.

I pulled into my garage. Opening it automatically and pulling in next to Barbara's Oldsmobile. She had wanted something big and comfortable, because of the drive into the city to go to graduate school.

I stepped outside and looked around the street. The light was still on in the Redfield bedroom. But Bea had either gone to sleep or was over there with the girls. I turned to the Siegals. The Siegal. Nothing. I wondered how Elizabeth had managed to put up with the other three women. They were all so humorless. Except Elizabeth. She was the only one who could laugh lately. Who didn't take everything so seriously. But, still, it was her particular murder . . . killing . . . that had started everything.

"Jack?"

I jumped. Turned around in the air and assumed a karate position.

"Who is it. Who is it?"

"Shhhh." The voice was Elizabeth's. A little slurred, but hers.

I tried to focus. To calm myself and find Elizabeth Siegal in the heavy darkness. Another "shh" helped me locate her. I walked toward the voice. She grabbed me before I saw her. Held my arm and swung me around to face her. I could see her now. We were five inches apart. It was hard not to be aware of her. And her breath. Gin.

"Jackie, Jackie," she kept saying as she narrowed the space between us. "Jackie, Jackie. Poor little Jackie." She had pressed herself against me. I could feel the floating breasts as they rubbed against my chest. I was sweating. Really sweating now. Even if it had been January I would be sweating. And still she kept saying, "Jackie, Jackie, Jackie." Her fingers stroked my cheek. Patted it and then slowly let go. I tried smiling. She just shook her head and stepped back, away. Trying to lean against something. I caught her before she fell. Grabbed her around the waist as she fell back. We must have looked like a bad tango duo. I tried pulling her upright. But she seemed perfectly happy to lay back, with me leaning over her. Her face was tilted up. Toward the cloudy sky. She was smiling at it. And I was trying to get her back up. I leaned forward and, with a heave, started pulling her forward, toward me. Reluctantly, her limp body agreed to become upright.

"Elizabeth," I grunted, "Please, help. Please."

"Jack, Jackie, Jackie," she slurred. "Come down here." She tried to pull me, but I wasn't about to land on the grass with her. Fear gave me strength. With a mighty tug we were upright. It seemed to wake her. I let go and instead of falling back, she actually remained steady. I stood there, looking unsmilingly at her.

"Widows get horny," she explained.

"I understand." I moved back a bit.

"It's nothing personal."

"I understand." It was hard to think of new words. The wine and all that butter were churning around inside my stomach. I could taste too much of what had gone down. I thought of how I should end the scene.

"Jack," she began before I could figure it out. ". . . please be careful."

I got cold.

She looked over my shoulder toward the Redfields. I turned around too. The lights were going off in the bedroom as I watched. There was a faint glow coming from the window next to the bedroom. I thought it was the hallway. Jane must have left a night-light on. I turned back to Elizabeth, who was staring at me. "What's going on over there, Elizabeth?"

"Nothing, really."

"Something is." I was feeling woozy. "Let's sit down." I lowered myself to the ground. The grass was almost hard, it was so dry. Elizabeth stood over me for a second and then, tucking her white skirt underneath her, sat on the grass alongside me. She leaned forward, thoughtful, concerned about something. I didn't want to know what.

"Well, it's hard to say."

"Tell me . . ."

Elizabeth dropped her head forward. All I could see were curls. She kept talking to the ground. "It's nothing specific, hon. Nothing I can put my finger on."

"Did Bea . . . Frank? Did Jane . . . Dave?"

She raised her head and stared over my shoulder, toward where Jane and Barbara were sleeping. "I . . . don't know." She turned toward me. She looked sad, a lot sadder than when she had killed her own husband.

"But you've got to know, Elizabeth. You're with them . . ."

"We don't talk about it, Jack."

"You must."

She slid herself forward. Our knees were almost touching.

She leaned forward and put her arms around my neck. I still hadn't touched her.

"Jack, let's just go away." She said it as if she were suggesting a visit to Disneyland.

I didn't change position. "I can't, just tell me what's going on."

"I don't know, but"—she looked up and over my head toward the house that had only one hallway light on, and then returned to me.—". . . you and I are the only ones around here who are thinking . . . normally."

"What are they doing Elizabeth, you have to tell me."

I reached over to touch her face. Briefly. "Please."

She let go of me with a sigh. "We just talk, Jack. A lot. All day."

"About what?"

"Men." She didn't say anything else for a while. ". . . husbands," she finally, grudgingly, got out.

"Dead or live ones, Elizabeth."

". . . live ones, Jack."

"Like . . . me?"

Elizabeth leaned forward and kissed me on the cheeks. Slowly, gently. She didn't say anything.

"Elizabeth, tell me."

She moved over to my mouth. Kissing it sweetly, softly. She had her eyes closed. Her head was weaving, drifting. I tried not to respond. I failed. She opened her eyes and smiled.

"You like it more subtle, huh Jackie?"

I tried to move back. But her arms around my neck kept me from pushing my body too far away. I kissed back. This time the mouths opened. A little. Not much tongue. But plenty of soft lip action. Well, if I was going to die, at least I was going to have fun before I went. I put my arms around Elizabeth's body and pressed her into me. She felt larger than Barbara. No bones. Her breasts squeezed against me. There was something so sweet about what we were doing. Even though I was getting an erection. A very large, very obvious erection. Too big to hide.

"Wowee, Jackeee." Elizabeth was looking down at my crotch.

I put my hand over her mouth and turned around to look across the street. No more lights went on in Jane's house. No windows flew open. No screams came hurtling down the block toward the practically adulterers. Adulterer.

"Elizabeth, listen." I moved away. She just stared down at my crotch some more. Slowly, I removed my hand from her mouth. She looked up at me with a large smile. Almost as big as my erection.

"Can I touch it?" she asked, with that grin growing larger all the time.

"No," I whispered loudly. I tried holding her hands, which seemed to be moving dangerously downward in spite of my half-hearted attempts to hold onto her. Finally, she gave up. But she kept on looking. "Listen, somebody might see us."

She shook her head. I held onto her hands. Gently, softly. I even rubbed them a little.

"I think we should go home."

She looked up. "Mine or yours?"

The lights in the Redfield house hadn't changed. Nobody appeared to be looking out the windows. I turned back to Elizabeth, who had given up her erection watch and decided to stare at me with a grin. "You're going home . . ."

"Sounds good to me."

". . . and I'm going home."

Her mouth turned down. She looked like one of my daughters who had just been denied a second dessert. "That's not fair, Jackie."

"Elizabeth . . . I don't fool around."

She tilted her head. All her gestures seemed like a little child's. "Yeah, but this is different."

"Why is it different?"

She let go of me. Placing her hands on her knees. She seemed to be trying to act more adult. A child playing at being a grown-up. "Well, for one thing, you and Barbara are . . . are . . .

having . . ." she seemed to hunt for the word for a second ". . . problems."

"We are?" I felt my face twisting into a "funny look."

"Didn't you know?"

I shook my head.

Elizabeth nodded. "Yeah, last few days all we've been talking about is you."

"Why me?"

She put on her sweet look. Her "Poor Jack" look. "Who else? There's nobody else left."

"How about each other?"

"Oh, Jack." She leaned over to stroke my face. Then followed it with a sweet little kiss. This time I didn't respond. "We talk about men."

"You all have fathers, and brothers and first cousins." I could hear my voice rising. "What's wrong with them. Did Barbara ever tell you about her Uncle Isadore? A pervert, the man—"

She kissed me again. It stopped me. "Husbands, Jack. That's who we talk about."

I let out some air. A soft whoosh. ". . . and I'm . . ."

". . . the only one left."

I nodded. "Barbara didn't say anything . . ."

". . . sure she did." Elizabeth was stroking my face. Talking seriously, and yet, touching me gently. I didn't touch her back.

"Nothing, I'm telling you. She hasn't said anything about us having problems."

"That's all she talks about, Jackie. You got to start listening."

"Men," I said assertively. "She puts down men. Not me, Elizabeth."

She took my head in her hands and brought it toward her. "Poor Jack Klein. You really are a shmuck sometimes."

"It's getting . . . weird."

"So what are you going to do?" She was still touching me. With her fingers.

"Talk to her?"

Elizabeth responded with a definite shake of her head.

"What do you think?" I held her hand. Took it away from my face and held it in the air.

"Be careful." She leaned over to kiss me once again. This time we both gave it equal emphasis. It took a while. And when it was over we drew back and looked at each other.

"I never fooled around," I said softly.

"I know." She smiled. "I can tell."

"I don't think I'd be good at it."

"Aw, come on, Barbara says you're terrific in bed." She reached down to cup her breasts. "And with a pair like these, you'd keep that . . ." she gestured toward my crotch with her head. ". . . up for days. Trust me, Jackie." She patted my crotch gently.

"Wait." I realized what she had said. "You mean Barbara has been talking about our sex life?"

Elizabeth smiled. "Yeah, for a long time now. You were the best. On the street that is. Not that it was all that hard to be champ of Apple Tree Lane. I mean, Frank wouldn't take his pajamas off, Dave had to wait until it was dark outside and there was no moon, and Marty . . ." she sighed. ". . . well, Marty was your basic one shot. Know what I mean?"

I nodded. "But when do you talk about . . ."

She sighed. "I'm getting hot, Jack. I mean the temperature must be close to ninety. You want to come over?"

"I don't think so."

"If you change your mind during the night . . ." She started to get up. I waited for her to stand and then pushed myself off the ground. Neither one of us moved. Finally, she reached over to wipe my forehead.

"Elizabeth, it's not that I'm not . . ."

"I know, I know, it's not that you're not attracted to me, but . . ."

This time I finished. ". . . I'm a happily married man."

She shook her head. "Wanna bet, Jack?"

I reached over and put my arms around her. Drew her to me

and held onto her. Finally, she pulled back enough to look at me.

"Jack, either we do it or not. I'm getting hot out here."

I shook my head. "I don't know, Elizabeth. Things are so . . . so . . ."

"Jack . . ." she moved away, put her hands on her hips and looked at me so very seriously. ". . . come on, do something for a change."

"Not going to bed with you is doing something, Elizabeth."

She started to walk away, shaking her head. I ran after her. Grabbed her around the shoulders and turned her back to me. "I like you, Elizabeth. I really do."

"But you're a happily married man." She said it like a computer voice.

"That's not it." I let go, she didn't leave. "Look, three men are dead. Three guys have been killed . . ."

"One, Jack. Just one." She didn't look at me when she said it.

I shook my head. "Come on, Elizabeth. You know about Dave and Frank."

"What do I know?" She was moving her body away? Trying to find a place to disappear in the dark.

I reached over and held her by the elbow. Tight. So she couldn't get away. I needed to know. And Elizabeth was the only one to tell me. "You know."

"I don't." She tried to get away, I held on tighter.

"Please."

"Jack, I'm sorry. But there's nothing for you to know."

"Yes there is, Elizabeth. You and I both know."

"Jack"—she started to reach for me. I just held on and avoided her advances.

"Elizabeth, I want you to tell me."

She stopped reaching for me and let her hand drop. "It's too hot, Jack."

I let go and turned away. "Okay, forget it."

"Stop it."

I looked back. "What?"

"Stop *pouting*. I hate pouting. My first husband pouted. Marty pouted. Men who don't get what they want start pouting." She lowered her voice, but it was still shriller than before. "I hate it. Despise it."

"So tell me." I said it quickly. No pout.

She looked at me suspiciously. "We haven't talked about it—"

I interrupted her. "What do you mean, that's all you do is talk. You must have, you had to have talked about it. Three husbands are gone, Elizabeth, and you're telling me you haven't talked. Come on."

"When they're alive, Jack. When they're dead we don't say a word."

"What happened to murder therapy? Wasn't that what Barbara was doing after Marty . . . died?"

Elizabeth nodded a few times. "Yeah, we talked about how we wanted to kill all the men who screwed us, not literally, mind you." She smiled. "But that stopped after a couple sessions. It was more fun to talk about husbands. Frank, Dave . . ." She stopped.

"And killing them?"

"No." She said it emphatically. "We never talked about killing them. I promise. It was always just what assholes they were . . ."

". . . and how much better off you were without them?"

She waited. Thought about what to say, and then nodded.

I went on. "But divorce took too long?"

She just stood there.

"And they'd wind up with the money?"

Still nothing.

"So wouldn't it be nice if they had a stroke or a fast cancer or . . . a big piece of steak?"

No denial.

"And now . . .?"

"We only talk about you, Jack." She hugged me. Walked over

the few steps and held me in her arms. "Come home with me, honey." She gave my ass a long, gentle pat.

It felt good. The hugging, the presence of someone who actually wanted to make love with me. But more than that, there was somebody to hold on to. A warm, voluptuous woman, who I had always ignored.

"Okay, Jack," Elizabeth finally said. "We'll hug again soon."

She pushed away from me. We were both incredibly wet, unbelievably sweaty. We made a squishy noise as our bodies separated. The kind of noise you get after an evening of passionate love. Her pink shirt was dark with sweat. I looked down, my blue shirt was stuck to my body. Attached to me. "I wish . . ." I began.

"You never know, Jack." She turned and walked off. When she got to the beginning of her yard, she looked back and gave me one of her big, warm smiles. I didn't smile back. I was too busy thinking about too many things. Things I hadn't done. Fears I hadn't figured out. Deaths I tried to ignore.

Chapter Thirteen

BARBARA STILL spent all of her time at Jane's. And I thought of Elizabeth. Constantly. It made my life interesting. Because I was alone practically all the time.

"I have to be with the girls," Barbara told me a week later. She was in Jane's driveway. I was in ours. We were picking up our newspapers. It was six-thirty in the morning.

"Why? Tell me why you have to be with the girls?" I said it straight. No edge in the voice.

"You wouldn't understand."

I had just said "hello" and "when are you moving out of Jane's?" That was it. No cynicism. No smarmy innuendoes. And still, she went back into Jane's house. I hurried back to call Elizabeth Siegal. I didn't have to look up her number. I had memorized it. Looked at a phone hundreds of times in the past week with Elizabeth in mind.

The first time I reached over to call Elizabeth was the day I saw Barbara, Jane and Bea out power-walking. Striding down the middle of Apple Tree Lane at six o'clock at night. Arms pumping, stepping out in unison, the three of them ignored the heat, paid no attention to the humidity as they strode forward. Dressed in their shorts and sleeveless shirts, they walked toward some common goal with tight lips and taut faces. Woe to the car that tried to honk them into moving to the side of the road.

So I looked up Elizabeth Siegal's phone number. That's as far as I got. Intending to call her up and follow up on that one night of affection. And it remained an intention. Even when my phone calls to Jane's house were answered by Bea, who explained, "We're having a meeting." Even when I sat with my lousy steamed vegetables at the kitchen table. Soggy, overcooked vegetables I had left in the steamer too long while I went to mix my third martini of the night.

My life wasn't even funny enough to be a situation comedy. I didn't see enough of Barbara to start any kind of nasty dialogue. My world, which had always been rigidly ordered, strict in its predictability, was loosening at the edges. It was fraying.

The real problem, of course, was the nights. Waiting for something to happen. Waiting until all the daytime traffic on our block went to sleep. When it was just the girls . . . and me. Because when it came right down to it, I was almost relieved Barbara wasn't there.

So I slept alone. Huddled up in my corner of my bed. The windows open, so I could hear the typical sounds of evening. And to make sure no new sound intruded. I could tell the difference in the sounds, because I was awake most of the time. At least I thought I was awake. Most nights I would find I had drifted off sometime around two in the morning. But still, I wasn't getting more than three or four hours a night. Waiting to be a dead husband can kill you.

Now, though, it was morning.

After I came back in, I reached for the phone. Thought about dialing Elizabeth's number. But it was early. Maybe this evening. That was it. Dinner. I would ask her out for dinner. A normal thing to do. I glanced at the clock on the table next to

Barbara's former side of the bed. It was seven A.M. Elizabeth didn't strike me as an early riser.

By the time I was ready to leave, the power walkers were also about to head out. I watched Bea, Jane and Barbara walk out the door of Jane's house. Barbara in the middle, they moved down the street, down Apple Tree Lane. All of them seemed to have gotten thinner this summer. The heat had done wonders for Bea's cellulite. There was a lack of jiggling in her legs as she hurried to keep up with her taller companions. They were dressed for the heat: skimpy shorts and tight tank tops. I watched them through the living room window. They weren't looking my way. Only forward. I thought of quickly getting in my car and following them down the street. I'd honk a couple times and then, when they didn't move, I'd . . . no, no, forget it. Maybe somebody else would. Maybe, ironically, a woman on her way to exercise class would be talking on the car phone and run them down in her Audi—

Forget it. I turned away as they headed toward the corner. I tried to figure out when the best time would be to call Elizabeth. Maybe when the walkers were out for their early evening drill? No, no, that was too late. Too late to ask her out. By then, Bea or Jane would have already set the table for four. Too many questions would be asked. And knowing Elizabeth, she'd answer them.

Lunchtime. That's when I called her. Insulated from the ears of my nurse and my receptionist who were discussing silver patterns. Lately Mary and Shari had become co-conspirators in their discussions. Now when I walked into a room, catalogues would be closed, conversations would end. When she wasn't talking to my nurse, Shari would be on the phone. I always saw her hanging up as I came into the room.

"Elizabeth." I mumbled the word. I had my hand almost over the phone, even though the door was closed. Tightly.

"Who is this?"

I spoke up. "Me."

"Who's me?"

"Jack."

She waited a second and then answered in that voice everyone recognizes: "There's someone here who I don't want to know who is on the phone" voice. "Uh" was the next thing she said, followed by a "nice to hear from you."

"I'll call back later." I got ready to hang up.

Elizabeth stopped me. "No, no, no . . ." and then to whatever was near her, "Why don't the three of you go ahead then? I'll catch up."

Neither one of us said anything. I practically stopped breathing. Finally, Elizabeth spoke. "They just left."

"Who did?"

"All of them," she said, now in her usual confident tone. "They travel together, you know."

"I know . . . I know . . ." I pushed my foot against the door. It was closed.

"We're supposed to have lunch together," she explained.

"Well then . . ." I got ready to hang up. Now that I had her on the phone, it didn't seem like such a good idea. I mean, whose side was she on?

"How about dinner, Jack?"

"Wha . . .?"

"Isn't that why you called?" There was a smile in her voice.

"Well . . . yeah . . . sort of."

"Okay. What time?"

Now what? I hadn't figured this part. Do I go up to her front door and ring the bell? Getting in and out while the "gals" were out power-walking. Elizabeth figured it out for me.

"I'll make dinner," she said. There was an even bigger smile in her voice.

"I'll . . ." I didn't get to finish.

". . . come in the back door. That way nobody'll see you."

I tried to remember if either Bea's or Jane's house had a view of the Siegal's back door.

"Jack, I promise, they won't see you. Make it six-fifteen."

I nodded. "Power-walking?"

She laughed. "Yeah, they've been trying to get me to go with them."

"And . . ."

"Jack," she said quietly, "they're my friends. But I'll keep the arsenic out of the tuna fish." She giggled some more.

"I'm not worried. Really."

She got a good, deep laugh out of that. "Sure, Jack." She giggled again. "I'll whistle three times if the coast is clear."

"Just close the shades."

"In the bedroom, Jackie." And she hung up.

By the time I walked out the door, Shari and Mary had gone to lunch. It was twelve-thirty. I put on my suit jacket and walked over to The Lunch Box. The temperature seemed a bit more reasonable today. There were actually people on the street. People who weren't trying to find an air-conditioned store to run into. They were strolling as if it were a typical summer. Not one where an eighty-nine degree day seemed like spring.

I looked in the window at The Lunch Box. The men's table was empty. Even Harold wasn't there. But Ben Bracken was in a booth wooing Hilda Robins. And at the next table, Shari and Arnie were ignoring their food and breathing deeply. Both couples looked happy with each other. Neither one would want to see me. And I didn't feel like eating lunch alone.

So I kept on going. Just walking. Not particularly noticing anything or anybody as I went. I hadn't done this in a while. Not since summer began. When I first moved to Lake View, I used to walk all the time. Walk to work. Walk at lunch. I would notice the seasons, the flowers, the birds. But these days, the things around me had become so unthought of. In the heat of the summer I had lost that sense of where I was. In trying to figure out what had come loose in my life, I had ignored those things that I treasured. Once the daffodils died, I had stopped looking.

And so I kept on walking. Trying to pay attention to the geraniums the Garden Club had planted through the town. Noticing the watering of the median strip on the street. It all seemed like the Lake View as I had known it for the past fifteen years. The quiet, peaceful town I had left the anger and noise of Chicago for.

I could hear the sound of the squealing brakes before I could turn around to see the white Audi with the black, black windows come toward me. And I couldn't move. I just stood there in the middle of the street and watched the car careen at me. It was so big. And it got bigger as it came swerving toward me.

It stopped in time. Maybe two feet away. I started to say something. Yell something. And then the driver honked. A loud, long, angry honk that kept up as I slowly walked to the sidewalk. As I stood there, the driver, I couldn't see who it was, finished that single maddening honk, and then with a mean squeal of tires jumped ahead.

And still I stood there. I looked down at my hands and saw them shaking. Almost shivering in the heat. I turned around to walk back to my office. Forgot the flowers and the foliage and saw the women running into the stores. Pushing their way past me as they tried to get a good table at The Lunch Box. Ignoring this sweating, shivering man who looked, no doubt, just slightly mad. For what else would he be doing walking around Lake View on a hot August afternoon?

I saw the first poster as I left work that night. Stapled on the bulletin board in the lobby of my building. "**WOMEN WITHOUT MEN,**" it said in big bold letters. Underneath that it read, **"We want to help you get on with your life. Counseling. Advice. Support. Practical. Emotional. Call 321–0986. We're with you."**

It was Jane's number. I remembered that. And the poster looked handmade. I thought of ripping it off, but why? And then I noticed a woman standing next to me. She was writing down the number. Seriously scribbling the numbers on a piece of paper. I left. Quickly.

* * *

The coast was clear. Not that I skulked over or anything. Of course, I called up Barbara before I left the house to find out what her plans were.

"Lots of work," she kept repeating. "Lots." She took a deep breath to emphasize just how hard it all was. "You can't believe the response to the notices. Jane must have gotten twenty calls in about an hour."

"Great."

"It is," she said. She waited for me to say something. When I didn't say anything sarcastic, she went on.

"I can't talk. We have a lot of work. Our first client is coming over tonight."

"Bet you're excited." I raised my voice, trying to sound up.

"A lot of work. A lot of work." She was repeating everything now. She sounded like a sane David Redfield. "But I have to go."

I had to ask. "What about dinner?" I said it softly. Maybe she wouldn't hear it.

"Impossible. Impossible."

"I understand." I said it forcefully.

"Good." And then: "It's about time."

What should I say? I'm about to have dinner with another woman? Was I supposed to be angry, cynical? Defender of the honor and integrity of mankind. "See you later, honey." I said it like I meant it.

"Yeah . . . later."

Okay, okay. I made it. Now I had to look out the front window and wait for them to walk out of Jane's house.

They were precise. At 6:14 the front door opened and out came Jane and Barbara. By the time they got to the curb, Bea had joined them. I noticed the letters on the back of their tank tops. Three big black letters that jumped out against the whiteness of the shirts. **WWM**.

I was scurrying across the backyard by the time they got to the corner. Tiptoed scurrying, hugging the side of my house, and then looking both ways as I ran across the open space between the two homes. I made it to Elizabeth's back door, without anyone seeing me. But I was puffing like I had just run a mile.

Elizabeth had the back door open as I got there. I ran in. And fell into one of her kitchen chairs.

"Made it."

I looked up. I saw her breasts floating above me first. Stretching out her white T-shirt. And then I noticed her big grin. I hadn't seen a woman smile at me in days. It seemed like years. Oh, what the hell.

Now that was a body. The kind to sink into. To spend time touching and feeling and playing with. The kind where you didn't mind occasional ripples of flesh. Little handles around the hips and waist. They gave you something to hold onto. Something to grab when she was on top of you. Something to clutch when you were on top of her, trying for dear life to keep from falling off.

We stayed in bed most of the night. I could have played with her breasts for about a year and a half. Touched them. Licked them. Traced their roundness. And just admired them.

"They're really real," she explained around ten-fifteen.

"You sure?" I asked, as I gently stroked the left one.

"Lots of people think they're surgical," she explained, rubbing my stomach. Slow, sensuous circles that she did seemingly without thinking.

"They're truly..."

"I know," she smiled rubbing a little harder "... wonderful. Everybody says so."

"Of course..." I started getting embarrassed. For the first time in hours I started thinking about what I was doing. Who I was with. "... I think you're ... special ... Elizabeth."

She started giggling. She kept rubbing, but she was smiling and giggling like crazy. I took my fingers off her breast. She reached over with her free hand to put them back. "Come on, Jack, let's not make too much of a deal over this. You're scared. I'm horny..."

I leaned over to kiss her lightly on the lips. She reached up to pull me into her mouth and down her throat.

Forty-five minutes later I was looking down at her. She had her eyes closed. Not sleep closed. Relaxed closed. All I wanted to do was touch her. Her skin felt like a baby's. Even with its deep brown tan, it had a softness that I remembered from early parenting. And all I wanted to do was settle into it. Stay there and feel it as long as possible. I was safe here. Protected here.

"I love your skin, Elizabeth."

She opened her eyes and grinned.

"It's true. Really."

"Good." She kept on staring at me. Finally she reached up and stroked my cheek. "Because I know how surprised you are to be here."

"Yeah . . . well . . ." I reached over to hold her hand on my cheek. She let go, but we held onto each other.

"You never talked to me until a month ago." She didn't seem angry.

I could feel myself starting to blush. "Sure . . . sure . . . I did. We talked. At parties . . ."

"C'mon, Jack." She still smiled. "I was the bozo next door. Marty Siegal's little piece."

I tried to let go of her hand. She held on tighter. "Come on, Elizabeth, that's not true. Absolutely not true."

"Jack, you never listened to a word I said."

"Don't be silly, of course I did." I tried to remember some bon mot she had uttered. Something to say that showed I had paid attention. "I listened, Elizabeth." I tried to look serious, intense. "It's, it's, just, we never had much of a chance . . ."

"I know." She looked up at me very sweetly. "I guess I'm thinkin' how we never would have talked. Now tell me you ever dated anyone who majored in typing?"

"In college?"

"High school." She grinned and squeezed my hand.

"Okay." I fell back down on the bed. We laid there side by

side. Looking over at each other, still holding hands. "So I didn't date a lot of typists."

"Or sleep with your nurse?"

"Are you kidding?"

"See, Jack. The kind of guys I went out with loved to date typists. Typists screwed around. Drank a lot. Wore too much makeup. Lots of cleavage. That's what the guys figured. Now I'm not talking about your law school graduates. Guys like Marty. Hondlers. Looking for a fast buck. Loved typists like me. Big boobs, little brains they figured."

"It's not true, Elizabeth."

"What's not true, Jack?"

I tried not looking at her chest. "You're smart, Elizabeth. You really are."

"Because I'm in bed with you?"

I tried letting go of her hand, but she held on even tighter. "I'm sorry."

"About what?"

"Not dating you in high school?"

She laughed. That big, chest-heaving laugh. I stared at her heaving chest. "That's good, Jackie. I mean it. That's really good."

"Thanks, I'm not usually funny."

"I know, you're usually sort of . . . meek." She smiled.

"That's not true."

"Okay." She still had a big grin on her face. "You're shy. Out of bed that is."

"It's just that . . ." I tried to think of what it was that I was. ". . . I don't care for . . . conflicts."

"To put it mildly." She was looking at me seriously. "This is not something to laugh about, Jack."

"Who's laughing?"

"But you're not taking it seriously."

"At three in the morning, when I'm alone, I take it seriously, Elizabeth."

"I think we should go away, Jackie."

"We?"

She rubbed my arm. It felt absolutely wonderful. "We'll go away for the rest of August."

"Us?" It came out in a sort of whining tone.

"I think once the kids come back from camp, everything'll be okay. The end of August is dangerous."

"Elizabeth." I closed my eyes and felt her rub me very slowly. "I can't go. I've got my patients—"

"Oh, come on, Jack, what do you do. Stick a couple needles in their arms. Your nurse can do it. How about San Diego? Did you ever go to San Diego?"

If she wasn't rubbing my arm so wonderfully, I would have gotten upset over the demeaning of my profession. "Suppose somebody has an asthma attack . . ."

"Steroids," she said, as she moved down across my hip.

"Since when are you such an expert on allergy?"

"Everybody in Lake View is an expert on allergy. You think poor people in Chicago can afford to have hayfever? I didn't know anything about pollens and mold until I moved here. It's big stuff around this place. Now I'm an expert."

"See, you're a lot more than a typist."

She kissed me softly on the lips. "That's the nicest thing you've ever said to me." She kissed me again. "I might even fall in love with you if you keep saying stuff like that."

"I don't think—"

She kissed me once more. This time to shut me up. "Don't worry, you'll do something dumb to keep me from falling in love with you."

"Don't be so sure." I moved toward her. Pressed my body into hers.

It was a wonderfully soft body.

"Like not go away with me?"

"Elizabeth . . ."

"I know, I know, you can't."

"What do I tell Barbara?"

She moved her head back to look at me like I was out of my mind. "The woman is rapidly developing an allergy to you and you're worried what you're going to say to her?"

"Yeah . . ." How could I think of Barbara when Elizabeth's hard nipples were tickling my skin. Barbara's nipples hadn't gotten erect in ten years. Or at least I hadn't felt them get pointed. ". . . I still think she would figure it was strange, me going to San Diego for August. It is not a normal thing for me to do, Elizabeth."

"Jack. Jack. When are you going to realize nothing is normal. First you'll go away and then I'll meet you."

"Can Women Without Men do without Elizabeth Siegal?"

She nibbled my ear a couple times. I got chills. "Sure. I'm just sort of the hired help anyway. I'm the only one who can type. By the way, your ears taste good." She moved down to my neck. Nibbling and kissing. I was so happy. So very happy I almost forgot my problems. I had definitely forgotten I was married.

"Have I mentioned your breasts lately?"

Elizabeth moved back and looked down at them. They had squished away from my body. I still felt them. The nipples must have made indentations, permanent dents in my chest. "They are terrific." She squeezed back into me. "Typists usually have good chests," she explained, rubbing my neck.

I moved my hands down her back. Making all kinds of noises to express my joy. "I would have dated your breasts. I promise, Elizabeth."

She mumbled something and then drew back. Not too far back. Just far enough to look at me. "I'm worried about you, Jack."

"Me too."

"It's not a game."

I gestured toward the outside. "You mean out there?"

She kissed my chin. "I plan on spending more time in bed with you."

"Keep Barbara at Jane's, then."

"That's easy. It's keeping you . . ." She stopped and hugged me. Hard.

"I've got to stay here. In town."

I could hear her let out a deep breath. Neither one of us said anything for a while. We just held onto each other. Until we fell asleep.

I woke up first. I could see the sun come in the window. Sometime between five and six in the morning. I had slept well. That much I knew. But it wasn't until I looked over at the person next to me, that I remembered why I had slept so well.

"Oh, my." I whispered it. And then I saw the nipple sticking out from under the cover and in spite of myself I wanted to touch it. Ached to reach over and lick it. But I looked out the window again, and remembered that yesterday Barbara had come over to get some clothes. Come over at six in the morning to find me sleeping.

I ran across the yard at the speed of sound. All the time visions raced through my mind of Barbara waiting around the corner, every corner in the house, with a gun, maybe it was Elizabeth's gun. Maybe it was their gun. Bea's and Jane's and Elizabeth's and the leader of them all, Barbara. Maybe the whole thing was a set-up. The typist as volunteer for the evening. Sacrificing her body for the greater good. Making me feel good, no making me feel great, for the first time in so very long. Making me stop worrying about order, predictability, making me stop thinking. Stop considering. Stop arranging. No, no, it couldn't be. Please, don't let it be. So I just ran. In the house. Through the kitchen. Up the stairs. Ran into the bedroom, threw my clothes into the hamper and jumped onto the clean, neat, perfectly made bed.

Barbara arrived fifteen minutes later. Her empty bag slung around her shoulder. I kept my eyes shut. Tight. I listened as she slammed the drawers.

Slowly, deliberately, I opened my eyes. I tried to mumble.

"Wha? Wha?" I mumbled.

She turned away from the underwear to look over at me.

"Why are you sleeping on top of the covers?"

I stretched, yawned a few times, trying to look as natural as possible. "Tired." I yawned out. "Real tired."

She shrugged and threw some more underwear into her bag.

"What now?" I asked, trying to remember if I left any traces of Elizabeth. I looked for red hairs along my body.

"What do you mean?" It wasn't a question, more like a bullet.

I dodged it this time. "Just that I think you should start . . . uh . . . considering . . . soon . . . that is . . ." I could smell Elizabeth. Unfortunately it was on me. Barbara was too far away to notice. I hoped.

"Well?" she said impatiently, slinging the bag over her shoulder. "Say it already."

". . . when are you moving back . . .?"

Feet spread apart, finger pointing at my Elizabeth-smelling body, Barbara announced, "Listen, what I'm doing is important. Finally. You've made fun of me for years. Well, now I've found something. I—"

"I never said it wasn't important."

She paid no attention. ". . . women need me. I've something to contribute."

"I never said . . ."

"Women whose husbands left them alone. . . "

"I'm here . . ."

". . . alone, do you understand that?"

I nodded. "Maybe when you run out of underwear?" I regretted saying it out loud.

". . . when Jane thinks she can make it through the night." A pause. "I'll be back."

For some reason the thought sent chills through me, and the air-conditioning was off.

The best part of the summer lasted two weeks. Even the memories of the previous six weeks couldn't ruin those days of pleasure. Hostile phone conversations with Barbara, angry confrontations with Jane on the street, the longer and longer line of cars parked on our block each night. They caused me to wake up sweating, but at least when I did jump up, there was Elizabeth to cling to.

I had a new routine. Every night, after getting home from work, I would call Barbara. I would invite her for dinner. Then I would try to contain my pleasure at her increasingly strong refusals. At 6:13 I would be ready to head for Elizabeth's. At 6:14 and 30 seconds, I would make my ever faster dash to Elizabeth's, timing it so the three power walkers would be just turning the corner.

For the next twelve hours I felt safe.

Awaking from some chilling nightmare, I would bury myself in Elizabeth's body. Trying to squeeze myself into her. Then I could sleep. Some nights, of course, it seemed, she would be required to appear before the group. To inspire them with the glory of her past. The tales of her adventures with Marty and mommy.

Those nights, when Elizabeth was gone for a few hours, were not the best times of my day. I would sit by the window, in the dark, watching the cars arrive at Jane's. The latecomers would fairly run across the lawn to get there on time. And I would sit. And sit. And try not to imagine what was going on inside. I would never ask Elizabeth. And those times, when she would return at midnight, I didn't want to listen to any talk. I just cared about holding on to her, making love to her, forgetting everything that happened during the day, all the fears that disturbed my nights. Only Elizabeth could exorcise them for me.

The mornings were the worst part. The races across the lawn. The rumpling up of the bed. The hiding of the timer that turned my lights on and off each night. I would throw my clothes into the hamper and lie down for ten minutes. My heart was threatening to burst through my chest as I waited for Barbara to come back. But she didn't. She already had plenty of clothes, and so I just showered, dressed and prayed. And waited twelve more hours, of course.

By the middle of August, I was even forgetting some of my fears. Half-believing that soon everything would be fine. And then I would look out of the Siegal window. Watch the line of cars parked around the corner, and I would get that old feeling again. Until Elizabeth got into bed with me.

I was late this particular morning. I had actually taken a long shower. Maybe I was getting overconfident. Maybe I was starting to believe that this nightmare would fade with the end of August. Shari and Mary were already huddled together looking at a few brochures. Reluctantly they put them away.

I had spent a lot of time in the shower. Alternately trying to wash away Elizabeth Siegal's scent and then trying to relocate it. Mostly, though, I stood there, letting the water run over my face and down my body. Turning it hotter and hotter. I tried to feel guilty. Tried to remind myself I had never done this before. But it was tough. Guilt has to come to you naturally. Trying to impose it on yourself is difficult, especially when the person that is supposed to make you feel guilty is spending her time thinking of ways to get at men in general, and, perhaps, you in particular. In the service of a greater good, of course, as Barbara would put it.

Still, was I cheating because of Barbara, or because I was a cliche? The middle-aged menopauser. Or because I was scared? Of my own wife in search of a calling?

Or maybe, unbelievable as it seemed, because I was in love. Because I hadn't been in love, real love, mad passionate-screw-them-all kind of love in maybe fifteen years? I had a lot of choices. All I wanted to do was get back into bed with Elizabeth Siegal.

My two o'clock patient was a shock.

Shari ushered her into my office. "This is Dr. Klein, Mrs.

Siegal." Shari glanced at the chart in her hand. "Hey, you two live on the same street!" She looked up with a big grin. "Some coincidence, huh?" When neither one of us said anything, Shari rolled her eyes at the ignorance of the older generation and walked out, shutting the door behind her.

I just sat there. Looked up at Elizabeth Siegal in a light beige blouse and beige skirt. She walked over and kissed me gently on the forehead. Her breasts were smack dab in front of my eyes. I almost licked them. Through her blouse and bra.

Before I could get my tongue out, she took a seat.

"Want a Kleenex?" I asked, reaching for the box.

"Please," she said very properly.

I gave her a tissue. She just held onto it.

"You don't have to sneeze?"

She shook her head. "Not right now. Unless you want me to, of course."

"No, no, not if you don't feel like it."

"Okay."

"Elizabeth . . ." I began. I realized I sounded serious. Like a doctor.

She stopped me from going on. "I think you and I have to do something about what's going on?"

"Perhaps we should start talking divorce . . ."

"Jack, I'm not talking divorce, I'm talking serious."

"Right. Right." I looked around the room, trying to focus on something else.

She didn't let go. "Listen, I think you should hear what the girls are saying."

"Are we all going out for dinner again?" I shook my head. "I don't think it would be too terrific, Elizabeth. Not right now."

"Jack, did you ever hear of something called eavesdropping?" She was getting upset. She started tapping her fingers together.

I couldn't get over how crazy I was about her. I couldn't believe I used to think of her as that "bimbo" next door. The woman was beautiful, sexy, sensitive—

"Jack, you're not paying attention." She hit me on the wrist. A pat really. An affectionate pat.

"I was just thinking about—"

"I know," she said, touching me on the arm again. "But believe me, if you want to do more of that, you'd better do some serious eavesdropping."

I reached over to grab her hand. Then I leaned forward to kiss her, but she moved away. "Jack, stop it."

I let go, lowered my head. She didn't reach over to raise it and bestow a hundred-thousand kisses over my face. I looked up.

"That's better," she said. "Now, listen to me."

"I'm listening."

"Good. Anybody ever tell you that you look like Gary Cooper?"

"Really?"

She cocked her head. "In a certain light." She looked at me for a second and then came back to the reason she had come. "Now listen, this afternoon, the girls are coming over."

"I gotta work."

"I know. I know. But the way I figure it is that you can sneak in the back way around five o'clock. We'll all be in the living room."

"Suppose someone decides to go into the kitchen for a drink? You don't think it's going to look a little suspicious—" The intercom buzzed.

Shari's voice. "Mr. Gordon is here, doctor."

"Tell him I'll be right there." I started to get up. "Listen, maybe some other day. . ."

Elizabeth stood up too. She kept talking. "Jack, I'm tellin' you, you've got to do something now."

"I've got to see Mr. Gordon, Elizabeth."

"You've got to come over at five." She reached in her purse to hand me a key. "I'll tell them I waxed the floor in the kitchen. That'll keep them out. Every woman respects waxed floors."

"They'll believe that?"

"Jack, if you're really worried you can sit on the top step of the basement stairs. You can hear into the living room from there. The living room wall is on the other side. It's real thin. Marty always went for lousy drywalls."

I looked at the key she was holding out toward me. "Okay." She put it into my shirt pocket. As she did I reached over to grab her. She pulled away.

"Elizabeth . . ."

"Jack, no nooky in the office." She smiled and opened the door. I noticed that she put the tissue up to her nose as she walked out, sniffling to impress Shari and Mary with her ragweed difficulties.

Chapter Fourteen

SITTING ON the top step of Elizabeth's basement stairs, the hot basement stairs, I started sweating long before I felt the moisture rise out of the dank, dark basement.

BARBARA: . . . and he is so resentful of the time I spend with you. All of you.

JANE: The same thing with Dave. He started getting more and more paranoid about things . . .

BEA: . . . Frank didn't know about paranoid. Screaming. That's all he could do. It killed him.

SOUNDS OF LAUGHTER. I DON'T HEAR ELIZABETH'S BELLY LAUGH.

ELIZABETH: I always thought of Jack as a nice guy.

JANE: You're doing it again, Elizabeth. Why do you feel this need to defend him?

ELIZABETH: He's cute?

BARBARA: See, you still think of men in sexual situations.

BEA: That's the way they think of us.

BARBARA: Right, and so we have traditionally given in to their childish needs. The fact that Jack is cute, well, so was Ted Bundy.

ELIZABETH: I'd say Gary Cooper . . . that's what I think of him as.

BARBARA: Don't be absurd, Elizabeth. He is no longer attractive. The man's anger and resentment have changed his looks. His failure to comprehend what we're doing here has really changed his features.

ELIZABETH: What are we doing here?

BARBARA: (A GIANT SIGH) Elizabeth . . . when are you going to understand that we are helping each other . . .

JANE: It was you who started it, Elizabeth . . .

ELIZABETH: I didn't mean to, Janie. I mean, I was aiming for his crotch . . .

BARBARA: Now, Elizabeth, it may have been an accident . . .

BEA: . . . but an inspired one.

SILENCE. LOTS OF SILENCE. A BIG COUGH. MAYBE BARBARA.

BARBARA: The point is, if men are going to force us to be alone, we're going to have to learn how to take care of each other.

BEA: . . . each other. That's the point.

JANE: Why aren't you walking with us?

BEA: Or putting up posters?

BARBARA: Now, now . . . remember Elizabeth is not the enemy.

AFTER A FEW SECONDS OF GLASSES MOVING AROUND THE COFFEE TABLE BARBARA SPEAKS.

BARBARA: I think we have to start getting our priorities straight.

BEA: I agree.

JANE: You don't realize the seriousness of our work, Elizabeth.

BEA: You've got to spend more time with us, Elizabeth. We need to be together.

BARBARA: (VERY, VERY CALMLY) I think Bea has hit on it, Elizabeth. Men *can't* be together.
JANE: . . . emotionally, that is.
BARBARA: (I HAD A FEELING BARBARA WAS GIVING JANE ONE OF HER LOOKS) Thank you, Janie. Yes, we've talked a lot lately about how men find themselves unable to connect with each other. Competition is all they can relate to. Winning and losing. Winning and losing. That's all they care about. Women can help each other.
BEA: That's why we need you, Elizabeth. To help other women.
JANE: Now that our kids are practically grown.—
BEA: They don't really need us now. Not as much as other women do.
ELIZABETH: It's not that I don't want to help . . .
BARBARA: That's all we're asking, Elizabeth.
JANE: Be a part of us, Liz.
BARBARA: You can help women like *you* cope with being alone.
BEA: Because they're not alone.
BARBARA: Elizabeth, Elizabeth. (I THOUGHT SHE MIGHT BE PATTING HER ON THE BACK. SHE HAD THAT SOOTHING TONE IN HER VOICE) You need to make some sort of commitment. You don't have a . . . man . . . in your life anymore to force you to commit to him. (I ALMOST FELL DOWN THE STAIRS)
ELIZABETH: Okay, okay. You know I still haven't decided what to do yet. About staying here in Lake View, that is. If I do . . .
JANE: We need you, Liz.
THEY ALL TALK AT ONCE. BARBARA'S VOICE RISES ABOVE THE DIN.
BARBARA: Stop. Elizabeth needs time.
ELIZABETH: Right, yeah, time. I need it . . .
BARBARA: About Jack, Elizabeth. He doesn't understand, won't take even me seriously—
ELIZABETH: Maybe you should talk to him . . .

BARBARA: I've tried. Believe me, I've tried. (THE VOICE LOWERED)

ELIZABETH: I always thought you and Jack had a good relationship . . .

BARBARA: So did I, Liz, so did I. And that's what's so sad. I assumed the relationship was good because it was on his terms only. The doctor as husband. Keeping his silly wife in school looking for degrees. Keeping his life in order. Like his nurse, his children, *his sock drawer*. Let me tell you about that damn sock drawer. It was arranged . . .

(I NOTED THE PAST TENSE)

BARBARA: It's the most anal thing.

BEA: I always thought Jack was *incredibly* neat.

JANE: Sick neat.

BARBARA: I think there's evidence in the literature for your evaluation, Jane. And I was like a pair of his dark blue socks, which I might add were always separate from the black socks. And that's me. Old dark blue Barbara. Never to be thought of as brown or beige. Well, he's going to have to learn.

BEA: Take it from me, men don't learn. Frank never did . . .

(ELIZABETH HADN'T SAID A WORD)

BARBARA: Jack is not important.

JANE: In my mind he doesn't exist. (LIKE DAVE AND FRANK)

Nobody said anything. But I could imagine a lot of nodding in agreement. I just crouched there, so very uneasy. But don't, I told myself, overreact, Jack. Nobody, after all, had said off the damned allergist . . .

I don't think the sex was as good as the night before. That's not to say it was bad. I just think I was too preoccupied with the conversation to really get into it with my heart, soul and fingertips.

"Jack, Jack . . ." Elizabeth kept saying, "you've got to do something." She said it again. And then again. And on into the evening.

We had dinner, of sorts, around ten. I made her get dressed, just in case one of the "girls" dropped by. "Suppose they want to have another session," I said as she found a housecoat to slip over her naked body.

"They don't come out at night, Jack." She went ahead of me to the kitchen.

I was tying my tie as she put a plate of cheese and crackers, a bowl of fruit, and a bottle of wine on the white counter. We sat next to each other on the white and chrome stools.

"You've got to talk about this," Elizabeth said as she uncorked the bottle and reached into the cabinet above us for a pair of glasses that were made for juice.

"What's there to say." I took a nectarine and bit into it. It was too sour. I left it on my plate.

"Only that your own wife is probably out to get rid of you. And I don't mean divorce."

"I wouldn't go that far," I said, looking into the bowl for an alternative to the rotten nectarine. Maybe a plum. "She just doesn't want to remember that I exist. There's a difference, Elizabeth. Also, I'm not hot for her mother, don't need my meat cut up for me—"

"Jack, you were scared when I opened the basement door."

I found a couple strawberries. "Well, I'm claustrophobic." The first strawberry was good. The second wasn't. I drank some wine. It was also sour but I didn't want to say anything.

"You know what I'm saying but you want to deny it. Well go home, doctor. Stay alone in your bed tonight. Alone. And then try and deny it."

I tried to concentrate on something else. I looked at Elizabeth. She made me feel good. I reached over to touch her. She held my hand.

"Jack, what are you going to do?" She said it gently. Evenly. Calmly.

"I can't just make love to you?"

"Jack." She stared at me and let go of my hand. "Barbara taught us all about denial. We learned this early in the sessions.

And what you're doin' is what she says is your typical denial of bad stuff. You know it's there but you're not going to do anything about it. And that's *dumb.*" She leaned closer. "You either got to confront the situation or get out of it. I got a feeling your best bet is avoiding it. For real that is. Get out of here. You want me to not come with you, that's fine, but for goodness sakes, get far away from here for a few weeks. By that time things will have calmed down."

I poured myself some more wine. So what if it was sour. I cut a hunk of cheese. It helped the wine go down. "Maybe if I talked to her—"

I didn't get a chance to finish. Elizabeth grabbed me by the elbow and pulled me off the stool. "Here, I'll show you what good talking will do." She guided me through the kitchen and into the living room. It was dark, and Elizabeth pulled me through the chairs and couches towards the big window that looked out onto Apple Tree Lane.

"Elizabeth, they might see us," I said as we got closer to the lights from either the street or the Redfield house across the street.

"They won't notice, believe me Jack, they won't notice."

"I'm telling you . . ." And then I saw the cars. There must have been hundreds of them. The lights came from Jane's house. It was lit up. A beacon.

"A meeting," Elizabeth said to me as if I were a baby. "It's not some game anymore. It's for real, Jack. And you ain't a part of it."

I shook my head and stared out at the Mercedes and Audis and Volvos and the occasional station wagon parked on Apple Tree Lane. I forgot that someone might see us. I just stared at the cars and the house and tried to figure out what was going on inside.

"Barbara's on a roll, Jack. She finally got something to do with her life." Elizabeth was talking to me sweetly. "She is going to make Women Without Men major league. I'm not talking old-fashioned women's lib, now, that's milksop stuff."

I kept staring at the house. As if, somehow, it would help me figure out why everything had turned out the way it had. Why the easy banality of my life had ceased. Why the equanimity of my existence had suddenly gone haywire. And why, especially, my fears had turned into denials. Why I had gone from being obsessed with events to ignoring them.

"People do that," Arnie explained. We were having drinks together. At Chez Schwartz. It was early. Just past five. The next day. The five-thirty seating hadn't arrived yet. Eddie Schwartz was in the kitchen and his surly French bartender was behind the counter. I had practically demanded that Arnie see me. I would have paid for his couch, but he just asked me to buy him a drink. He sipped his wine and went on. "When a problem gets closer to you, rather than actually deal with it you, people, that is, will often tend to deny that it's there. That it relates to them."

"So what do I do?" I took a big swallow of my wine. I hadn't mentioned Elizabeth.

He shrugged. "Who knows?"

"Thanks, Arnie. A lot."

He gave me one of his nice warm smiles. "No, no, what I meant was that maybe your inability to do anything comes from a realization that there really is nothing to do. Maybe you've figured that everything that happened on your block this summer is entirely coincidental."

"Come on, Arnie."

Arnie nodded once. "Then again maybe not."

"Thanks." I turned away from him and stared at the bartender, who was staring at nothing in particular.

Arnie tapped me on the shoulder. "Look, you may be right. Your turn may be next. But . . ."

I glanced away from the bartender and looked at Arnie, trying to be sincere.

". . . I don't think you should make that assumption. From what you've told me, Barbara is a rational person. Talk to her,

I'm sure that if you do, things will get better. They have to." He gave my shoulder a squeeze. "Now about me . . ."

"Wait a minute. Arnie, suppose, just suppose, the whole thing is true. Suppose Barbara is going to follow the lead of Bea and Jane. Suppose, just suppose, Arnie."

He tried looking serious. Puckering his lips. Rubbing his hands through his hair. "I guess you could call the police."

"Forget it. I have nothing to tell them. Nothing they'd listen to."

He nodded. "Okay, then I suppose if your paranoia had some basis . . ." he tried to look like he was considering the possibility. ". . . you could take some kind of action."

"Like what, Arnie?"

I could see by his eyes that his mind was starting to wander. To think about Shari. "The problem is that you and Barbara have to get back into love."

"What does that mean?" I took another sip of wine. I noticed a party of six come into the restaurant.

"That I've come to realize that passion does make the world go round."

"Wha'?"

"I know. I know. I sound like some pop psychologist, but it's true."

"You're in love, Arnie."

"Yeah, but passion is really the determiner of mental health." He held up his right hand. "Used positively, it allows us to feel love and hope." He held up his left hand. "Used destructively, it becomes a force for evil. But, Jack,"—he clapped the hands together—"it's what motivates people. Passion about causes, passion about men and women. Right now, your wife is passionate about a cause. And you . . ."

I tried to look away from him, at the party being seated by Eddie Schwartz's proud mother. He didn't notice my embarrassment.

". . . you're the odd man out here. You need passion in *your* life, Jack. Desire, madness, that sort of thing." He started to get up from his stool. "Help any?"

"No."

He smiled and gave me another one of those manly shoulder clasps. "C'mon, Jack, you're taking this all too seriously."

"So did you, Arnie. Remember how a month ago you were going crazy about the womanization of the suburbs? Remember that? Remember how bitter you were about your ex-wife and how the men in Lake View were second-class citizens."

He didn't seem disturbed by my memories. In fact his grin grew larger as he leaned on the back of the stool. "Jack, Jack, that's the point, I was like you. Then I discovered personally that life was driven by . . . desire." He leaned back, away from the bar, ready to go off to another night of passion. "That's all we need, us poor slobs, some love in our lives." He stood up. Ready to leave.

"Thanks, Arnie." It was no use. Shari had turned him into mush.

"Glad to help, Jack." He gave me a wave and went off into the night.

I left a bit later. It was just six and the rain that we had been waiting for all summer long had finally arrived. A hard, mean rain. But it was still blisteringly hot, and when the water hit the street, you could see the steam rise. Another miserable night, only it was wet and miserable. I ran through the rain to my car. I tried skipping around the puddles, trying to avoid getting my pants wet. But it was no use. I was soaked. And the car was hot. Steaming. I turned on the engine and waited for the air conditioner to start working.

Finally, it was cool inside the car. I headed home. The beads of sweat on my forehead were frozen. The shirt, wet from sweat and rain, stuck to my body. But, for once, I liked air-conditioning. It protected me from all that was going on outside.

When I was a kid I used to love to ride in the old Buick

Special in the rain. A green behemoth of a car that, even without air-conditioning, protected me from all that lay outside. A car to sink into, with a back seat that kept me far away from my parents and sister as I stared out the window at the rain that couldn't touch us. I loved to watch the water falling down my window. Sheets of rain that kept me from seeing but a few feet.

It was growing dark now. Not because the sun was setting, but because all the clouds that had skirted Lake View this summer, had, at last, joined together to make early evening seem like midnight.

There weren't many cars on the road. People seemed to be staying home. All the tennis buffs had hidden inside. All games called off because of unexpected rain. Even the commuters had hurried home. My Saab was one of the few cars out.

I heard the Audi before I saw it in the rearview mirror. Heard, over the rain and the squeaking wipers, the sound of a car barreling through the rain on the deserted side street. I had decided to take a short cut home. Avoiding Broadway and the larger, stop-lighted main streets of Lake View.

I thought it must be a commuter, racing from the station. Trying to get to his family. As the dark-colored Audi got closer, I saw it was speeding along as if in an emergency. A paramedic squad without the siren. Nobody passed cars in Lake View. But this one was, pulling over as it got ready to overtake me. I moved closer to the puddle-filled curb. I could hear my car make a series of splashes as I gave the Audi all the room it needed.

I tried to look over as it came abreast. Tried to find out who was in such a hurry to get home.

I noticed she was on the phone. It was in her right hand as she gripped the wheel in her left. The phone hid her face. I didn't recognize the blonde ponytail. And then, as I turned back to look at the road, I heard a screech of tires. Quickly, I looked over. She hadn't passed me, hadn't kept up her speed, hadn't tried to leave me behind. Instead, she seemed to be moving over toward me. Maybe she was looking at me out of the corner of her eyes, but she was staring straight ahead. And yet, the car was moving toward me. Edging toward mine. I slowed down. From thirty to twenty. And then she slowed down. Let me pull even with her and drove alongside of me for another half block. And still her eyes were glued to the road ahead. Still, she kept the phone close to her ear.

She swerved over just when I turned back to look at the road. A swerve that I avoided only because I heard its screech. The noise from the tires on the water. My tires hit the curb but I had managed to slam down on my brakes so that the Audi also hit the curb right in front of me.

Both of us were out of control. Sliding on the water, bumping the curb, wrestling with our wheels to get back onto the street.

I did it first. Turned the wheel gently to the left, feeling the tires grip the cement. And I brought the car to a stop. Waited while the larger blacker Audi in front of me regained its equilibrium. It stopped too. Waiting. Both of us stayed very still. The sound of my windshield wipers seemed to grow louder. And then, suddenly, just as I was ready to back up, she took off. In a rush. Down the road and into the rain. A black creature disappearing in the dark.

I laid my head against the wheel. Let it drop there. Stay there while I shut my eyes and tried to figure out what had happened.

I took a deep breath and slowly blew it out. Why? Who was it? And why? It wasn't Bea or Jane or Barbara. An anonymous woman. On her car phone. Why? Was I just an anonymous man to be hurled to the side of the road to pay penance for something her husband had done to her? Or was it me? Not a symbol of man, but a specific one.

I must have sat there for three minutes. Waiting for my heart to stop pounding. And then, very, very, slowly I began to drive down the street. Inching, crawling, moving at the pace of a little old lady in a '55 Ford down the block, I made my turn. A wide, safe right turn onto Pierce, half a mile from home. I concentrated on the rain. Once again I felt the freezing air inside the car as I hunched over the wheel, peered out the window for the

Audi. But driveways all over Lake View were filled with Audis. Still, I looked for a clue, for the blonde woman trying to run me off the road.

I didn't know the car was behind me until I felt the bump. The seatbelt kept me from going through the window. Throwing me up to the steering wheel, but holding me back at the very moment before impact. I couldn't look behind because there was a second bump a moment later. I was holding onto the steering wheel when this one came. Holding on hard. Arms stiff. Pushing myself back into the seat. I took off, skidding, but, somehow, staying in control. The car behind me took a while to get into gear, but then it too skidded down the street. A Volvo. A big one. I couldn't see who was driving it, except that as it got closer, I deliberately slowed down, trying to glance up in the rearview mirror.

I was sweating again, forgetting the coldness of the car and just feeling the sweat falling down my forehead, slipping down my nose.

She was on the phone. That was all I could tell. She was talking on the phone and staring straight ahead. At me. And picking up speed.

I didn't know whether a Saab could beat a Volvo, but I was sure trying. I kept looking back in the mirror. All I could see was the phone. The phone pressed to her face. She was gaining on me. I didn't know what she was doing, but I could see her lights were getting closer. And closer. And still there were no other cars on the road, and the rain was coming down as hard as ever and there was nowhere else to go.

I stopped. Quickly. Suddenly. Without warning I slammed on the brakes. In the mirror I could see the phone fall away from her face as she realized that if she hit me, it wasn't going to be me that was going to get it the worst.

I took off a moment before she was ready to slam into my rear. Instead she swerved, off the road, up the grass and into a very thin very young tree. I watched the Volvo stay there, half off the road as I hurried away down Pierce.

A car passed me. A station wagon. American. And I crouched down. Hid because I wasn't sure if it was going to swerve into me. But it passed. Slowly, evenly, and I saw children in the car.

I turned on the radio. Switched to the news station. As if what had just happened to me was going to be reported. On the air. Instant news. But it wasn't there. Just the story of basements flooding all over town.

A car in the distance, two blocks away, turned into a driveway. I slowed down. Waited until I could see its lights go off, and picked up speed.

I wiped my eyes. Shook my head. Tried to get back to reality. A summer of coincidences. And now an evening of . . .

. . . a rocket was coming toward me. Aimed at me. A lo-slung sports car, splashing through the puddles, its yellow headlights making it look like an enormous, angry animal. I moved my car to the left. Slowed down and hugged the curb, feeling my wheels scrape along the side. The speeding car slid over. Moving along seemingly without fear. I couldn't judge how far away it was. But I knew there was no place to escape. No side of the road to hug in safety. It was like watching a make-believe vehicle in a video game. As if it were controlled by some distant source, by somebody at the arcade who was turning the wheel and looking at the screen. I looked for driveways to turn into, streets to turn off. But there were only ravines on either side to plunge down. And the car kept coming toward me. Racing, racing, speeding. Targeted onto my fragilely built Saab.

Her top was down. It made no sense, but the top of the convertible was down. I could see, even from far away, a woman's head peer over the top of the windshield. Phone in hand, she looked at me through the rain. Checked my position before sitting back down in her seat. No seatbelt held her, gave her a chance when the inevitable collision occurred. And then I understood. She was going to jump. Somehow the car was going to go the last few feet alone. Into me, as she took her chances with the muddy grass.

A couple hundred feet. I could see her door open. And still I was looking around for escape. The sports car swerved slightly as the driver, phone in hand, seemed to be edging out. One hand holding the wheel as she stepped halfway out. Fifty feet, that was all, fifty feet as I tried to swerve to the other side of the road. But she followed me. Twenty feet and she was almost out, the phone dropped. With one hand on the wheel she looked to see if there was grass to leap onto. Then looked back, stared back at me, watching to see if I would move. I slowed down. Waited until she was almost out of the car and pressed down on the horn.

She hesitated. Turned back. It was all I needed. That moment of not being sure let me swerve to the left. Feel my wheels climb onto the curb. She tried to move back to me. But it was too late. By the time she could get her wheel around, we had already passed. I had pressed my foot all the way down on the gas. In my rearview mirror I could see her car careen down the road. Make a zigzag as it tried to right itself. As I turned the corner I could see the convertible top start to rise again.

I made a series of turns. Rights and lefts, without design, that took me down streets that led me nowhere. I wasn't thinking. Wasn't trying to figure out where I was going. Just away. That's all I needed to know. Get away. Far from the women on the phones. From cars that would be destroyed to eliminate me. It was like the Manson family. Sending out their followers to kill mindlessly. But this was Lake View. Dumb, ordinary Lake View. The place I had chosen to fit into the orderliness of my life. And now there was only messiness.

I was just a few blocks from home. But there was only one way into Apple Tree Lane. Only one way to get from where I was to my home. To Elizabeth's actually. My house wasn't safe. But hers was. She was one of them and so, when I was with her I was all right, protected.

I inched down Haven Road. Moved, oh-so-slowly to the corner. There was no alternative to getting to Apple Tree Lane. By now the women on the car phones must have told each other that. They must have figured out how to keep me from getting to my destination. Assigned positions to the cars. So that there would be no way for me to escape. They must have figured it out by now. Figured out how to keep me from getting away. But who was "they"?

I had to make a run for it. Somehow get into Apple Tree Lane and turn into Elizabeth's driveway. They wouldn't be waiting for me there. Maybe they were in my driveway already. That I could believe. Lights off, waiting to crash into me as I drove up to my house. A crash on the driver's side of the car. An accident. The weather. Lots of witnesses to verify that her car slipped. Maybe his car had done the slipping. Whatever, it was an accident. Like Frank's asphyxiation and David's bleeding to death, the car crash of Jack Klein, once a well-known North Shore allergist, was going to be an accident.

I wished I had put a phone in my car. I wished. And I drove surreptitiously down the block. In the rain. And tried to figure out a way to get in.

Of course I could always go back. Back to my office. Or Chez Schwartz. Or even Chicago. But really, there was no place to go. No place that would make me feel safe. Except Elizabeth's.

Turn the lights off. That's what I should do. Turn off the headlights and creep quietly into Apple Tree Lane. And so I drove gently. Down the block. Trying to keep my splashes from splashing too hard. Trying to shrink behind the wheel. Cursing the color of my Saab. Red was not very hideable. Black, beige, but not bright, jarring red. My one act of indulgence, the one time I picked a color that didn't blend into the traffic. The one time I picked a color that wouldn't get lost in supermarket parking lots. I made it so easy to find. Unfortunately. Because now, there sure wouldn't be a lot of red cars on the road. In the rain. If I had only opted for an Audi, I could probably sneak home unnoticed. Just another German car running through the rain. But a red Saab stood out like a pink-and-white polka-dotted Studebaker.

And the rain still came splashing down. Sheets of it. Making a water-slide out of my hood.

I was chilled now. But I was also sweating. Sweating and shivering. No doubt a common shock phenomenon that I had forgotten about. Whatever the cause, I was gripping the steering wheel with white knuckles. Holding it so tight that my fingers would have to be pried off. Separated one by one by whomever found me in the wreck.

Of course I could always turn off into a driveway. Just pull into an empty driveway whose houselights were off and wait for morning. But they'd find me. Lake View had more divorced women with car phones than streets, so eventually, inevitably, they'd discover me cowering inside my loud red Saab. Soon, before morning, maybe when I was fast asleep, still gripping the steering wheel and shivering and sweating, they'd find me and crash into me. There was no escape. No way out of this wet, hot mess. So I drove on. On and onward. Toward some kind of inevitability. Toward a messy ending for an incredibly neat life. A disorderly finish to an orderly existence.

I was a doctor who purposely chose a bloodless specialty ending up covered with the stuff. A joke, on me, some kind of medical laugh riot, imposed upon me by the gods of Medicine. "You don't like the stuff, buddy? Okay, then, here it comes. Start spurting all you arteries. Har-de-har."

I slowed down. From ten to five miles an hour. And tried to use what was left of my brain to figure out how to avoid, for the moment, the blood-spurting inevitability of my demise. Tried thinking of how I could make a run, a dash, a drag race of half a block or so to my driveway, or Elizabeth's driveway. Past Corvettes and Maseratis and Audis and a fleet of Mercedes, BMWs, and maybe even a couple Rolls Royces, all talking to each other at a rate of a dollar a minute, but not caring because, after all, the important thing about a car phone is that it must be used, must be seen, or why else would you have it? I wondered, though, who was at the controls? Barbara? Bea? Maybe Jane. Jane's anger seemed to be much more translatable into action.

Barbara was above it all. Way too high up. Jane was her Ollie North. Translating her leader's feelings into intricate plots.

About two blocks away. Two right turns. Two minutes away from something.

Make a run for it. That was the only thing I could figure out to do. Make some kind of mad run for Apple Tree Lane.

I made my way stealthily along the street. Hugging the curb. Making little splashes through big puddles. There were no other vehicles in sight. Nobody else in front or back. So I gradually put my foot down on the accelerator. Moved the car toward the middle of the street. Switched on my lights. Hell, why not try to just go for it. For once in my life do something dramatic, something that was not measured and studied. So I put my foot down harder. Felt the car pick up speed. Felt the power as it rammed through the water. Turned up the windshield wipers. Mario Andretti, watch out, Jack Klein, voted outstanding Chicago Allergist two years ago by his peers, was laying rubber.

But there was nothing in the way. No cars to attack me as I hurried toward Apple Tree Lane. No lurking ladies watching for the approach of the red Saab. It was all too easy. Too easy for me as I made the first of the turns. Down another empty street. No cars hiding behind bushes, no Corvettes waiting to run me off the road. Just me and the rain.

It should have made me suspicious, but then, I wasn't quite used to this. Quite used to being chased by women on car phones.

By the time I hit Maple I was drenched in sweat and confidence. I was driving much too fast for conditions, but I didn't care. I was free. And then I noticed the four headlights in the rearview mirror. Two pair. They seemed to have emerged from driveways. Driveways that I had just driven past. Driveways that seemed to be empty at the time. Garages. That's what they had come out of. Hidden in garages, phones pressed to their ears, they must have been waiting. Cued by several recent divorcées who had been watching for me as I drove with more and more confidence toward Apple Tree Lane. Dummy. Dummy. I kept saying it again and again as the light behind me came closer. And then I saw Apple Tree Lane ahead.

The cars hadn't turned on their lights yet. But there was no hiding them. And they weren't trying. They were right out there, waiting in line like a Panzer division. Their Bavarian bodies gleaming in the rain. There were cars everywhere. If I tried to avoid Apple Tree, tried to go straight on Maple, I'd run right into the row of Mercedes that were blocking that street three deep. Stopping would be just as futile. And all the driveways were blocked by parked cars. Cars standing there with their headlights off. I looked at one of them as I sped past. Another woman. Eyes forward. Phone pressed to her cheek.

Fuck it. I'm going home.

I screeched around the corner. The headlights turned on the moment I made my move. We started toward each other. Like fighters coming at each other in the ring. Only there were lots of them and just one of me. As I glanced in the rearview mirror, at the cars coming behind me, I had a feeling that the lucky one wasn't going to be me . . . I might make it through a head-first crash and maybe a rear-end crackup. But both at the same time would not be good odds. If I stopped, it would certainly be all over. Waiting for them to crash into me was not a pleasant thought. I was Frank with that steak in his throat. Dave seeing his father's bow tie coming toward him and going through the window to grab it . . . him. Even Marty falling to his knees to beg for forgiveness, survival. I was a man. Enough.

I saw Elizabeth's car hurtling out of the driveway when I was about fifty feet away. Horn blaring, lights flashing, she backed out into the middle of the street, backed her tugboat of a Cadillac out into the middle of Apple Tree Lane and calmly awaited the crash.

I slammed on the brakes. Slammed so hard that I could feel the floor beneath my foot. All around me, underneath the blare of Elizabeth's honk, I could hear the screech of brakes. Everyone was trying to avoid hurting Elizabeth Siegal's Cadillac. Within five seconds Apple Tree Lane was filled with cars halted in mid-crash. Some up on lawns, one or two across driveways, and four within a foot of Elizabeth. And still she honked. Still she flashed her lights. My head was resting on the dashboard. It had fallen there with exhaustion when the final screech had screeched. Till only the sounds from Elizabeth Siegal's car interrupted the rain.

Finally, the horn died out. I looked up. It was a still-life of madness. Nobody seemed hurt. No car appeared to have even a dent. But it all looked like part of a battle. A black-and-white photograph. Only the tanks were made by BMW.

One by one the cars backed off. Slowly the cars retreated. I watched in my mirror as they headed away. Watched as they headed back down Apple Tree toward Maple. I could see the car phones put away. I noticed one blonde in a Mercedes slam the receiver back down as she zoomed backward. The battlefield was clearing. The cars on the other side of Elizabeth's Caddy waited for her to leave. Instead, she rolled down her window.

"You all right?" she yelled loud enough for me to hear over the rain.

I just nodded and dropped my head to the steering wheel. It hit with a bang.

Chapter Fifteen

I COULDN'T STOP kissing her. Big wet kisses. The kind children give to their mothers. I stood in the kitchen, far away from the living room picture windows, and held onto that wonderfully soft, incredibly kind, body.

"Thank you." I kept on saying it. In between kisses. "You actually saved my life. You did."

She smiled a lot. Looked at me and let me envelop her in hugs and kisses.

Finally, eventually, I pulled away. She had practically pulled me out of the car. Like a traffic cop. Waiting until I was safe in her driveway, then driving her car in back of mine. Protecting it from the incursions of Mercedes. We both waited until the cars had left the street, driving slowly past us. I never turned around, but just watched the retreat of the German machines as they slowly wound their way down Apple Tree Lane. Only when they were all gone, did Elizabeth come to get me. It couldn't have been more than a couple minutes, but it already seemed like part of a previous lifetime's nightmare.

"How did . . . you . . . know." I finally got out. I looked down at the puddles I had made on the kitchen floor. For once I didn't think about getting a rag to wipe them up.

"I was just going out to the store. Nothin' dramatic, Jack."

"But why then? It couldn't have been a coincidence." I reached over to touch her face, to make sure she was real. Oh boy, was she real.

"I saw all those cars lining up on the block. It looked like they were getting ready for an invasion. All those broads talking on phones and waiting. I figured that something was up."

I kissed her a few thousand more times.

"I got to keep my sex symbol happy. Us forty-year-olds only get so many chances." She said it seriously.

I touched her cheek, held my hand against its softness. She kissed me lightly, gracefully, on the lips. I couldn't think of anything to say.

"No big deal, Jackie. I save lives all the time. Certain lives, that is. Now Frank Bernstein, I wouldn't have done a lot for, but you," she held my arm and squeezed it. "For you I'm pleased to run interference."

The doorbell rang before I could think of anything to say. I jumped back, trying to see if anybody could have looked in the window. It rang again before either one of us could move toward it.

"I'll get it," Elizabeth said as she ran her fingers through her hair and tried to rearrange her rainsoaked blouse. I looked down to make sure that my erection wasn't too obvious. When I realized it was, I decided to sit down on one of the chrome-and-white chairs.

"I'll wait here. I'll lay low."

"We'll do that later, hon." And she left the room.

I could hear some women's voices. I thought of looking for a couple of butcher knives. Hiding them in my socks, but it was too late. Barbara was in the room before I could figure out which drawer to go for.

"What's going on?" she asked as she strode into the kitchen. "I saw your car in Elizabeth's driveway."

Elizabeth walked in behind her. Struggled to look like I just happened to drop by.

"I almost got killed." I looked at Barbara's face as she stopped a few feet from me.

She looked down at me. "What are you talking about?"

"The cars." I tried finding some sympathy somewhere in her face.

"What cars? Talk, Jack."

"They tried to kill me—"

"Who? Who tried to kill you?"

"Women."

"*What* women?"

"In the cars. They were chasing me, Barbara. They were waiting for me to come home."

"You're crazy."

I nodded. "Yeah, but they were still trying to crash into me."

Barbara turned to Elizabeth. "He's nuts, right?"

Elizabeth just shrugged.

Barbara looked back at me. "Why should they want to kill you, Jack? It makes no sense. No sense."

I looked down at the floor. Noticed that the puddles were still there and looked back up at Barbara.

"Come on, come on, Jack. Out with it." She didn't point her finger at me, but the effect was the same.

That's when I realized it. Realized that whatever there was between Barbara and myself had been lost. Maybe long before this. Maybe years ago when the kids were off at school all day and she careened from one graduate program to another trying to find something to make her happy. Something to make her feel whole, complete. Now, now that she had found the elusive "it" she didn't need to hold onto whatever threads held our relationship together.

It was my fault, too. My fault that we had stopped saying new things. We had created orderliness in our lives. Patterns that were rigid and unyielding. But so fragile that one tiny rip tore them all into shreds.

"Forget it, Barbara." I looked away from her. Not at Elizabeth. Just away.

"No, I want to hear all about this, all about these so-called killer women."

"I said to forget it."

"You heard him, Elizabeth, he said all these women were out to kill him. Any reason, Jack? Any reason why they should want to kill you? Because you're too neat? A capital crime?"

I looked up at her. At the smile with no humor. She was dry. The rain hadn't touched her. It was as if she were protected by some screen. Or maybe lots of women holding umbrellas over their leader. Over the one who had brought them to The Promised Land. Were they waiting outside in the rain? For her? For me?

I tried to speak calmly. "Listen, Barbara, I don't know why, but tonight a lot of women, in a lot of cars, tried to run me over—"

"Why, Jack? Tell me, why?"

"If it wasn't for Elizabeth . . ." We both looked at her, and I knew right away I'd made a mistake.

Elizabeth seemed uncomfortable. Barbara finally turned back to look at me.

"I would be dead, Barbara. You understand that?"

"I don't, Jack. I just don't understand anything you're saying."

"It could have been a bad . . . accident," Elizabeth offered quietly, caught between.

Barbara kept on looking at me. "Listen to her, Jack. An accident. That's all it was. Make that could have been. It could have been an accident. The word is *could*. It's the right weather for crashes."

"Fine, Barbara, Elizabeth saved me from a terrible accident."

She turned around. "Thank you."

Elizabeth nodded.

I stood up. Barbara stepped back. Away from me. As if I were going to hit her. Or maybe kiss her.

"I'm going home," I announced.

Elizabeth crossed her arms. Barbara looked at her for a second and then back at me. "I hope you'll stop making accusations about people."

"Which people, Barb?"

"Women."

"Okay." I waited. "I won't accuse women of trying to kill me."

Silence.

"Only certain women."

She stepped back . . . "You're out of your mind," she whispered.

I stood there and waited. Finally, I broke the noisy silence.

"Sure, I'm being driven out of my mind, just like . . ."

"Stop it," she said before I could finish. Before I could say any more about Dave Redfield. "You're crazy, nuts. Two men die . . ."

"Three," I said, trying not to look at Elizabeth.

"That's their problem."

"No question it is now. Which is my point."

Elizabeth coughed. Barbara turned and walked over to her. She gave her a hug. "This is a fine woman."

Elizabeth tried getting away. No use. "Come on, Barb."

"No, Elizabeth, I'm serious. When you shot Marty, you helped more of us than you know."

"Didn't do too much for their husbands," I said, girding myself.

"Their husbands? You want me to have sympathy for those impotent assholes. You think I should feel sorry for them? When did they feel sorry for their wives? Name me one man who ever cared, ever thought about what his wife thought. When she hurt. When she needed him. You got one, Jack?"

I turned away. "You don't listen, Barb."

She came toward me. Stood in my path so that I couldn't walk out the door. "I'm sick of this, Jack, do you understand, I am *sick* of all this . . . crap."

I tried whispering. "What crap?"

She waved away my question. Looked at Elizabeth, who tried to turn away. And then looked back toward me. "Why? Why, Jack? What do you want me to tell you that you won't listen to?"

"Tell me what I've done. I'll listen." I thought of reaching out for her. Just to touch her once. But I didn't. And she didn't try to move toward me.

She shook her head. Evenly. Slowly. "Forget it, Jack. Let's forget it, okay?"

I nodded. I didn't want to say any more.

Barbara turned to Elizabeth. "There's a meeting at Jane's tonight. The four of us. You'll be there."

I watched Elizabeth nod. Reluctantly, I thought. But still she nodded. Agreed with Barbara? What was going on? Who was she with? Why would she go with them?

Barbara looked back at me. "I hope you don't plan to go around town telling that ridiculous story."

"Nobody'd believe me," I said softly.

"It's dumb."

"Yeah, like Frank and Dave dying was dumb. Same dumb, Barbara."

"Accidents, they were all accidents, you heard Elizabeth."

I looked at Elizabeth. She seemed to want to disappear. I looked back at Barbara. "Twenty cars chasing me wasn't an accident, but we've been through that Barb, I—"

"Since when are you calling me Barb?"

"Jane calls you Barb. Bea calls you Barb."

"That's them, you're you."

I threw up my hands. "Fine, next time I'll clear it with the Politburo."

"You're not funny."

"Nothing is these days."

She turned to Elizabeth. And announced:

"I'm moving out."

"You already did."

"Well, now it's official. It's your house . . ."

Somehow it sounded like it was on a string, with the action end in her hand. She walked out of the kitchen, took hold of Elizabeth's hand and went out of the room with her.

It took Elizabeth a couple minutes to return. She moved back into the room and walked over to one of the stools.

"You're in major trouble."

"Thank you."

"I'm serious, Jack."

"I think we should go upstairs."

She shook her head.

I walked over and touched her face. She didn't look up. I stopped stroking her. "I really think we should go upstairs. I could use it, Elizabeth."

She looked up at me angrily. "I'm not some sexual therapist, Jack. You understand? Don't start dealin' with me like that. Marty used to do that. He got scared of somethin' and figured a good screw would make it all better. Make him forget what was botherin' him." She pointed a lacquered fingernail at my face. "So don't try that stuff with me. Okay?"

I turned away. Walked away. Toward the kitchen door. "No, I don't get it." As I reached the door, I looked back. She was staring at the floor. "The only thing I think I know is my wife wants to do away with me and . . ." I tried to think of the approriate word. It didn't appear. ". . . you are mad at me because . . ."

"Because I'm some lousy surrogate. You like that word, Jack?" She wasn't smiling. "'Cause that's how you happen to be treatin' me. Like an expensive hooker."

I thought of going back to her. Hugging her. But she didn't want to be hugged by me. She held onto herself. Protecting her body against any attempts by me to touch it. "Elizabeth." I said her name so quietly, I wasn't sure she heard it. She didn't look up. "Elizabeth." A little louder. "You're what I have." Still nothing. "Except for my kids, you're it. That's why I want to be with you."

She shook her head, to herself. "I'm a body, Jack. A warm soft body. Just another body."

"You're not. I promise."

She nodded. Not a believable nod. "Sure." She got up. Ran her fingers through her hair and straightened her tank top, making sure it covered every bit of cleavage. "I gotta go, Jack. Sorry."

"Elizabeth . . ."

She waved away any further conversation. "We'll talk about it."

"Elizabeth . . . believe me . . . I need you. Not just a . . ."

She never let me finish. "Just go, Jack. Please."

"But . . ."

For the first time ever, I heard her raise her voice to me. "Get. Out. Of. Here."

I tried smiling. It didn't make any difference. "Sure. Sure."

I locked the house up as best I could. I pushed chairs against doors that Barbara had the keys to. I slept in Martha's room. Underneath the Prince poster. But before that, I stared out the living room window. In the dark, holding onto a bottle of beer for both sustenance and protection, I watched Elizabeth go over to Jane's house. Watched Bea scoot across the street underneath her umbrella. And then I waited. Ran off to get myself another half-dozen beers, but mostly I waited. It was eleven o'clock when Elizabeth left. When she ran to her house. She looked adorable. But she didn't give my house a glance. Didn't seem to care if I was inside or out, safe or not.

I think I slept with my eyes open. Listening for sounds that were different than usual. Looking around the room to try and remember life as it had been before the heat had come. How it had been when the girls were home. When we all left in the morning for school or work and then came back together in the evening for dinner and sleep. A boring, familiar series of events that, looking back now, seems so idyllic. So full of joy and peace. It was to dream of. Hope for. Pretend that the heat and bitterness of summer had never happened. That it was all but a moment in time that had no permanent place in life.

The rain stopped around one in the morning. And after that, all I could hear were the drips. I even turned the air-conditioning off. So I sweated. Lay there in my underpants and listened. And sweated.

The doorbell woke me. The relentless ringing and pounding brought me out of bed.

By the time I got downstairs, dressed in my soaking undershorts, the noise had grown. Women's voices, loud voices that accompanied each pounding on the front door of the house.

I ran to the living room window. Past the chest I had pushed into the front door to keep it from opening. All three were standing on the front steps. Jane seemed to be doing most of the yelling. Bea the pushing, and Barbara a serious leader.

By the time I got back to the hallway, Bea and Barbara had managed to shove open the door a crack. I could hear Bea groan as she tried to move the heavy wooden chest aside.

"Wait a second," I called out.

I thought about not moving the chest. About waiting until Jane stopped carrying on. But they weren't going to knife me in broad daylight. Or were they? After all, they were the only witnesses.

"Missy?" I heard it over their sounds. It was a wonderful sound. Berta's question, directed, no doubt, at Barbara.

Everything stopped. And then Barbara, in her warmest sweetest tones "Hello, Berta. The door seems to be stuck."

"Missy home?" Berta was confused.

I moved to push the chest full of old books out of the way. Giving it enough of a shove to let the door be opened.

"He's in his shorts," declared Jane.

I didn't move. Didn't even look down to see how much of me was exposed. "Breaking and entering gets you fifteen years."

Barbara stepped forward. "It's my house. Remember? The way I see it, you were trying to keep me out of my own house."

Berta rubbed her head fiercely. "Missy no home?" she asked worriedly.

"Missy no home," I said firmly. I ignored Jane. Bea shuffled uneasily. She had backed away from the front door and was rubbing the shoulder that she had laid into the door.

"Missy wants to be home," Barbara explained. Both of us were now talking to Berta as if she actually understood what was going on.

"Ah, Missy no home," Berta exclaimed proudly.

"Missy home," Jane shouted. "Mister no home."

"Missy home?" Berta rubbed her head some more.

"Missy want to be home," Jane said loudly. "Mister won't let her."

Berta stared at me. I shrugged. "Missy no want to be home."

"Because I need protection to get into my house," Barbara said.

"You need protection?"

Barbara turned to the other two women. "See what I'm talking about. The man is paranoid. Paranoid."

Bea and Jane shook their heads almost as if on cue. They appeared ready to sign the commitment papers.

Barbara looked back at me with a "I'm talking to a madman" glare. "I came to get some clothes. That's *all."*

I pointed at the chorus. "And what about them."

"Did you ever think that I might need protection? Who knew what you were going to do. You were crazy last night. Talking about cars out to get you."

"You want some breakfast, Berta?" I asked, ignoring the women.

Berta nodded. She always understood the words for meals.

Walking up to the door, she gave it a mighty heave and the chest crashed into the wall. The hallway and I were now completely exposed.

I made sure Berta was cleaning upstairs when I showered. In fact, I basically hid behind her substantial bulk all the time Bea, Jane and Barbara were in the house packing more of Barbara's clothes. Nobody spoke. Nobody acknowledged the other's existence. It was like being in a silent film.

I waited them out. Selecting my shirt and tie so slowly I was afraid I was going to miss my first appointment. But I wasn't going to leave them alone. Even though I knew Barbara could come back any time she wanted. To set whatever booby traps she cared to set. But I wanted her out. Out of my house. Because at least for now it was mine. There was nowhere else to go.

They left before me. I looked out the bedroom window and watched the three of them carrying Barbara's clothes across the street. To Jane's.

Berta shook her head sadly at me as I walked out the door. "Missy no . . ." She couldn't finish, but stood there shoulders heaving, tears running down her chubby cheeks. I waved weakly. She didn't wave back.

My car looked all right. It was still in Elizabeth's driveway. And it didn't seem like anything had been done to it. No bomb wires stuck out. No shards of glass glared in the sunlight. Elizabeth had moved hers onto the street sometime during the night.

The rain had cooled things a bit. But these days every degree less than ninety was a blessing. At least the ground was wet. The brownish grass of this particularly brutish summer hadn't changed color, but the dirt was black. The footing softer than usual. And the cracks in the lawn had gone.

I looked up at Elizabeth's window. Looked for a sign of her. But the shades were drawn and there was no reason to think she would be looking for me. I opened the car door slowly. Waited for whatever bomb was there to go off and, when nothing happened, sat down gently.

I drove toward my office at ten miles an hour. But there were no sounds to force me to stop. No time bombs ticking. No cars waiting to ambush me.

It seemed like just another day in Lake View. Another typical day of allergy shots and tennis games.

Chapter Sixteen

STAYING ALIVE was not a skill taught to me by my parents. Learning how to recognize booby traps and guerrilla tactics was not part of my background. It wasn't even part of my street learning. That was confined to discovering the intricacies of yo-yoing and dirty phrases. So even though I walked from my car to my office as if I were pretending to be strolling through the jungles of Southeast Asia, the greenest guerrilla could, no doubt, easily have picked me off.

I considered hiring a bodyguard. Or at least putting a security team to work figuring out how to wire my house against any incursions. But my musings upon protecting my person against the onslaughts of known and unknown females were broken up by the whistlings of love.

Arnie Melton was trilling some tuneless song as he tried to imitate Gene Kelly. Or maybe it was Fred Astaire. Whatever it was, he was moving down the street as if in a movie, touching lampposts, even twirling around garbage cans, and in general making a major fool of himself. No one was watching, of course. Just me, in coat and tie.

"Jack, Jack . . ." he crooned as he came up to me. "I have found it. Discovered it."

I tried to stay calm. Not twitch in nervousness. "Yes, you told me."

"The secret, Jack." He sang out the words.

I didn't say anything.

He gave me a toothsome smile. "Shari, I just met a gal named Shari . . ."

I took a breath. A deep one. "Now let me tell you a secret, Arnie." Venom flowed onto each word as it emerged.

He just kept grinning. I noticed he wasn't wearing socks. A sport coat, shirt, tie and no socks. Brown loafers and no socks. "I want to tell you what happened last night."

"You fell in love." A bigger, if that was possible, grin.

"Fifteen women tried to ambush and kill me."

He gave me a nudge and a wink. "Great, great, Jack, some kind of guy."

He was about to break into another whistle when I grabbed his arm. He looked down as if I had hurt him. "This is no joke, Arnie. After I left the restaurant last night, at least fifteen cars tried to run me down."

Still smiling, although rubbing his arm, Arnie Melton, Dr. Arnold Melton, spoke to me as if I were an idiot patient. "Right, Jack. Sure they did."

"Arnie . . ." The presence of violence in my voice must have alerted him to the possible danger that lay ahead if he continued to condescend.

He held up his hands. Palms up. "Okay, Jack. I believe you. But . . . it was a wet night. Lots of cars slipping. Probably whole bunch of accidents." He patted me. "Now, then . . ." He grabbed my arm and started to lead me into the building. For once, the air-conditioned hallway didn't startle me. The inside and outside temperatures were close together. But Arnie wasn't noticing anything, except himself. "I got to tell you. I never realized it could be like this."

"Yes." I only got one word in.

"Love. It was never like this, Jack. That's what my problem has been as a psychiatrist. My patients' inability to love has always been something that I thought I understood."

"And now you—"

"Now I realize what it really was, was my own personal inability to love. That's what my relationship with my wife was all about. You see, the difficulty with that, was that we tried to have similar roles. We were the same. Equal. And so we were always fighting for ascendancy. Whose job was more important. Whose needs came first."

"And now—"

A large smile. He put his arm around my waist and squeezed. "Now, Jackie, Shari wants to be . . ."

I found the word for him. "Shari."

"That's it. She is perfectly happy being herself. She wants to shop . . ."

"And . . .?"

He looked at me with a non-psychiatric shit-eater of a grin. "That's it Jackie. She wants to shop. She recognizes that shopping gives her the most pleasure. Next to me, of course. So she doesn't fight it. Doesn't try to do things that society expects a woman to do these days."

"Like think?"

He paid no attention to the cynicism. I wasn't sure he heard. "Shari has gone beyond feminism. Way beyond. She appreciates the differences in our roles rather than the similarities. The distinctions are what make it work."

We were in front of my office. I tried to go in, but Arnie held onto me. He wasn't through. "It's really changed my whole attitude toward psychiatry."

"I'm glad."

On and on he went. "The idea is that the differences between men and women are the basis for love. How can you fall in love with someone like yourself? You've already got yourself, you don't need a competitor."

Now it was my turn to look at him as if he were crazy. But he paid no attention. I wondered if his patients were able to get a word in. Maybe he paid them to listen?

"Shari and I are able to love because we're able to accept our different roles. Totally different. It's opened us up."

I reached for my door. He let go. "I think that's what's wrong with you and Barbara. You're not comfortable with the similarities in your roles."

I stopped and turned back to him. "Barbara is not comfortable with *any* role of mine."

"Jack, Jack. The problem is you two talk more than you love."

"Who's *talking,* Arnie? She's trying to kill me."

"Jack, c'mon now, Barbara is ready to love—"

"You reading Kahlil Gibran?"

A short punch to my arm. "Hey, Jack, be open. Be ready for . . ."

I opened the door quickly, but before I could run inside he called out at me ". . . love, Jack. Think about it."

I slammed the office door. It wasn't much better inside. Shari was looking at me as I walked in. She was peeking out of the receptionist's window. "Morning, Dr. Klein."

"Morning, Shari," I said, hoping to make it inside without having to talk to her. No such luck, of course.

"Did you see Arnie on your way in?"

I smiled. "Yes, Shari." I reached the door to the offices but she got me before I could open it.

"He's a wonderful man."

I nodded and grabbed the handle.

"He's taught me how to love."

I opened the door.

"He likes it when I do what I like. Like shop. Really."

I stepped into the hallway.

"So I'm quitting."

It stopped me. I looked back over my shoulder at Shari, who was checking out the length of her nails. "I don't understand?"

"Arnie thinks I should get ready for the wedding." She frowned at her index fingernail.

"I didn't realize it was that soon."

"It's not." She studied the finger, and then, finally, looked up at me. "But Arnie feels I should take my time . . ." She smiled with such happiness that even I felt good. "I have a lot of shopping to do—"

"I'm sure."

"Arnie even likes to watch me shop."

"I heard."

"Well," she sighed, "I really enjoyed working here."

I gave her a smile back. "We were really glad to have you, Shari."

We smiled at each other as I closed the door and dreamed of, fantasized Arnie's death. Some healer, that one.

I don't know if it was my imagination or just paranoia, like the women claimed, but walking into The Lunch Box was not the same. Usually the women would ignore me. Except, of course, for my patients or their mothers. But today, I had the feeling that most of the eyes turned in my direction as I entered the place. I checked my suit for enormous stains. Nothing. And yet, they stared. I *knew* they were staring. I felt my face turning red as I walked to the table. The noise wasn't that much lower, and the stares weren't the obvious kind that greet the handicapped or the flamboyant. No, these were subtle stares, slightly raised eyebrows, quick glances. And so I made my way quickly to the table.

It was gone. Disappeared. The big round table that had dominated the center of the room for so many years was nowhere to be found. There was nothing to indicate where it might have been. Just a couple more square tables for four that were already occupied by women in T-shirts and tennis dresses. I stood there, looking around for someone to recognize, or at least somebody to recognize me. I felt the eyes directed at me, but every time I tried to catch someone's look, they turned away.

"Jack!" Finally, at last, a male voice. I turned and looked for it.

"Jack!" It was a faint plea over the din. A chubby hand appeared out of the sea of foursomes. "Over here," Harold Goldberg called. "I'm here. I'm here."

I ran through the room. Past women, who I would swear, looked at me with loathing. I could feel hate in the air. Hate, not for men in general, just for me.

By the time I reached Harold I was more angry than embarrassed. "What's going on?"

His face was redder than ever. "Camille said we were taking up too much space."

"So this is where she's putting us?"

He shook his head. Held up a cherry tomato and pointed to the mob at the door. "No, we have to stand in line like everybody else."

I looked around for Camille Grasso. She was holding court at the front of the restaurant. Her back to us. I tried to get her attention but she refused to look my way. I sat down at the depressing table. "What's gotten into her?"

"I don't know. I walked in and the table was gone."

"Did you say anything to her?"

"I did. I did. But she wouldn't listen. I don't know"—he looked across the room where Camille was standing—"this place gives me the creeps."

"But why. . .?

Harold shook his head.

"But we've been coming here for years."

"It's over." Harold sighed. "Maybe we should move over to that Tea Cozy place?"

"You got to be kidding."

He speared a radish from his salad and then looked at it despairingly before tossing it into his mouth. "What difference does it make. Wilted lettuce is wilted lettuce. You think maybe we came here because Camille was serving terrific food?" He played with his salad for a few seconds. "We came here for each other." He looked around the room. I turned and stared with him. "And now you and I are each other, Jack. We're all we got. There's no one else."

"Arnie Melton . . ." I started, but Harold stuck his fork angrily in my direction.

"Shmuck," he said loudly. A table of older women behind us looked disapprovingly at him. He couldn't see them. "The guy stopped by the other day with his little friend."

"Shari?"

Harold nodded. "Yeah, that Herman tramp. He asks to see some sport coats. Something in linen, she tells me. I got this nice rayon and linen weave, but do you think she'd even let him look at it?"

He didn't wait for me to nod or shake my head.

"Of course not. That one has got him by the nuts." He lowered his voice again. "If you know what I mean."

This time I nodded.

"Wouldn't even let him look at anything with rayon in it. Can you believe it? Walked right out the store."

"Terrible."

"Eh." He waved away my sincerity and pushed his salad bowl to the wall. "What good does it do? This town isn't the same." He pointed a chubby finger at me. "You like it here, Jack? You happy these days?"

I tried to find a waitress. None of them seemed to want to notice me. I looked back at Harold. "No, I'm not happy. It hasn't been a good summer, Harold."

"No kidding, Jack. Sales are down 20 percent from last year . . ."

"Also, people are dying, Harold. Men people." I could feel my voice growing thin and taut.

"Sure, but you got to look at things in perspective. Economically . . ."

"Harold. We are talking about living and dying . . ."

He nodded and pointed with his fork to his salad bowl. "Yeah, I know, I'm trying to cut down on fats and sodium, Jack."

"Harold. We are in danger."

He started to get nervous. "Of what, Jack?"

I near-whispered the word. "Women."

He looked at me, examined me. "They're difficult, Jack, I'll admit that they're difficult. But . . ."

". . . they're what's scary about this summer. Not blends of rayon and linen."

"Jack, Jack . . ." He was talking to a child having a tantrum.

I sat back. It wouldn't do any good. It was like Arnie all over again. "Forget it, Harold. You got your own problems." I stared at a new waitress until she noticed me. Arlene was across the room. She probably wasn't permitted near us.

He relaxed. "You're right, Jack."

The waitress approached me. "Menu?"

"Just a tuna salad."

"Plate or sandwich."

I looked up. She had no idea who I was. And didn't care. Every other waitress at The Lunch Box knew I got a tuna plate. I always got the plate and not the sandwich. But this one wouldn't remember if I ordered it fifty times in a row.

"Plate or sandwich?" she repeated, impatient now.

"He'll have the plate," Harold said gently. "And an iced Sanka."

The waitress wrote it all down and went off.

"You always have a plate," he explained.

I nodded.

"I thought you should have something cold to drink. You look bushed. Heat's getting to you."

I nodded again.

"Maybe you should get away." He looked concerned. He may have been the only one.

"Soon, Harold, soon."

"Why are we here?" The voice interrupted.

I looked up. Ben Bracken was standing there in a suit and tie. "Where is our table?"

Harold pointed to Camille. "Ask her."

"I did," Ben said as he sat down. "She told me we have to wait like everyone else." He seemed more shocked than angry. "Then she told me that you two were back here." Ben looked at the big container of sugar substitute. "Thirty-five years there's been a table at The Lunch Box. A table for the men who work in town." He looked at me like an old man trying to understand some modern improvement. "Thirty-five years, Jack. Before you ever came to Lake View, there's been a big round table for us. And now..." he just shook his head. "... we got this."

"It's cozy," Harold replied, trying hard to say something nice, but Ben Bracken wasn't going to sit still for it.

He pounded the table with his strong eighty-year-old fist. "It's stupid, Goldberg."

Harold seemed to back away from the table. "Well, yeah, Ben, in that sense . . . I just thought . . ."

Ben was paying no attention, just getting angry. "Do you understand that they're taking away what little rights we men have, Harold? We're the Negroes of Lake View. Second-class citizens. Visitors to the homes we purchased. Because we've given it all to them." Harold kept nodding. "Given them our houses, our businesses, this town. That's really what we gave them. This town. It's theirs now, and the only men welcome in it are hairdressers or tennis coaches." He turned to me. "And your wife, Jack Klein, isn't helping any."

"The organization?"

"What organization?" Harold asked, interested in hearing about something he hadn't heard of.

"Women Without Men." I mumbled, in case a member was nearby.

"Yeah, yeah." Harold said knowingly. "Nobody gets to have dinner on the table when they come home anymore."

Ben Bracken looked seriously at Harold. "Harold Goldberg, if you could only see over your stomach. It's not a question of meals on the table. What's important is what's to become of you."

"I'm doing okay, Ben. I mean business may be down . . ."

Ben gave Harold Goldberg a look. "Harold, shut up."

A chastened Harold returned to his salad bowl, attacking a piece of lettuce.

I tried to calm the conversation. "I think Ben means, Harold, that these women are potentially dangerous."

Ben looked at me. "You're right, Jack, the end result of this kind of organization is to do without men. Now, that's fine. Unless, of course, you happen to be a man. Then you're an alien. A foreign being to be eliminated."

I'm sure Ben wasn't using the term "eliminated" in its literal meaning, but nonetheless . . . I stood up. I had to get out of there. Away.

"I got to go." I announced. I didn't want to look around the room. Didn't want to see those people, some of whom could very well have been trying to run me over twenty-four hours earlier. So I just stared down at the table. "I . . . I . . . have to do something."

"I'm going with you," Ben announced.

"I thought we guys had to stick together," Harold said. "Isn't that what you've been telling me, Benny? That we gotta take care of each other?"

"I'm going to take care of Jack."

The waitress arrived with my tuna plate. She looked at me. I pointed to Harold. "He'll eat it."

Harold looked happy as Ben guided me out of the restaurant.

Ben took me by the arm and started walking down the street. It was cooler than usual. Bearable for a change. The kind of weather when people walked. For once, we weren't the only ones outside. There were even a couple women who nodded as we passed. Most, though, paid no attention.

"See," Ben said as a group pushed around us, without even acknowledging our existence. "We don't even exist any more. I'm not blaming your wife, Jack . . ."

"That's okay, Ben. She blames me. You might as well blame her."

"It's the same with Hilda."

"Hilda's trying to kill you?"

Ben stopped. "What are you talking about?"

I slowed down and waited for Ben to start walking and catch up to me. "I think . . . I know you think I'm crazy, Ben . . . but I really think Barbara's trying to kill me."

He didn't laugh. Didn't call for the paranoid squad. He just kept walking. I waited until he decided what to say.

"It's not beyond belief."

Once again I lowered my voice, afraid of even a passerby hearing what I was going to say. "Last night, I almost got killed, Ben. A whole bunch of women tried to crash into me, run me down on the way home."

"Did you call the police?"

"What was I going to say, Ben? There weren't any witnesses. They'd think I was out of my mind."

He looked over at me and then gave me a pat on the back. "That's one of your problems, Jack. You want to be so normal. So ordinary. You don't want anyone to think you're different. Can't stand to be different. That's one of your problems." He nodded to himself.

"One of my problems?"

"I'm sure there are others. But the big one is your trying to fit in without anyone noticing you. It might have been fine thirty, forty years ago. But these days, trying to act normal is almost impossible. When a world has gone mad, the sane person seems crazy. This town . . ." He looked up and down the street, at store windows filled with women's clothes. At stationery stores stocked with colored note paper. At fur salons and jewelry shops. At ice cream parlors that sold only frozen yogurt. At restaurants where men weren't seen until five-thirty. Ben made a sweeping gesture with his arm. ". . . this place is now a different country. I don't speak its language. And neither do you."

"But you keep coming back."

"No more. I'm staying in Arizona. Maybe go up to Sedona for the summer. It's a little cooler there. Got to be better than here."

"What about Hilda?"

"What about her?" He didn't sound happy to hear her name.

"Are you going to get married?"

He shook his head.

"What happened?"

"Says she doesn't need me anymore."

"You're kidding?"

He shook his head. "Wish I was. But she's got herself involved in this new group of old ladies."

"I'm sure they have groups of old ladies in Arizona."

"Lots of 'em. All of 'em tryin' to figure out how to have a couple more husbands before they die. But the one here tells these old ladies that they should be happy not to have men any more."

"Sounds like my wife's . . ."

He didn't let me finish. His voice rose. I noticed that his fist clenched. "Yeah, it was her organization that did it. Decided to come up with this group called Happy Widows."

I almost said you're kidding but stopped myself. Ben wasn't amused. Neither was I.

"Stupid," he mumbled, and then didn't say anything until we reached the corner. Ben Bracken's house was about a block away. I remembered how he used to walk to work in five minutes when he owned the stationery store. Now he stopped and pointed in the direction of his Victorian home. "There's nothing here for me anymore, Jack. Nothing at all. No table at The Lunch Box. Book store sells wrapping paper. And Hilda's lost. At least she says she's happy. Somebody ought to be. So I'm going to sell. The teacher who rents it from me during the winter wants it."

"Things'll be different, Ben. Next year all this nuttiness will be over. It's the weather. All the heat is driving people nuts." I tried smiling. Patting him on the back. Talking to myself.

"Keep thinking that, Jack. Keep thinking it."

An Audi came hurtling past. Going forty in a twenty-mile-an-hour zone. The woman at the wheel, sun-goggled and tennis-dressed, was talking on her car phone. The woman in the seat next to her was talking on another car phone. "What am I going to do, Ben?" Ben didn't look at me. Just straight ahead.

"Don't really know." He turned to me. "Come to Sedona with me, Jack. Your girls aren't back from camp yet."

"I don't know, Ben, my patients . . ."

"Jack, they'll still be sneezing and wheezing when you come back."

I tried to figure out why I should stay. Elizabeth came to mind. "I'll make it through the next week, Ben."

His eyebrows rose. "Hope so." We shook hands and after looking both ways, he crossed the street.

I spent the rest of the day acting paranoid. I hugged walls. Jumped every time the door opened. I would only feel comfortable with male patients. Talking to them in the hope that my female patients would go away. But they didn't. When one came in, I would try to figure out if she could have driven one of the cars that had come after me.

Most of them ignored my nervousness. One or two did look at me warily. But whether it was because I appeared strange, or because they knew something I didn't know, I couldn't be sure. Only Susan Abt said anything. And it wasn't about me.

"You're a very lucky man, doctor," she informed me as she walked into the office.

"I am?" I looked warily at Susan. She was somewhere in her thirties, allergic to ragweed. A housewife I would occasionally see at The Lunch Box.

"You must be very, very proud of your wife." She stood there, waiting for me to answer.

". . . yes . . . yes . . ." The two words took a long time getting out.

"I attended my first meeting yesterday."

"I didn't know..." I was about to say something about her marital situation. She stopped me.

"Oh, I'm still married, if that's what you were referring to." A tone was creeping into her voice. That same edgy tone that Jane and Barbara used when talking to me.

I just nodded and looked at her chart. But still, she didn't sit down. It was as if she were trying on an attitude. And on who better than her leader's hubby.

"Barbara, she asked me to call her Barbara..."

I nodded and bit my lip too hard.

"...Barbara feels that, in a sense, all women are without men." The voice started to rise, the parvenu evangelist in her voice, a tone that I recognized from the women on Apple Tree Lane, took over. "...we need each other because only we can understand each other's needs."

"Good slogan," I said pleasantly.

Susan Abt looked down at me. "It's not a slogan...Klein."

I handed her chart over to Mary and left the room. My hands were too unsteady to give an injection.

I sat on the toilet in the men's room. It was the only place in Lake View I felt safe. My house, my office, even my restaurant was unsafe.

I had to approach things calmly. Figure out exactly what to do. Not just hope and pray and wait for Elizabeth to save me—that hardly seemed likely now, remembering how she had turned on me. Maybe a snowstorm in summer. No, this had to be me doing something. Something. Anything.

Whistling. Happy whistling. Unconcerned with me. Or my problems. It could be anyone's. Any woman's. Jane's on her way to... Or even some unknown divorcée who, for practice, would take on the task of eliminating Barbara's hubby.

I wasn't going to look. I wasn't going to peek under or over the door. No, I would just sit. And hope.

And the whistling continued. I didn't hear any toilet flushes. Or water running. Just that same joyful whistle. Waiting for me.

While someone else stood guard outside. Keeping other men out. The unsuspecting men of Lake View. The poor dumb men who didn't know what was about to hit them. Marty hadn't known. Frank hadn't. Only Dave had understood. And now me.

I wasn't going to move. I would wait them out. Wait until they tried something.

I could hear feet shuffle. Big feet. Not tennis-shoed or high-heeled feet. No, these feet had real shoes on them. And then there was a voice. Humming. Just as tunelessly. But it was a male hum. A man's hum. An Arnie Melton hum.

The asshole was probably looking in the mirror. Checking out his tie, and hair and shirt collar and smile.

I could run out and talk to him. Grab him by the shoulders and shake him until he realized what was going on. But, of course, he wouldn't. He was in love. In passionate love. Women were great. Women were wonderful. They loved him. Asshole.

I stayed in the bathroom after he left. Letting my anger at Arnie build until it drove out all the thoughts of the women who were attacking me. Trying to eliminate me from Barbara's existence. He was the jerk. Letting sex drive out reality. Wait until it happened to him. Wait until Shari discovered another passion besides shopping and sex.

I didn't bother looking at myself in the mirror before leaving. Didn't bother straightening my hair, or making sure my tie wasn't off-center. Suddenly it didn't matter any more.

Chapter Seventeen

ONE MORE week. One more week. Just one more week.

I kept saying it. Repeating it. All day long. It kept me from thinking of what they were planning for me. What was waiting for me during the final week of summer vacation when all the children would pour back into Lake View.

I looked up the travel agent's number. Then forgot it and looked it up again. I could go visit my parents in Palm Springs. Or just get out of town. Hole up somewhere for the next seven days. Arrive at the airport at the same time as the girls. Our planes touching down simultaneously, so I could ride home with them.

But I was going to stay. Because, ultimately, what I realized was that there was really no place to go. This was my home. Unlike those commuters who visited Lake View, this is where I lived and worked. I wasn't going to be chased out. I wasn't going to give up what I had created for myself. This was my world. Even if it was now disheveled and chaotic it was what I had. What I was damned if I was going to give up.

So instead of calling the travel agent I called my wife. She was at Jane's.

"I'm staying," I announced. It was five.

"What else is new?" It sounded like she was talking to a group, not just me.

"I mean I'm not leaving town, Barbara."

"Keep it down," she said as the buzz behind her softened. "Now what was that, Jack?"

"I said, I'm staying in Lake View."

"Wonderful." I heard some louder sounds in the background again. "Merle Gordon, would you please keep it down. Thank you."

I waited a second. "I'll be at home."

"You'll be at home, Jack." She sounded distracted. Not even hateful or angry, just not paying attention to what I was saying.

"I think when the girls get home we should talk."

"About what?"

"Barbara, this is ridiculous."

Another voice in the background. "We'll discuss it later," she said. "Jack, I don't have time for this nonsense."

I took a deep breath. "I just wanted you to know . . ."

"Yes?"

". . . that I'm . . . going to have a barbecue on Labor Day." I smiled at the idea.

Now she paused. "That's . . . wonderful." I could picture her pressing her lips together. "Am I invited?"

"Alone."

"What is that supposed to mean?"

"That I don't want you to bring anyone else."

The clamor in back was rising again. "Sylvia . . . please . . ." Barbara said in warmer tones, then the voice lowered again. ". . . listen, Jack we'll talk later."

"When?"

She hung up. I disconnected and then dialed Elizabeth's number. Nobody answered.

She must have been with Barbara.

The pollen count was in the eight hundreds over the weekend. Which actually helped me get through it. Both figuratively and literally. I was at the hospital almost all day Saturday and Sunday. Ten of my patients came into the emergency room. Three of them wound up staying for the weekend. One of them needed me there with her most of the time. So I slept on a cot Saturday and Sunday nights. The only time I left was to go to the country club for Sunday brunch.

I don't know why I did it. Why I left the safety of Lake View hospital for the streets of town. An act of defiance? A slight attempt, on my part, to assert myself?

I didn't go there for dinner. That would have been too much. The dark held too many possibilities. I wanted to be back in the hospital before five.

Brunch on Sundays was one of the reasons people joined the Elm Wood Country Club. For nine dollars you could stuff yourself with eggs, waffles, fish, cheese, bagels, coffee cakes, fruits and assorted hot dishes. I took some carrot sticks from the buffet table.

The dining room was crowded. A lot of families. None of whom I knew well enough to join.

"Hey, Jack . . ." It was a voice from during the week. Harold.

He was with a bunch of men. Four of them, all in bright pants and T-shirts. Golfers. I hurried over.

"You guys know Jack Klein." Harold gestured to the others, Irwin Levy, Bud Friedman, Paul Lehman and Bob Rush, who nodded. Only Harold was interested in talking. The others ignored me. Pointedly, I thought. But I didn't care. I was safe here between Harold and Bud Friedman.

"How was golf, Harold?" I was determined to make conversation.

"Terrible, terrible, I don't know why I play."

"So you can complain," Bud Friedman mumbled between swallows. He never looked up from his plate. In fact, everyone except Harold and me was staring down at his plate. These were normally talkative men, who now seemed hellbent on finishing up their meals and getting away.

I looked over at Harold, even he seemed slightly abashed.

"What's wrong?" I said to the table at large. "What have I done?"

The men kept eating. Only Harold glanced over at me.

"It's your . . ." he took a deep breath " . . . wife. You know why we're here?" he added.

"No."

Irwin Levy looked up, his forkful of salmon pointed at my eyes. "Because our wives are at another one of those damned meetings. That's what they do these days. Meet. They meet before they can get us breakfast. They meet instead of making dinner. They meet instead of—"

Bud Friedman was nodding furiously." . . . sex. That's what they meet instead of . . ."

Harold shook his head. "Big deal, that I can live with, or without, but I got nobody to talk to. Adele hasn't said two words to me in a week."

"That's two more words than I got." Bob Rush took off his glasses and wiped his forehead. "Grunts is what I have. Like she didn't hear me."

Paul Lehman said, "we all work hard and love our family. What's so terrible about us, Jack?"

"We're men, Paul." I said it very quietly.

"So?" Paul kept on stroking his beard.

"So, we're the bad guys."

"But why me?"

"I don't know."

Irwin put down his fork and then pointed a shaking finger in my direction. "Well, you better find out, Jack. It's your wife."

"Talk to her." Paul said. "Ronna and I used to be happy. I

swear. Two weeks ago we were the happiest couple I knew. We were the envy of our friends."

Harold grunted in agreement. "Absolutely."

"And now. . ." Paul seemed so sad he couldn't finish.

Irwin finished for him. "Now I'm sleeping in the den, Jack. And I don't know why. Tell me, Jack, why am I sleeping in the den?"

"Barbara's not even sleeping at home. I'm alone too."

They all started talking to me at once. Bud's voice rose over the others. They quieted down. "Jack, this is serious."

I nodded. I looked at my plate. I wasn't hungry.

"It's not getting any better," Bud said.

"Are you scared too?" I asked.

Bud looked at me strangely. "Of what?"

"Of them."

"We're scared of not getting dinner, Jack."

"No, I mean . . ." Oh, what the hell, I figured. ". . . of them . . . hurting you?"

They all looked at me strangely. Harold grabbed my arm and held it tightly. Almost to keep me from talking. "Jack's had a rough summer. You know, with Marty Siegal and then Frank Bernstein and Dave Redfield . . ."

Irwin Levy sorted it out. "You don't actually think that their wives . . . ?"

I sat there. I didn't want to nod. Nobody said anything for a minute. Finally Bud broke the tension. "Jack, have you talked to anybody . . . the police?"

"What am I going to say, Bud. We all know how Marty got killed. Frank choked on a piece of meat and Dave jumped through a plate glass window at an alleged apparition."

"See," Harold said, squeezing my arm. "A coincidence."

I shook my head. "No, no, that's the point. It isn't a coincidence. Did you guys ever hear of a *folie à deux?*"

"Some kind of disease?" Bob asked. He took off his glasses and started playing with them.

"Like something in the water?" Harold seemed grateful to be

talking about something else. "I heard about that once. Minerals. Too many minerals. Maybe it affects—"

"Shut up, Harold." Bud said. "Let Jack explain."

Harold let go of my arm and sat back. Everybody else leaned forward. At me.

"Well, I don't know much about it, but basically it's this term psychiatrists use when you have people imitating certain kinds of neurotic behavor. Like two sisters in the same house who are anorexic."

They all nodded. Even Harold.

I went on. "Or a sorority where there are a bunch of kleptomaniacs."

"So they sit around and talk about it . . ." Irwin began.

I interrupted. "No, no, that's the point. They don't sit around and talk about it. It's as if they do it automatically. It becomes accepted behavior."

"Like not making dinner?" said Bud.

Bob put on his glasses. "Or not having sex."

Irwin seemed to understand. "Or . . . killing your husband. Is *that* it, Jack?"

They stared at me. "That's it, Irwin."

Harold patted my arm again. "C'mon, Jack, you don't believe that . . ."

"Yes, I do, Harold."

Bud coughed. "Jack, I know it's been a strain . . ."

Irwin jumped in. "If it had been happening on any of our blocks I don't know how we'd have handled it either. Right?"

Nobody agreed. They all were looking away. Paul Lehman pushed his half-eaten plate away and stood up.

"Listen, guys, I gotta be runnin'. Take care, Jack." He sounded like he meant it. I nodded.

Bud and Bob followed quickly. They seemed flustered, and practically ran out the room. Harold squirmed some in his seat before mumbling his good-byes and going. Only Irwin didn't move. "You really serious about the murder stuff, Jack?"

"I'm serious, Irwin. Also scared."

He leaned toward me. "Listen, my brother-in-law has this problem . . ." the voice lowered, he leaned across the table ". . . it's his sex life, not as good as it could be, anyway he sees this therapist . . ."

I jumped up from the table before he could finish. "I got to go, Irwin, I really do, I really do."

He just stared up at me. "Jack, believe me . . . this person helped him a lot. Melton. Arnie Melton is the guy's name."

He must have thought I was crazy. I laughed for the first time in days. All the way out of the club I laughed. All the way to the hospital. I even got three hours of semi-sleep.

Monday morning, one of the nurses woke me.

"Dr. Klein, Dr. Klein . . ." I could hear her voice vaguely through my dreams of mountains and snow. It was very cold in my dream, and I didn't want to leave it. But the voice was not letting me stay there.

"Dr. Klein. I think you should get up."

So I opened my eyes. Oh, how I didn't want to. How I wanted to keep them closed until the kids came home.

"Dr. Klein . . ." I looked up into a very young face. There were a few pimples on the girl's chin, but she had such an eager look to her that I knew whatever the emergency, it wasn't life threatening. "Dr. Klein, Mrs. Klein, your wife, is on television." She fairly beamed.

By the time I got a pair of pants and a shirt on and walked into the staff lounge, it was practically six-thirty. Three other nurses and a couple of doctors were entranced by the screen. Barbara was being interviewed. Sitting in a high-backed chair next to the host, she seemed to be in the middle of a monologue. I noticed the interviewer kept glancing forlornly at the camera.

I stood in back.

I picked up Barbara in the middle of her lecture. ". . . so it's really not our problem as much as men's. That's why we feel divorce is a symptom of a greater malaise. It doesn't solve the difficulties men and women have in getting along."

"So you don't think"—the host smiling at the camera before turning to Barbara—"men and women were"—another grin—"meant to coexist." A near-wink.

Barbara must have seen it too. I could see her lips thin out before she spoke. "That's the problem. Winks and leers and grins."

The host tried a sincere smile.

She ignored his attempt. "You don't get it . . . do you?" She shook her head sadly. "But why should you be different." She leaned forward, talking to the camera. "Listen, all we're trying to do in Women Without Men is get women to understand that ultimately, eventually, most are without men, alone. We're just trying to help them be alone together."

The host, who obviously hadn't heard a word, gave Barbara a smile before turning to the camera. She didn't smile back.

"Our guest on *Wake Up Chicago* has been Ms. Barbara Klein, head of Women Without Men. Tomorrow morning . . ."

Everybody turned around and saw me standing there. Nobody smiled. Nobody congratulated me on my wife. I left the room as fast as possible.

I discharged two of the three patients before I left for work. The third was finally breathing on her own, and I could let her go the next morning.

I had to borrow a shirt from one of the other doctors. A white shirt that was too big for me. I was wearing the same pair of slacks I had worn to the hospital on Saturday. At least I had showered, but I didn't feel like me as I walked outside.

The temperature was way up again. After spending the weekend in air-conditioning I was surprised summer was still here. It was climbing, the car radio told me. Upper nineties by the end of the week.

Hilda Robins wasn't there when I got to the office. She arrived at nine. On time for her appointment, but half an hour later than usual. She was also quiet.

"Any problems, Mrs. Robins?"

"No." Quick. Curt. Not a glance in my direction.

"Pollen was up this weekend."

A nod.

I looked at her face. She was staring over my shoulder. Like Jane. And Bea. And Barbara. And now, Elizabeth.

"Have you seen Ben?"

She lowered her eyes. And stared at me for a while. "He's left town, Klein."

I turned away to put the vials of serum back on the desk. "You're not marrying him, Hilda?"

It was the first time I had ever called her by her first name. It made her stare at me. "No. I don't need him." She waited before finishing, waited till my tush started to squirm. "I have become more satisfied with myself, Klein. And I am no longer lonely."

I decided to pay no attention to her cant. "I like Ben. I'm going to miss him."

She stood up. "I've spent too many years without a man to have one now." She started out.

"We're not that terrible . . . Hilda."

She turned around and tried to smile. It seemed like an effort. "As I remember, some of you were not quite so terrible."

Monday at noon I drove home to tell Berta we needed her to come in every day.

"Missy no home?"

I nodded and she nodded back. I got out of there quickly. There were a lot of cars in front of Jane's house. Elizabeth did not answer her back door.

I brought lunch back to the office. The vision of Harold sitting there alone with his vegetable platter made me more depressed.

I called Elizabeth from the office at five. She answered, I didn't say hello.

"Elizabeth, you have to talk to me."

"Damn it, Jack, would you please leave me alone."

"They're there? Right? I can understand you can't talk out loud. Just say 'yes' if you love me."

"No, Jack."

She hung up the phone before I could ask another question.

Shari was still in the office when I started to leave. She was just finishing packing up. We walked out together. She and her shopping bags. Me and my building hysteria.

"Are you all right, Dr. Klein?" She waited while I turned off the lights.

"Sure, sure."

"You seem nervous."

She opened the door for me. I looked both ways before walking out of it. The corridor was empty.

"I'm fine. I'm fine. How's everything . . . with you." I locked the door. Shari waited for me to finish up. Then the two of us made our way out of the building. I stood closer to her than usual. I was brushing up against her shopping bag.

Talking about herself made her forget me. I noticed a big smile on her face. "Oh, I'm great, Dr. Klein. Since I met Arnie, that is."

"Good. Good." I saw a pair of women in the distance. Coming toward us. They were talking to each other. Seriously. And then they looked up at us. I couldn't see the expressions on their faces. They turned into an office. But still I stayed close to Shari.

"He's a wonderful man, Dr. Klein."

"Good. Good."

"I think this time it'll work."

I tried to figure out why the two women were going into a doctor's office together. They were the same age. It wasn't mother and daughter. Unless, of course, they were after me and seeing me with a woman . . .Then I remembered Shari. "What . . .?"

She looked up at me strangely. "Marriage. Arnie and I. I think this time it'll work out for both of us."

I nodded as we came to the outside doors. "Uh-huh. Sure."

Arnie was sitting in Shari's convertible. Waiting in his parking space. His coat was off. His tie loosened. He was whistling.

Shari saw him too. "I've got to run, Dr. Klein." She scampered out the door before I could say anything. Arnie didn't notice me as I walked after her. So I just stood there on the sidewalk and watched them kiss. I turned away before they were done. Anxious to get out of there before the two women came after me. In a car or on foot.

"Jack. Jack" he called as I started off.

I looked back. They were holding tightly onto each other.

"Listen, Jack . . . what're you doing tonight?"

I shrugged. "Not much."

"Want to go shopping?" Was he being kind?

I thought of the alternatives. There were none.

"We're getting Shari's wedding dress at Neiman-Marcus," Arnie explained as we drove toward the Mall. "Shari loves Neiman's." He turned to me in the back seat. He wasn't joking. I tried to smile. I couldn't begin to match the wattage of his grin.

I stuck close to them. Huddling next to Arnie as we made our way through Neiman-Marcus. I sat next to him in the wedding dress section as we waited for Shari to come out.

"Pretty exciting, right, Jack?" I moved closer.

The store was practically deserted. The usual flock of women was nowhere to be seen. Even in the summer, Neiman-Marcus had its loyal customers. Its cadre of regulars. I had never seen it so empty. "Where is everybody?"

Arnie didn't care. "You're going to love this dress, Jack. It's got this high collar . . . "

"Where could they be . . . ?" I looked around for anyone who wasn't a salesperson. I couldn't find one.

"Who? Who is they?"

"The women. The people who shop here. The ones who drive the Audis and Jaguars and Volvos . . ." I could hear my voice beginning to rise, tried to contract it.

He lowered his voice. Leaned into me. "Jack, Jack. Come on. You're doing it again."

"Arnie, there's no one here." I tried to stay calm. "They should be here."

"It's summer, Jack. Lots of people don't shop in the summer."

"These people do. They should be here, Arnie, do you understand that. Do you?"

He patted me soothingly. "Jack, listen, it's time for dinner. People are home with their families."

I didn't answer. He didn't know what was happening. Only I knew. Only I cared. I turned away.

"It's fabulous!" Arnie's voice rose three octaves as Shari paraded toward us. It was a wedding dress. The young saleswoman walked proudly behind her.

Shari smiled sweetly at her Arnie. "You really like it?"

"I love it. I love it."

Nobody looked at me. Not even the saleswoman.

"You sure, Arnie?"

"It's the best!"

Everyone beamed. Except me. Nobody noticed I wasn't smiling.

"She is a beauty, Dr. Melton," the saleswoman said. She looked to be almost as serious a shopper as Shari.

"Isn't she gorgeous, Jack?" Arnie said, never taking his eyes off his fiancée.

"Great," I answered. Nobody was coming in the doors. Nobody was strolling through the dress sections. It was just the three of us. And the saleswoman. Where were they? Damn it all, where were they?

"I think the dress sets off her cheekbones," the saleswoman said.

They all nodded. Nobody noticed I wasn't looking at them. A man walked in. Holding a little girl's hand. They came in from the outside and started walking through the store. I wanted to ask him where his wife was. But I sat there, trying not to think of the things that lay in wait for me.

"What do you think, Jack?" Arnie was now trying to include me.

"Good cheekbones," I mumbled. The father and daughter passed through the dress section and went in the toy department. Maybe he was divorced? Could this be his one night out with his daughter? And where was his wife? Attending . . . "Excuse me." They turned my way. "Where is everybody?" I said to the saleswoman.

"A big meeting," she said. "An organization . . ."

". . . your wife's," Shari explained. "It's at the gym. Everybody is there."

"You're not," I said quietly.

"I'm busy." She beamed at Arnie. "But everybody else is going."

"Is *your* wife, Barbara Klein?" The saleswoman looked at me for the first time.

"Yes." I answered quietly.

"A wonderful woman. She has done amazing things for this community."

I just sat there and thought of the cars of twenty-four hours ago.

The saleswoman went on. "You're a lucky man. I hope you realize that."

I tried to nod but couldn't. The saleswoman turned back to Shari. I looked at Arnie. He was also looking at Shari. Again, nobody noticed me.

They didn't invite me out to dinner. I wasn't sure whether it was because they wanted to be alone, or if I just had become too depressing for them. They dropped me off in front of the building. At my car. I watched as they sped away.

I had no place to go. So I walked. Close to the buildings. Away from the curb. Far away from any cars. There were a few people on the street. I stared at them. But they didn't notice me. Even though I knew how different I looked. How messy my shirt was, how askew my tie had become, how rumpled my suit appeared. I knew it without having to look in a mirror. I didn't care. I wanted to be outside. In view. In public. My car was going to stay in front of my office for the next five days. Until I drove it to the airport. It wasn't going to trap me. Hold me penned up for some Mercedes to bash it again, and again, and one last time.

I walked past Harold Goldberg's. He was fitting someone's pants. He wasn't looking out the window. So I kept on. Past the stores. I saw Ben Bracken's house coming up on the right. But by the time I got there, I could see that no one was home. There was no one at all. And so I kept walking. It was getting dark. I walked faster.

I selected a strange route home. Crossing half-a-dozen backyards to get to my house. I utilized bushes for cover. Avoided houses where people were sitting outside. Listened for unusual car noises. It took me an hour to cover half a mile.

The street, of course,was deserted. Black. But still, just in case, I came to my house the back way. Skirted the side of the house and, sliding against the wall, made my way inside. I locked every door. And then went to Martha's bedroom to look out over the street. I sat there with my tuna fish sandwich and orange juice, the air-conditioner off because I didn't want to miss any meaningful sounds. I sat there in my underpants. Oh so hot. The sweat poured off me.

The car came back around midnight. Just one car, Jane's, pulling into her driveway. The four of them got out and went into the house. An hour later Bea and Elizabeth left. I followed Elizabeth. Watched her go home. She didn't look up at me. Ignored me and the house. I thought about calling her. Letting the phone ring until she had to answer it. Until she had to hear much I missed her. But I didn't. Because I knew I had toget to 7:05 Friday bight. When the plane ws going to arrive. That's when my misery would be over.

For three days nothing happened. Barbara didn't try to come over. And I sweated. The sound of Berta coming in the back door each morning made me feel safe. Safe enough to shower and get dressed.

Even getting dressed had changed. It used to take me just a few minutes. I always decided the night before what I was going to wear the next day. Then I would lay out the clothes. My underwear was on top of my shirt, my socks right next to them. The tie next to the socks. Now, I had to rush around to find clean clothes. Berta was doing my socks and underwear, but I was running out of clean shirts. I was paying less and less attention to matching striped shirts and ties. So long as it was clean, I wore it.

Thursday, August the thirtieth.

I checked the time every thirty seconds. I even looked at the calender a few times an hour in case it really was Friday. I was planning to go to the airport after work the next day. I wanted to be early. I wanted to see my children.

Arnie called before lunch. "I've got to talk to you, Jack."

We ate in his office. He had sent out for fruit salads and iced Sankas. I sat on the couch. He put a table between his chair and the couch so we could have some place to eat. But, he wasn't eating.

"Jack, I know how you feel that I haven't been exactly. . ."

". . . sympathetic?"

He nodded. "Yes, well, I want you to know I feel badly."

I didn't say anything.

"But you know how it is." He still hadn't looked at me.

"When you're in love?"

He just stared at his fruit plate. He hadn't touched it. Finally he looked up at me. "Yes, well, I sort of wanted to ask you something about . . ."

I waited. Watching him be uncomfortable. Why should I be the only one who was having problems?

". . . you see Shari went to this meeting the other night . . ."

Bingo.

". . . and ever since then . . ."

". . . she tried to knife you in bed?"

He looked up. "No, no, it's just that she isn't quite as . . ."

". . . sweet? Innocent? Childlike? Loving?"

"Jack, stop it." He regained some of his composure as I was losing mine. "It's not that bad."

"Sure, sure, Arnie, that's why you wanted to have lunch with me. So you could tell me how great everything was."

"Jack, now come on . . ." He was trying to be warm.

I wasn't buying it. "For the last two months, Arnie, I've been trying to tell you what was going on in my life . . ."

He put a hand up to stop me.

". . . and what you did was tell me how much in love you were. Remember Jack the crazy allergist? Mr. Paranoid? Remember him?"

He nodded. "I wasn't quite as understanding as I could have been."

"Arnie, I'm being assaulted by coveys of women and you told me how passion makes the world go round."

"Okay, I'm sorry, but I felt that the best thing I could do for you . . ."

"Is be a friend?"

I reached for a piece of pineapple and threw it into my mouth. Chewed angrily.

"About this meeting."

I leaned back. I was going to enjoy something about the week.

"Remember the other night when we went shopping?"

I nodded.

"Well, after we dropped you off, we passed the gym. Lots of cars. Women." He said it as if I didn't know.

"I figured."

"Well, to make a long story short . . ." He was wringing his hands. "I dropped her off there. She said she could get a ride home."

"And . . ."

". . . she wants to get more involved in the organization."

"She take out a hunting license?"

He tried looking stern. He only appeared worried. "No, no, I'm serious, Jack."

"So am I, Arnie. These people want to get rid of us."

He kept staring at his fruit. "Not, Shari, Jack. She just wants to work for them."

"For who?"

"For your wife." He glanced up at me. "Says she can work part time for Barbara, doing her typing and stuff, and still get ready for the wedding."

The anger, the almost-pleasure of watching him squirm evaporated. "Was this Barbara's idea?"

He nodded. "Shari told her about leaving your office. But what really worries me . . ." He paused. I waited for him. ". . . what bothers me is that she's starting to be angry. So alien to her . . ."

"Like your first wife, Arn?"

"Sort of. Except she was angry at people like the Contras and the Republican Party."

"And Shari?"

"Her father, a little."

"What about him?"

"I guess he fools around. Flies off to see some woman in New York every couple months."

"And Shari says she'd like to kill him?"

"Not exactly . . . she's just getting angrier . . ."

"Isn't that normal, Arnie?" I wasn't sure what role I was playing.

"Sure, sure, but like I said, this kind of anger isn't like her. She's not normally that kind of person."

"Neither was Bea Bernstein, Arnie, or Jane Redfield . . ."

He looked up. "Or Barbara?"

"Uh-huh. Got any ideas."

He shook his head. "I don't know what's going on, Jack."

"But something's going on?"

He nodded.

"What are you going to do about it?"

"Marry Shari and get the hell out of town."

"How soon?"

"Soon."

I stood up. He had his own problems. He couldn't help me. "Hope you make it."

He reached up with his hand. "You too." He said it seriously.

I spent a lot of time looking at Shari that afternoon, but she seemed no different than usual. No angrier, no more determined. She didn't resemble Barbara or Bea or Jane. She seemed like Shari. Except she didn't hang around after work waiting for Arnie. Neither did I.

I took an entirely different route home. Coming in from across the street. Through the woods in back of Jane's house.

I made it.

I thought.

Apple Tree Lane looked the same. Although for once there were no cars lined up in front of Jane's. In fact the street looked like a picture. The cars were all in garages. Nobody was outside. Nobody was watering the grass. And, of course, there was absolutely no wind, no breeze. The one-hundred mark had been reached. And even though the shirt stuck to my back, I was so grateful to be home that I didn't mind it. I leaned against the kitchen table. Out of breath from my hundred-yard dash. Berta had left the air-conditioning on. The house was cold. Reluctantly, I walked over to turn it off. Click off the noise. And the air. Only then did I go to the refrigerator for my juice. Afterward I checked my watch with the kitchen clock and took my tuna fish upstairs.

I chose Mandy's room for my last night. It had the best view of the street. I could see Bea's and Jane's houses perfectly. I'd have to go to the far window to check Elizabeth's, but I didn't think I had to worry as much about that direction. She may have turned, but not that much . . .

Nothing moved on the street. All night long, nothing moved. No leaves. No cars. No people. A still life of a hot night in August. People had stopped barbecuing. It was that hot. The only sound was the occasional car speeding down the next block. But that was a faraway sound, and by ten it too had virtually disappeared, as parents all over town made plans to welcome their children back from camp. And still I sat and sweated and dreamed of Elizabeth.

When you sit up and fall asleep, you find that you wake up a lot. The heat only added to my discomfort, so every few minutes I jarred myself awake with my own movement. And still there were no sounds. No lights. Maybe they had come home while I was asleep. But I couldn't see any sign that they had. The street was dead.

At two I went to the bathroom. Ran there. Just to throw some cold water on my face. I was back in seconds. Sat down on the soaking sheet and looked again out of the window. I had brought a glass of water back with me and slowly drank out of it. I put it on the window ledge and then watched some more. And waited. And slept.

The heat woke me up again. Heat that seemed to be rising from the house. A scorching, searing heat that was like the one that arrived at noon. But it was two-thirty in the morning. And then I smelled something. I had been so aware of listening for sounds I had forgotten about smells. It was the smell that made me realize the heat wasn't coming from outside. And then I heard it. A crackling noise. A series of sparks. From down below me. From my house. And now there was smoke. I could see it coming up the stairs. And as I ran toward the hallway, as I looked around the corner, I saw the flames climbing. Rising, as if ordered, up, up and toward me.

I ran to the far end of the hallway. The back stairs. Next to the maid's room. There was another way. If the fire was coming up the front I'd go down the back. Take that. I'd show them. I was going to that damned airport tomorrow. I was going to walk down that stairway, run down that stairway, and get out of the house. I was going to get out of there. Jack Klein was going to make it. No matter what they tried to do to him, he was smarter, he was going to make it.

The back stairs were on fire. A bitch of a fire. Coming right toward me. Blocking me off.

I ran back to my bedroom. Down the hallway, past the front stairs, now virtually gone, and into my room. There was a window on the side of the room. Off the bathroom. If I could get to that window I could at least jump. Onto the garage. The garage was one floor below me. I might break a leg, or sprain an ankle but I would be alive. I could jump to the ground from the roof of the garage.

I looked out the front window of the bedroom on my way toward the bathroom window. And I stopped. Amidst the heat and smoke and noise and pain I stopped.

The three were looking out from Jane's window. Barbara and Jane and Bea. They stared. Stared at the fire. And at me. I thought, for a second, that Barbara looked away, but she hadn't. And then I turned away, and kept running.

The garage was starting to burn. The flames from the side of the house had reached the garage. But the roof was still there, and so I climbed out onto the ledge. I looked down, ready to jump. I could hear the noise behind me. The smoke was coming into the bathroom. The heat was beyond belief. And then I heard.

"Jack, here. I'm over here."

Elizabeth.

I waited. Waited to see where she was. Hiding. Laying in wait to pass her initiation into the sisterhood of Lake View. Two murders in one year. Two gold stars. Because she must have set it. Set it while they watched. Set it to prove that indeed she was committed to them, despite an earlier lapse.

The gun totally convinced me. The gun that she was holding as I saw her looking up at me from the driveway. The gun that she had probably shot Marty with. And now me.

"Jack, come down," she yelled it at me.

I looked back. Watched the flames engulf my dresser. Watched as they came toward me. I jumped back. Into the bathroom. Closed the door and turned on the water. The shower water. The sink water. Just water. Fill it up. I closed the drains. Let the room flood.

"Please, Jack." It was a harsh voice that pierced the noise of the fire. "Come down, come down," it hollered. But I was too busy making the water flood the bathroom. It wasn't enough. The door was almost gone. And now the flames were on their way toward me, ignoring the water. I backed away. To the window. Climbed up and looked at the fire that was destroying everything around me.

Elizabeth's voice rose above everything. So I turned. Looked and saw that the garage was now totally in flames and the only way I could jump was two floors. Down to the ground. Two broken legs. But of course I'd never know that, because the gun was in Elizabeth's hand.

"Jack. Please."

I didn't look back but down at Elizabeth, whose face was red, whose hair was sticking out, Elizabeth in her nightgown waving her revolver. And in spite of what I knew she was there for, in spite of it all, I jumped to her. Straight into her arms.

Chapter Eighteen

I TOLD JACK *that he overreacted. I mean, if he'd ever* thought *about it he would have figured out that I was just doing an acting job on the girls. The way I analyzed it, they were definitely going to knock him off. The only way I could stop it was to get in good with them. And so I had to cut him off. Give him the business. But the big lug was so damned sensitive he never figured it out. Take the gun, for instance. Here I am, trying to make sure that the girls don't come running across the street with butcher knives, and he thinks I'm going to shoot him. I ask you, would I get off with temporary insanity a second time? No way. So I'm holding onto the revolver trying to keep crazy Barb and company from murdering my Jack, and he can't decide if he should jump. And then, when he does jump, he falls right on top of me. Can't even aim for the bushes. My back hasn't been the same. Six months now, and I still can't lift. Of course the guy did have a couple broken arms, but he's fine now.*

In case you didn't know, we're in Vail. That's in Colorado. Jack wanted to go somewhere cold. Said he never wanted to see a day over seventy again. He says that we'll summer in Alaska.

We even have the kids. There wasn't a heck of a lot Barbara could do about it when I casually mentioned that I was about to turn state's evidence on her. They love it here. And Jack loves the kids.

He's working here. Sort of a general practice. Said he's tired of shooting people up with pollen. So he's actually dealing with sick people for a change.

He's much better now. Even mixes up his black and brown socks once in a while. Can't stop holding onto me. Not that I mind. He's got his daughters and me. As for me . . . well, I guess I got Jack. Could do a lot worse. And so far things are really swell . . .

FOR IMMEDIATE RELEASE—

Barbara Klein, president of Women Without Men, announces that the organization will open branches in three cities this spring. There are now 2200 members in the Chicago Chapter.

Starting April fifteenth there will be Chapters in Miami, Seattle and Denver. Ms. Klein will be based with the Denver group for six months. She intends to set up groups in the outlying cities and suburbs. Including Aspen and Vail.

For more information: Contact Women Without Men. 100 Apple Tree Lane, Lake View, IL.

Shari Herman-Melton, Director of Information.